"Anothe[...] [...]day cozy. The *Upstairs, Downstairs* class difference just before WWI comes alive, as it always does in the Pennyfoot saga, in this exciting amateur sleuth."
—*Midwest Book Review*

"Kingsbury continues to delight fans with well-thought-out mysteries that will challenge and entertain for hours."
—*Debbie's Book Bag*

Mistletoe and Mayhem

"Full of wonderful characters, a welcoming home setting, and many surprises, this one is a keeper . . . These are characters you will want to visit time and time again!"
—*The Romance Readers Connection*

Decked with Folly

"Kingsbury expertly strews red herrings to suggest plenty of others had reason to wish Ian dead . . . This makes the perfect stocking stuffer for the cozy fan in your life."
—*Publishers Weekly*

Ringing in Murder

"*Ringing in Murder* combines the feel of an Agatha Christie whodunit with a taste of *Upstairs, Downstairs*."
—*Cozy Library*

"Engaging . . . Cozy fans will be pleased to ring in the New Year with this cheerful Kingsbury trifle."
—*Publishers Weekly*

continued . . .

Berkley Prime Crime titles by Kate Kingsbury

Manor House Mysteries

A BICYCLE BUILT FOR MURDER
DEATH IS IN THE AIR
FOR WHOM DEATH TOLLS
DIG DEEP FOR MURDER
PAINT BY MURDER
BERRIED ALIVE
FIRE WHEN READY
WEDDING ROWS
AN UNMENTIONABLE MURDER

Pennyfoot Hotel Mysteries

ROOM WITH A CLUE
DO NOT DISTURB
SERVICE FOR TWO
EAT, DRINK, AND BE BURIED
CHECK-OUT TIME
GROUNDS FOR MURDER
PAY THE PIPER
CHIVALRY IS DEAD
RING FOR TOMB SERVICE
DEATH WITH RESERVATIONS
DYING ROOM ONLY
MAID TO MURDER

Holiday Pennyfoot Hotel Mysteries

NO CLUE AT THE INN
SLAY BELLS
SHROUDS OF HOLLY
RINGING IN MURDER
DECKED WITH FOLLY
MISTLETOE AND MAYHEM
HERALD OF DEATH
THE CLUE IS IN THE PUDDING
MULLED MURDER

Titles by Kate Kingsbury writing as Rebecca Kent

HIGH MARKS FOR MURDER
FINISHED OFF
MURDER HAS NO CLASS

MULLED MURDER

KATE KINGSBURY

BERKLEY PRIME CRIME, NEW YORK

THE BERKLEY PUBLISHING GROUP
Published by the Penguin Group
Penguin Group (USA) LLC
375 Hudson Street, New York, New York 10014

USA • Canada • UK • Ireland • Australia • New Zealand • India • South Africa • China

penguin.com

A Penguin Random House Company

This book is an original publication of The Berkley Publishing Group.

Berkley Prime Crime Books are published by The Berkley Publishing Group.
BERKLEY® PRIME CRIME and the PRIME CRIME logo are trademarks of
Penguin Group (USA) LLC.

Library of Congress Cataloging-in-Publication Data

Kingsbury, Kate.
Mulled murder / Kate Kingsbury.—Berkley Prime Crime trade paperback edition.
pages cm.—(Pennyfoot holiday mysteries)
ISBN 978-0-425-26291-7 (pbk.)
1. Baxter, Cecily Sinclair (Fictitious character)—Fiction.
2. Hotelkeepers—Fiction.   3. Pennyfoot Hotel (England : Imaginary place)—Fiction.
4. Murder—Investigation—Fiction.   5. Christmas stories.   I. Title.
PR9199.3.K44228M58 2013
813'.54—dc23

PUBLISHING HISTORY
Berkley Prime Crime trade paperback edition / November 2013

PRINTED IN THE UNITED STATES OF AMERICA

10 9 8 7 6 5 4 3 2 1

Cover illustrations by Dan Craig.
Cover design by Judith Lagerman.

To my husband, Bill,
who has given me twenty years of
pure happiness and contentment.
I will always love you.

ACKNOWLEDGMENTS

To my editor, Faith Black. Thank you for all the wonderful suggestions, ideas, and great titles. It has been a huge pleasure to work with you. We have been on the same page since day one, and you will always be in my memories of my Pennyfoot family.

To my agent, Paige Wheeler. Thank you for your help, your consideration, and your friendship. It means a lot to me to have someone in my corner I can trust.

To Bill, for always understanding when I drift off into my "other world."

To Ann Wraight, for all the wonderful magazines and research that helped so much in writing the series.

To my readers:

I'm sad to say that this book will be the last in the Pennyfoot Hotel Mysteries. Most of the characters are looking forward to new lives, and it's time to let them go. It wasn't an easy decision to make, but I feel it's the right one.

I will miss my family in Badgers End, and my beloved Pennyfoot Hotel. But I leave them knowing they are going on to better lives. When I first created them, I had no idea we would be together so long. It has been a great pleasure and a privilege to tell you about their adventures.

I want to thank you, dear readers, for all your wonderful letters and e-mails. You are the ones I have to thank for keeping the series alive. For the past twenty-two years I have enjoyed a delightful correspondence with you, and

ACKNOWLEDGMENTS

many of you have become close friends. For me, that is the best reward I could have.

I wish you all a very merry Christmas, and a healthy, happy New Year filled with love and laughter. I'm not giving up writing, and Kate Kingsbury will strive to entertain you well into the future.

Bless you all,

Doreen

aka Kate Kingsbury

CHAPTER 1

"Really, Frederick! I do wish you wouldn't dawdle so." A playful wind tugged at Phoebe Carter-Holmes Fortescue's hat, and she snatched at the wide brim before it could be whisked off her head.

Her husband had paused at the railing that divided the deserted beach from the Esplanade, his gaze fixed on something beyond her sight.

Glancing at the sea, Phoebe could see nothing but gray green water churning toward shore, and a lone ship too far out to discern anything unusual about it. "Whatever are you staring at?"

He declined to answer, and she drew back her thin shoulders to take a deep breath. Much as she adored her husband, he could, at times, try her patience dearly. It was her decided opinion that in deference to his service in His Majesty's armed forces, people gave Frederick far too much leeway.

True, his experiences had left him somewhat addled in the head, but Phoebe had no doubt that Colonel Frederick Fortescue had far more gumption than people gave him credit for, and delighted in the attention gained by his erratic behavior.

At that moment, however, he seemed transfixed, his back as straight as a tent pole.

Murmuring her displeasure under her breath, Phoebe joined him at the railing to see what had taken such hold of his interest.

At first, all she noticed was the smooth golden sand and the thin line of seaweed left by the retreating waves. Then she spotted what appeared to be a bundle of clothing lying just beyond the edge of the water. "Goodness!" She narrowed her eyes, trying to see more clearly. "It looks as though someone has discarded their castoffs in the ocean."

The colonel snapped awake. "Just what I was thinking, m'dear. I think I'll take a closer look. There might be something there worth salvaging."

Phoebe uttered a shriek of horror. "You'll do no such thing, Frederick. Those disgusting . . . *things* could be full of germs. You could catch some deadly disease. Besides, why on earth would you want some poor peasant's hand-me-downs? We have more than enough fine clothes to wear. Really, if you think—"

She broke off as her husband uttered a sharp exclamation, then dashed off toward the steps leading to the sands.

Phoebe had learned from bitter experience that when

Freddie acted on impulse, more often than not he ended up in serious trouble unless she was there to control the situation. After a moment's hesitation, she picked up her skirt and chased after him.

She reached the top of the steps at the same time her husband leapt onto the sand. Keeping a wary gaze on her buttoned boots while she scrambled down the gritty steps, she slid one hand down the rail to steady herself. She reached the bottom with the dismal thought that at least one of her white kid gloves was beyond repair.

Her feet sank into the soft sand, and she had trouble following in the colonel's footsteps. Her temper rising, she clutched her umbrella like a weapon as she advanced on him. The wind from the ocean bit into her face with icy fingers, and she could feel the chill right down to her bones. Frederick would have to pay for this outrage, she vowed, as she finally reached his side.

He stood quite still, looking down at the bundle. She followed his gaze.

At first glance she noticed only that the clothes had belonged to a man. Her next glance confirmed what her mind had at first refused to accept. The owner of the clothes was still inside them and, judging from his gray shriveled face, he no longer had any need of them.

With a little sigh, Phoebe closed her eyes and let the darkness take her.

With the advent of Edward VII on the throne shortly after the turn of the twentieth century, British subjects shrugged off the heavy blanket of decorum and constraint dictated by the late Queen Victoria, and embraced a new age of decadence. Lavish banquets, high jinks on the racecourses, and most especially jaunts to the seaside had become the custom for the wealthy, and the Pennyfoot Country Club was in high demand.

No sooner had Cecily Sinclair Baxter recovered from the busy summer season, during which London's aristocrats had arrived in droves to bask in the clean, balmy air of England's southeast coast, than she was almost immediately thrown into the frantic preparations for yet another Christmas season at the Pennyfoot.

It seemed to her that the holiday season arrived earlier each year. Either that, or time was flying past faster than ever before. Gazing at the profusion of holly and fir adorning the mantelpiece, she found it hard to believe that Christmas Eve was just four days away.

She remarked to her husband, who was seated in front of a roaring fire with his feet propped up on the fender, "Why is it that no matter how early we begin to make plans for Christmas, invariably we end up racing against the clock to complete them?"

Absorbed in his newspaper, Baxter appeared not to hear her.

Cecily leaned forward in her chair and tapped him on the knee. "Darling?"

Baxter slowly lowered the newspaper. "Did you say something?"

"It must be an interesting story."

"Just some drivel about the impact of exhaust fumes from

motorcars on pedestrians' lungs. Good Lord, why do people waste time on such nonsense? It's not as if we walk behind exhaust pipes breathing in the smoke."

"No, dear, but I imagine some of that smoke gets mixed in with the air that we do breathe."

Baxter grunted. "There's nothing but depressing news in the paper these days." He shook the page at her. "Look at this. The price of everything is going up, there was a fire in Whitehall and paintings stolen from the National Gallery, and they want to raise taxes on spirits. Can't we ever get good news in the newspaper?" He frowned. "What was it you were saying?"

"I was saying that sometimes I wonder how we manage to get everything done in time for Christmas."

"By *we* I assume you are referring to our staff, and not including me in that observance?"

Cecily smiled. "Of course I meant the staff, dear. I wouldn't dream of expecting you to involve yourself in all this chaos."

Baxter narrowed his eyes. "Do I detect a touch of sarcasm in that sweet voice?"

"Why, darling, what on earth gave you that impression?"

Sighing, Baxter folded his newspaper. "Very well. What is it you wish me to do?"

Cecily gave him a suspicious stare. It wasn't like her husband to volunteer his services unless she was in dire need. Especially when he was so comfortably ensconced in his favorite armchair in the quiet privacy of their suite.

When she'd agreed to take over the management of the country club, she'd been resigned to the fact that Baxter had his own business to take care of, and would have neither the time nor the inclination to help with her duties. To be fair, there had been occasions when he had stepped in admirably when she most needed it, but the day-to-day chores of running an efficient establishment were hers to supervise.

To be even fairer, she preferred it that way.

Nevertheless, Baxter's offer of help was so rare, she couldn't possibly refuse for fear he may never offer again. "Well, now that you mention it," she murmured, "I do need someone to make sure the new stable manager's assistant is suitable for the position. He's working on a probationary status at the moment. I've been meaning to talk to Charlie Muggins about him."

Baxter frowned. "What does Charlie have to do with anything?"

"Don't you remember, dear? Charlie Muggins took over from Samuel when he left. He's now our stable manager and Henry Simmons is his new assistant. He's a little fragile—Henry, that is—and rather on the short side, but he seems intelligent and certainly appears to know a lot about motorcar engines."

Baxter shook his head. "All this change going on. It's no wonder I can't keep anything straight. I can't believe Samuel's gone. He'd been with us so long. How's he doing, anyway?"

Cecily winced. She missed her former stable manager dreadfully, and any mention of him gave her fresh pain. "From what I hear, the motorcar repair shop he opened up with Gilbert is doing quite well. Which is just as well, seeing that Samuel is marrying Pansy in a few days."

"So I suppose Pansy will be leaving us as well, then?"

"Yes, dear. Right after the wedding. I've already found a housemaid to replace her. Lilly Green seems to be a very nice young woman. Pansy is training her. She's most anxious to please, and I think she'll work out well."

"And our maintenance man?"

"Clive's new toy shop is doing extremely well, so I've heard. Of course, it's Christmastime, so I imagine he's been quite busy of late. Things are bound to slow down a bit after the New Year."

"I meant the new chap. What's his name?"

"Jacob Pinstone." Cecily held her hands out to the fire to warm her chilled fingers. "I'm not so confident about him. I hired him out of desperation. I had just three applicants for Clive's job, and Jacob was the lesser of the evils, I'm afraid. Apparently he used to be in the Royal Navy, but when I inquired about it he seemed most reluctant to discuss it. Still, he seems to be competent enough, though I do miss Clive."

Baxter grunted. "I don't know why everyone had to leave at once. It puts the whole place in a state of upheaval."

Cecily raised her chin. "I think we manage everything quite well, all things considered. The guests seem happy enough."

Baxter leaned forward and patted her hand. "Of course, of course. I didn't mean that the operation of the country club is any less efficient or gratifying. I simply meant that it made things more difficult for you, having to deal with all these changes in our staff. In spite of everything, you've managed to carry on as usual, in a most admirable way."

Compliments from her husband were rare, and Cecily smiled her pleasure. "Thank you, darling. I do—"

A sharp rapping on the door interrupted her. Rising to her feet she murmured, "That's most likely Phoebe. She's coming over this afternoon to prepare the ballroom for her presentation."

Baxter groaned. "Not another fiasco."

"Now, now, dear." Cecily headed for the door. "Phoebe's pantomimes provide a great deal of entertainment for our guests."

"Only because they're waiting to see how badly she can foul things up."

Cecily wisely decided not to answer that. Instead, she pulled open the door and smiled at the young woman waiting outside.

Lilly Green was taller than the rest of the maids, with the exception of Gertie McBride, the Pennyfoot's chief housemaid. Gertie not only had the benefit of height over the rest of the downstairs staff, she had the girth as well, which would have made her quite formidable had it not been for her jovial nature.

Lilly, on the other hand, was so painfully thin, Baxter had been heard to remark that if the maid turned sideways only her nose would be visible.

At that moment she appeared somewhat distressed, and Cecily was quick to respond. "What is it, Lilly? Has something happened?"

Behind her she heard Baxter groan. Not that she could blame him. It seemed that every Christmas season something tragic happened at the Pennyfoot. In fact, the misfortune had become so prevalent, the staff referred to it as the Christmas curse.

Judging from the expression on Lilly's scrawny face, it seemed likely the curse had struck again. Her voice was barely above a whisper when she answered. "I believe it's a friend of yours, m'm. The gentleman she's with has white hair and a bushy beard. He's not making much sense. He carried her into the lobby, but I gathered from what he said that he can't carry her up the stairs."

Cecily's chill robbed her of speech for a moment.

"What is it?" Baxter demanded from across the room.

Clutching the doorjamb, Cecily said faintly, "I believe something is wrong with Phoebe. We must go downstairs at once."

"Of course." Baxter arrived at her side and took her arm.

"Thank you, Lilly," Cecily murmured, as the maid curtsied. "We'll take care of things."

"Yes, m'm." Looking relieved, Lilly scurried off.

Cecily looked up at her husband. "Oh, Bax, whatever can be wrong with Phoebe? I couldn't bear it if . . ." She let her voice trail off, unable to put her fears into words.

He gave her arm a little squeeze. "I suggest we go down and find out."

She allowed him to lead her along the hallway to the stairs. Her mind seemed incapable of functioning. Phoebe had been one of her two closest friends for a good many years. The other, Madeline Pengrath Prestwick, would be just as devastated if something dreadful were to happen to dear Phoebe. The two of them invariably bickered with each other when they met, but underneath the feuding, Cecily knew, was a bond that would never be broken.

Her eyes misted as she hurried down the stairs, with

Baxter close behind. Life without Phoebe was just unthinkable.

She couldn't control a cry of dismay when she reached the lobby and saw her longtime friend seated on the floor, her back propped up by the wall. Phoebe's chin rested on her chest, and her hat had tilted forward, obscuring her face. Its wide brim held a trio of white doves nestled among swirling blue chiffon and velvet ribbons. It looked a little pathetic perched on its owner's slumped head.

Standing at her side, Colonel Fortescue seemed bewildered, staring helplessly down at his wife.

Cecily hurried forward, calling out to Baxter, "Could you give Kevin Prestwick a ring, please? Ask him to come here as soon as possible."

She didn't hear his answer. At the sound of her voice, the colonel switched his gaze to her face. "She fainted dead away, old bean. One minute she was standing there, the next she was on the sand."

Cecily blinked. "The sand? You were on the beach in this weather?" She dropped to the floor and gently tilted Phoebe's hat up. Her friend's face was as gray as parchment and her eyes were tightly closed. She appeared to be breathing, however, which eased Cecily's mind somewhat.

"We went down there to see what was in the castoffs, old girl." The colonel seemed to suddenly remember he was wearing a hat, and pulled it from his head.

Cecily frowned. "Castoffs?"

"Well, that's what we thought they were. Never expected to find what we did." The colonel rocked back on his heels and stared up at the ceiling. "Reminds me of when I was in—"

Cecily surged upright. "Enough, Colonel! I need you to tell me exactly what happened."

The colonel's mouth snapped shut. Obviously he wasn't used to being so rudely interrupted.

Cecily felt a moment's regret then quickly suppressed it. Colonel Fortescue was notorious for launching into one of his war stories at the slightest opportunity, and once he was in full stride nothing short of a shotgun to the head would stop him. "I'm sorry, Colonel," she added, "but it's imperative you tell me exactly what happened on that beach."

The colonel shook his head, as if trying to clear his mind. "What happened? Dashed if I know, old bean. She took one look at the body and dropped to the ground."

Cecily swallowed. "Body?"

"Yes, old girl. That's what was in the castoffs. Though I suppose they're not really castoffs if the chap is still wearing them. Even if he is deader than a doornail, what what?"

Cecily felt like sinking to the floor herself. She spoke carefully, making sure to enunciate every word. "Are you telling me, Colonel, that there's a dead body on the beach?"

"Well, of course I am." A look of uncertainty crossed his face. "I mean, I suppose he's still there. I just picked up the old girl and carried her up here." He looked down at his wife. "She might not look all that heavy but it felt like I was carrying a blasted elephant."

"I heard that."

At the sound of the weak voice, Cecily looked down at

11

her friend. To her immense relief, Phoebe's eyes were not only open, they were glaring up at her husband, reassuring Cecily that Phoebe was not at death's door after all.

"Phoebe!" Cecily squatted down again. "Are you all right?"

"I will be when I can get up off this dratted floor." She scowled at the lobby, which, fortunately for everyone, was deserted. "Get me up this instant, before someone comes in and sees me in this ridiculous position."

Cecily grabbed her under an arm, and signaled to the colonel to take hold of the other. Between them they hauled Phoebe to her feet. She immediately tugged at her hat to straighten it, then slapped at her skirts to get rid of the sand that still clung to the folds.

Just then Baxter strode into the lobby. "I rang Prestwick—oh!" He raised his eyebrows at Phoebe. "The lady seems to have recovered."

Before Phoebe could answer, Cecily cut in. "You'll have to ring him again, I'm afraid. As well as P.C. Northcott."

Baxter stared at her. "You want me to ring for a police constable?"

"Yes, Baxter. Tell them both there's a dead body on the beach." She turned to the colonel. "Whereabouts would you say it is, Colonel?"

The colonel waved his arm at the door. "Just a few yards down from the steps. Looked like it washed up from the ocean. Better tell them to hurry before the tide takes it out to sea again."

Cecily felt sick as she watched her husband disappear back down the hallway leading to her office. She took a deep breath, telling herself that just because a body was on the beach didn't mean that it had anything to do with the Pennyfoot. Even so, she couldn't shake the uneasy feeling that there was a connection somewhere, and that sooner or later, she'd be in the thick of it.

She looked up as the front door opened and a slim woman with flowing black hair sailed in on a blast of wind, followed by two footmen carrying large boxes. Catching sight of the small group at the foot of the stairs, she floated toward them, bare toes peeking out of open mesh sandals beneath the hem of her billowing yellow skirt.

"Mercy, this is all we need," Phoebe muttered, and tugged on her long gloves to cover her elbows.

Cecily greeted the newcomer with a wave of her hand. "Madeline! I forgot you were coming here today."

"I brought the last of the decorations." Madeline glanced at the bare branches of the tall Christmas tree standing in the corner. "I still have that tree and the one in the library to decorate." She signaled with a wave of her hand, and the footmen placed the boxes at the foot of the tree, then disappeared out the door.

Cecily managed a wan smile. Madeline had been decorating the Pennyfoot for Christmas ever since it had originally opened as a hotel. Until she had married Dr. Kevin Prestwick, she had lived in a small cottage at the edge of the woods and handpicked the holly, mistletoe, and greenery that she used so abundantly.

An expert with herbs and flowers, she had often mixed potions to cure the local villagers of an array of ailments, and many a husband had benefited greatly from her passion potions, as she called them. Her skills went beyond the herbal remedies, however, and in many households, her unusual abilities had earned her a reputation of a witch.

Some feared her because of it, but those who made use of her talents were loath to question her methods. Since she had married Dr. Kevin Prestwick and become a mother, her standing in the village had improved dramatically. Most chose to ignore the mystery that surrounded the respected doctor's wife, and that suited Madeline just fine.

Right now, she was gazing at Phoebe as if trying to read her mind. "You have had a nasty shock," she said at last.

Phoebe raised her chin. "I had a small mishap, that's all." She peered up at the colonel, who was beaming at Madeline and paying no attention to his wife. "Frederick. I thought you were planning a visit to the bar."

Hearing the magic word, the colonel shot a glance at Phoebe. "By Jove, old girl. You're absolutely right. High time I toddled off. Cheerio!" Apparently happily dismissing everything that had happened earlier that afternoon, he headed for the hallway and vanished.

Phoebe fanned her face with her gloved hand. "I really would like to sit down. Preferably somewhere warm."

"Of course." Cecily glanced at Madeline. "We'll go up to my suite. Would you care to join us?"

Madeline nodded at the Christmas tree. "I must get started on that tree. I promised little Angelina's nanny I would be home for supper. Heaven knows when Kevin will be home."

Cecily felt a little stab of guilt. "Goodness. I should have mentioned this before. Baxter is ringing Kevin right now.

Phoebe and the colonel found a dead body on the beach. I imagine Kevin will be calling in here after he's examined the body. No doubt Sam Northcott will be with him."

Madeline had gone very still. Her dark eyes seemed to burn brightly in her face when she answered. "Oh dear. I'm afraid this means more trouble for you, Cecily."

Cecily felt a tug of apprehension. "What do you mean?"

Phoebe clicked her tongue. "She's off again. Pay no attention to her, Cecily. All that mumbo jumbo. She makes mountains out of molehills."

Madeline turned her intense gaze on Phoebe. "I would hardly call a dead body a molehill."

Phoebe had the grace to look uncomfortable. "Well, of course not. I merely meant that this couldn't possibly have anything to do with Cecily. It's a body that washed up on the beach. Heaven knows where it went in the ocean. It could have been way up north for all we know." She shuddered. "It certainly looked as if it had been in the water awhile."

Madeline appeared to ignore that. She turned back to Cecily, murmuring, "Be on your guard, Cecily. I could be wrong, but I have a feeling the Pennyfoot is involved somehow."

Fully aware that Madeline's "feelings" often transpired to be facts, Cecily's fears intensified. "I certainly hope you are wrong." She turned to Phoebe. "Come. We'll go up to my suite and I'll order some brandy. You still look pinched from the cold."

Phoebe rubbed her arms. "I am frozen stiff. I need to discuss the preparations for the pantomime before I get started, anyway."

Madeline drifted off toward the tree, and Cecily began

climbing the stairs with Phoebe puffing behind her. Madeline's words kept coming back to her. *The Pennyfoot is involved somehow.* Surely not, she thought, as she rounded the landing on the first floor and began to climb the second set of stairs. Not again.

Just a dead body on the beach. Phoebe was right. It could well have been a nasty accident, and the poor man could have fallen into the ocean anywhere.

Still, she wouldn't relax until she heard from Kevin Prestwick that the death had nothing to do with the country club. And that news couldn't come soon enough.

CHAPTER
❀ 2 ❀

There was rarely a quiet moment in the Pennyfoot's kitchen. One only had to pause in the hallway outside to hear the clatter of dishes, the crashing of pans, the chopping of knives, and the raised voices of the harried staff struggling to keep things running smoothly.

Most of the racket could be attributed to Michel, the country club's chef, who often displayed his displeasure by slinging his kitchenware around with as much gusto as he could muster. When fully aggravated, or after imbibing a generous amount of brandy, he would at times lose the French accent he'd spent years polishing, thus revealing his less than desirable origins, which is why he perfected the accent in the first place.

Right now he was voicing his irritation with a mixture of French words and the occasional Cockney curse.

Pansy Watson rolled her eyes as she pushed open the kitchen door and plunged into the pandemonium that usually prevailed in the busy hours before the evening meal was served.

Michel was at the enormous black stove, where pans bubbled and spit their contents onto the shiny surface. The delicious aroma of spiced goose and garden herbs was marred by the smell of burning gravy. The chef's tall white hat bobbed up and down as he darted back and forth, brandishing a large wooden spoon and yelling words no gentleman would ever use.

Mrs. Chubb, the efficient cook/housekeeper, spared a moment from the pie pastry she was using to cover a plate of sliced apples and glared at the chef. "Michel, watch your tongue. We have young ladies in here."

Michel swung around, dark eyes blazing. "*Ladeez?* I see no ladies. Kitchen staff, that's what I see. *Non?* Where are the ladies?"

Mrs. Chubb dropped the pastry and folded her arms across her buxom bosom. "They are young girls, Michel, and do not need to hear filthy words coming out of your mouth."

Pansy hunched her shoulders, braced for the explosion.

There was a long pause, while Michel glared at the housekeeper, anger smoldering in his thin face. Then he flung down his spoon, dragged off his hat, and threw it on the floor. "You do not like what I say? Then I go. You do not hear me anymore. *Au revoir* and bloody good riddance." With that he shoved past Pansy and stormed out.

Gertie stood at the sink, her back to the housekeeper, as if paying no attention to the mayhem going on behind her.

Pansy could see her friend's shoulders shaking, however, and knew she was trying to control her laughter.

The next moment Gertie turned and looked at Mrs. Chubb. "Now you've bleeding gone and done it."

The housekeeper scowled. "He'll be back. Meanwhile, Gertie McBride, what I said to him goes for you, too. Enough of that bad language. I won't tolerate it in my kitchen."

Seemingly unperturbed, Gertie shrugged. "You should be used to it by now. Everyone else flipping is."

Mrs. Chubb opened her mouth to answer, then apparently thought better of it. "Get over to the stove," she muttered, "and stir that gravy before we lose any more of it."

Gertie wiped her hands on her apron and walked over to the stove.

Pansy jumped as the housekeeper turned to her. "What on earth are you standing there gawking at? Why aren't you upstairs in the dining room? Aren't you supposed to be laying the tables?"

"Yes, Mrs. Chubb." Pansy glanced around the kitchen. "I came down to look for Lilly. She's supposed to be helping me."

"Well, she's not here." Mrs. Chubb spun around to look over at the dumbwaiter, where two maids stood loading china and silverware. "Where the blazes is she, then?"

"Oo," Gertie said softly, "what language!"

Ignoring her, Mrs. Chubb turned back to Pansy. "Get back to the dining room. I'll send someone to look for Lilly."

"Yes, Mrs. Chubb." Pansy turned away, then hesitated. She didn't like tattling on someone, especially another maid, but she felt compelled to say something. Looking back at the housekeeper, she took a deep breath. "There's something I've got to say about Lilly."

The housekeeper's stern expression did nothing to soothe Pansy's anxiety. Stumbling over her words she added, "There's something strange about her."

Mrs. Chubb folded her arms again. Never a good sign. "What do you mean, strange?"

Pansy swallowed. "I mean, she's really nervous. She jumps out of her skin every time I call out her name."

"She's new. Of course she's nervous. Give her time. She'll settle down." Mrs. Chubb leaned forward. "Just like you did."

"Yes, Mrs. Chubb." About to turn away, Pansy hesitated again. "It's just that, well, she says she grew up in an orphanage, and I grew up in one, too, so I know what it's like, but when I asked her about different things, she didn't seem to know nothing about it."

"Per'aps she don't want to talk about it," Gertie said. "You don't like talking about it, neither."

"I know but . . . she just seems . . ." Pansy lifted her hands and let them drop again. "I dunno. I just hope she's ready to take over my job by next week."

Mrs. Chubb's face softened. "For heaven's sake, child, stop worrying about that. You've done a fine job in training her to take your place. You just worry about being ready for your wedding. We'll take care of things here."

Pansy felt the dreaded tears pricking her eyes. Every time she thought about leaving the Pennyfoot, she started to cry. She loved Samuel with all of her heart, and had yearned to be his wife for so long, but she'd seen how upset he was when he left to open his own business. Much as she looked forward to getting married, she dreaded the day she'd walk out of the Pennyfoot for the last time.

Afraid if she tried to speak she'd bawl, she gave Mrs. Chubb a quick nod and fled from the kitchen.

The housekeeper was right, she told herself as she tore up the stairs. Mrs. Chubb and Gertie would take care of Lilly and see that she did a good job. Still, she wished she didn't have the feeling that something wasn't quite right about the new maid.

All she could hope was that it wasn't something that could cause trouble in the kitchen. The last thing she wanted was to leave problems behind because of her departing to get married. Thinking about the wedding cheered her up, however, and she was actually smiling as she headed for the dining room.

"I'm so excited about this year's pantomime," Phoebe declared, as she waited for Cecily to open the doors to the ballroom. "It's the first time we've done *Dick Whittington and His Cat*. I can't wait to see what Clive builds for the setting."

Cecily paused with one hand on the door. "Phoebe, did you forget? Clive is no longer with us. He opened a toy shop in Wellercombe two months ago."

Phoebe's mouth dropped open and her eyes mirrored her distress. "Oh my, I did forget. We had to employ that new janitor—what's his name?"

"Jacob Pinstone. I'm sure he'll be able to satisfy your requirements. He seems quite capable, and after all, we don't really need anything elaborate."

Phoebe's chin shot up, sending her hat rocking back and forth. "*Elaborate?* My dear Cecily, how could you have forgotten the marvelous ship that Clive built for *Peter Pan*, or the wonderful little stable he put up for last year's Nativity play?" She shook her head, and the doves trembled. "Elaborate? How can I possibly replace him? The man is a genius. That Pinstone fellow is not nearly as accommodating. He's quite surly, in fact. Are you quite sure he understood what I need for this presentation? He didn't seem too bright to me."

Fully aware of how much her former maintenance man was missed, Cecily pushed open the door with an impatient hand. "I explained to Jacob in great detail everything you told me you needed. I'm sure he'll do his best. We'll just have to manage somehow. We—" She broke off with a little gasp.

This was the first time she'd seen the ballroom since Madeline had worked her magic again. The spacious room had been turned into a Christmas wonderland. Madeline had hung huge boughs of holly and fragrant pine along the balcony. Wide swaths of red and green satin swooped along the walls, anchored in place by the cherubs that still clung to the pillars, having escaped the renovations when the hotel had been turned into a country club.

Long paper chains of red and gold crisscrossed below the ceiling, and garlands of holly framed every one of the tall, narrow windows. Glittering silver stars fell from the crystal chandeliers, slowly turning in the draft. Cecily couldn't wait to see them reflecting the brilliance when the gaslights were lit that evening.

"Oh my goodness," she murmured. "Madeline has outdone herself."

Phoebe sent a cursory glance around and sniffed. "Yes, very nice. A little pretentious, though, don't you think?"

Deciding it was time to change the subject, Cecily walked over to the stage. "Jacob has been working very hard and I'm quite certain you will be happy with the results."

"Well, I hope he's finished with everything by now. I'm holding a dress rehearsal here the day after tomorrow and we'll need the settings onstage. Setting the pantomime a day earlier this year has upset my schedule. I just hope I can be ready on time."

Cecily smiled. "I'm sure you will be. With Pansy's wedding on Christmas Eve, we had to push everything else forward a day. It's the only way we can fit everything in."

"Well, if you ask me, I think Pansy could have picked a better time for her wedding. She must know how busy everyone is this time of year."

Cecily secretly agreed with her friend, but wasn't about to admit it. "Samuel made Pansy a promise that they would get married by this Christmas. It has taken him this long to get his business started, and he wanted that on solid ground before he took a wife."

Phoebe shrugged. "Ah well, you always did treat your staff as though they were family. Personally I think you worry about them too much. You should be worrying about yourself, and how much extra work all this will put on you."

"I'm happy to do it," Cecily assured her, meaning every word. "We shall miss Pansy sorely, and we all want to give her the very best send-off we can manage. Holding her wedding reception here in the Pennyfoot has been a dream of hers since she first started working here, and we are all happy to give her that dream."

"Well, I—" Phoebe broke off as Lilly appeared in the doorway, her eyes wide with apprehension.

"I'm sorry to disturb you, m'm." She bent her knees in an awkward curtsey. "There's two gentlemen to see you." She slid her gaze sideways at Phoebe, then back again. "There's a *constable*, m'm."

She'd said it as if announcing the presence of the devil. Cecily felt a chill all the way down her back. Madeline's words rang in her head. *I could be wrong, but I have a feeling the Pennyfoot is involved somehow.*

"Thank you, Lilly," she said, doing her best to sound unaffected by the news. "Please see the gentlemen into the library and tell them I'll join them shortly."

"Yes, m'm." Looking worried, Lilly rushed off.

Phoebe sounded shaken when she spoke. "I suppose they're here with regards to the dead body on the beach."

Cecily nodded. "Sam Northcott will probably want to ask you and the colonel about what happened. Though, on second thought, it might be better if you talk to the constable alone. You know how confused the colonel can be at times. Especially after he's visited the bar."

Phoebe groaned. "I do, indeed. You're quite right, Cecily. I shall speak to P.C. Northcott alone. Though I must confess, I'm rather dreading the idea."

"I'll be there with you," Cecily said, leading her friend to the door. "Let us just hope that this whole tragic event can be dealt with quickly and quietly. The last thing we need is for our guests to hear of this."

"Oh, I couldn't agree more." Phoebe shuddered. "I shall

never forget the sight of that poor man all shriveled up and—"

"Phoebe!"

To Cecily's relief Phoebe closed her mouth and didn't speak again as they made their way to the library.

P.C. Northcott stood with his back to the fire when Cecily entered the room. His helmet lay on a chair close by. Kevin had seated himself, but jumped to his feet when the women appeared.

The constable was the first to speak, though he remained close to the fire, warming his backside. "Ah, Mrs. Baxter. Sorry to 'ave to meet again under these h'unfortunate circumstances."

"Yes, indeed, Sam." Cecily turned to Dr. Prestwick. "Kevin, it's good to see you."

"Cecily." Kevin nodded at Phoebe. "Good afternoon, Mrs. Fortescue."

Phoebe became flustered, as she usually did when addressed by Kevin. He was a handsome man, whose surgery was always full of women, most of whom faked ailments just for the opportunity to spend some time with the charming doctor.

There had been a time when Kevin Prestwick had pursued Cecily quite ardently, even though she'd given him not one speck of encouragement. Baxter had never forgotten that, and for a long while treated the doctor with disdain. When it became apparent, however, that Kevin had transferred his affections to Madeline, the tension had eased between them, and now she liked to think that the two men had become firm friends.

Right now Kevin's chiseled features wore a grave frown, intensifying Cecily's anxiety. He looked about to speak, but Sam Northcott was too quick for him.

"We 'ave identified the deceased discovered on the beach," the constable announced in his pompous voice of authority.

"At least we think we have," Kevin said, earning a scowl of annoyance from Northcott. "The chap was obviously killed by some vagrant who robbed him of everything of value. We found a name on a label inside his coat." Kevin's eyes were full of concern when he looked at Cecily. "The name is G. Evans."

Cecily's neck began to tingle. "We have a guest of that name. I saw him just this morning leaving the dining room after breakfast."

Kevin took a step forward. "Can you describe him?"

"Yes, I think so. Light brown hair, rather tall and thin. Oh, and he had a scar on his chin in the shape of a V. I remember wondering if he was hurt as a child."

Kevin exchanged a glance with the constable. "I'm sorry, Cecily. It appears the dead man was your guest."

"We surmised as much," Northcott said, "when we found a receipt for a bottle of scotch from your bar."

He might well have said that in the beginning, Cecily thought, struggling to remain calm. "I see. I'm so sorry. Was there any indication of how he died?"

"He was stabbed, m'm," Northcott announced with relish, putting any hope of an accident out of Cecily's mind. "Right in the heart. Whoever did it knew what he was doing."

Phoebe uttered a soft moan and clutched her throat.

Afraid the woman was about to faint again, Cecily forgot her own anxiety and helped her friend onto a chair.

Oblivious to Phoebe's distress, the constable blithely continued. "The killer must have shoved the poor blighter in the ocean hoping he'd go out to sea. Must not have realized the tide was coming in, not going out." Northcott shook his head. "They always slip up somehow, sooner or later."

Kevin shot the policeman a dark look. "Mr. Evans hadn't been in the water all that long. He was probably killed somewhere close by. I'd say the killer used a hunting knife. The victim was stabbed three times, once through the heart. We're going to need any paperwork you have concerning this man, Cecily, so that we may find out where he lives and inform his next of kin."

Cecily decided she needed to sit down as well. "There isn't any paperwork to speak of, I'm afraid. According to my reception manager, Mr. Gerald Evans walked into the Pennyfoot and asked for a room. He said he wasn't satisfied with the hotel he was staying at and was looking for somewhere else to stay. Luckily we'd had a cancellation so we were able to accommodate him. He signed the guest book, but I don't know if he wrote down his full address. You are welcome to take a look, of course."

Northcott cleared his throat and dragged a crumpled notebook out of his uniform pocket. From the other pocket he produced a well-worn pencil. After giving the end of it a quick lick, he started to scribble down words on the pad.

"Nah then, Mrs. B.," he said, peering down at Cecily, "just to set matters straight, I have to ask the following questions. Did the deceased have any communication with anyone else here in the hotel?"

"Country club," Cecily murmured. Baxter was always

correcting her when she called the Pennyfoot a hotel, a habit that she found totally unnecessary and somewhat annoying. It was even more irritating to find herself doing the same thing.

Before she could say anything else, Northcott said a little testily, "This h'establishment, then."

"Quite." She sighed. "No, Sam. As far as I know, the gentleman was here alone. He was alone when he arrived two days ago and he dined alone. I didn't see him speak to anyone else. Then again, I have no way of knowing what he did when he was out of sight. Except . . ." She paused, wondering if what she was about to say next would be significant.

The constable cleared his throat. "Except what?"

"I do know Mr. Evans was fond of walking on the beach. I noticed more than once that he left a trail of sand when he walked across the lobby. I was going to have a word with him about it, but I never got around to it."

"So the killer probably followed him on the beach and waited for a chance to attack him." Northcott scribbled furiously in his notebook. "Did he say which hotel he was staying in before he came here?"

"I don't think so, but Philip, my reception manager, might know."

He turned to Phoebe, who sat rocking back and forth, her hands clasped together as if in prayer. "Now, Mrs. Fortescue, per'aps you can tell me what you saw on the beach."

Phoebe answered in a quivering voice that was barely audible. "I saw what appeared to be a bundle of clothing. When I got closer, I saw it was a man." She visibly shuddered. "A dead man."

"Did you touch 'im?"

Phoebe sat up straight. "Are you completely insane? Why on earth would I touch that . . . *thing*. I took one look and fainted dead away. I don't remember anything else until I came to here in the lobby."

"What about the colonel, m'm? Did he touch anything?"

Phoebe's voice was getting stronger by the minute. "My good man." She struggled to her feet. "The *second* I fell, my husband scooped me up in his arms and carried me all the way to the Pennyfoot. I can assure you of that. No, he did not touch anything."

Northcott had backed up a step. He cleared his throat one more time. "Just had to make sure, m'm." He snapped his notebook shut and shoved it in his pocket. "That's all for now, then. I'd like to take a look at that guest book, and then I'll go down to the kitchen." He gave Cecily a meaningful look that she interpreted at once.

"While you're there, Sam, tell Mrs. Chubb that I offered you a taste of her mince pies."

The constable beamed as he reached for his helmet. "Thank you kindly, m'm. Much obliged, I'm sure."

"Not at all, Sam."

He hesitated, and she waited, wary of what he'd say next.

"There's just one more thing. If it's all right with you, m'm, I'd like to take a look at Mr. Evans's room. The h'inspector likes us to be thorough in our investigations."

It was the last thing Cecily wanted, but she could see no way to refuse. "Of course." She turned to Kevin. "Would you find Colonel Fortescue and ask him to come to the library, please? I think Phoebe should go home and rest. She's had quite a traumatic experience."

Phoebe raised a hand in protest. "But Cecily, dear, we haven't fully discussed the pantomime. I wanted to go over the entire production with you and hear your comments and suggestions before I make my preparations."

Knowing that all Phoebe really wanted was approval, Cecily clasped her friend's hand. "My dear Phoebe, I have complete faith in you. Your presentations are always impeccable in taste and highly entertaining. I'm quite sure that this year's pantomime will be no exception. Now, I'm sorry, but I must accompany P.C. Northcott to Mr. Evans's room. Go home and get some rest, and by tomorrow you will have all the energy and spirit you need.

Looking somewhat mollified, Phoebe nodded. "Oh, very well." She glanced at Kevin. "Please do not trouble yourself on my account, Dr. Prestwick. I know exactly where to find my husband and he will leave far more promptly if I'm there to drag him away from the bar."

Kevin's mouth twitched, but he looked perfectly serious when he answered. "Are you quite sure, Mrs. Fortescue? It's no trouble, I assure you."

"Quite sure, thank you." Phoebe reached for her umbrella. "Besides, I believe your wife is around somewhere, hoping you will take her home. She was decorating the tree in the lobby the last time I saw her."

"Then I shall go there to see if she is waiting for me. Thank you, Mrs. Fortescue."

Obviously dazzled by his smile, Phoebe dipped her head and scurried off to the door, calling over her shoulder, "Goodbye for now, Cecily. I hope you find out where that poor man lives. There must be someone waiting for him to come home."

"We'll do our best," Cecily promised. She looked at Northcott as the door closed behind her friend. "If you'd care to come with me, Sam, I'll take you to Mr. Evans's room. I just have to stop at the desk for the key. You can look at the guest book while we're there."

The constable nodded, picked up his helmet, nodded again at Kevin, and followed Cecily out the door.

Cecily didn't see the doctor leave. She noticed as she crossed the lobby that Madeline had finished decorating the tree. It looked magnificent as always, and she couldn't wait to examine it closely when she had more time.

Right now she had to search the room of a dead man—a man who had been a guest at the Pennyfoot when he was brutally murdered. As sad and unsettling as that was, at least this time she wouldn't have to be hot on the trail of a cold-blooded killer.

CHAPTER

❋ 3 ❋

If there was one thing Cecily couldn't abide it was watching
P.C. Northcott rummaging around in one of her guest rooms.
Even if that guest was no longer alive. Even more so in that
case. Sam Northcott tended to rifle through drawers full of
personal belongings with an avid curiosity that was far beyond
his official duty.

She watched him lift a pile of shirts from the drawer.
"Cheap material," he muttered, fingering the top garment.
"Must do his own laundry. These look like they've been
dragged around in the Thames."

To hasten the procedure, Cecily decided to take matters
into her own hands. "We really should inspect beneath the
bed," she told the constable, as he prepared to open yet another
drawer.

Northcott stared at her as if she'd lost her mind. "Under the bed, m'm?"

"Yes, Sam." She gave him an encouraging smile. "In the past when I've had occasion to search a room, I've found all sorts of interesting things hidden under the bed."

Northcott's eyes lit up. "Is that so? Well, then, I shall h'endeavor to get down on my knees and take a good look."

"Good." Cecily crossed the room to the chest of drawers. "Meanwhile, I'll finish searching the drawers for you."

"Oh, I don't know about that, Mrs. B. After all, it's my job to do the investigating."

Cecily pulled open a drawer. "Now, Sam, you know me well enough to know that I'm quite capable of conducting a thorough search. After all, I've done so many times before and, may I add, I've contributed to the capture of many a criminal in the process."

"You have that, m'm, but—"

"You know, if we don't finish up here shortly, it might be too late for you to have a taste of Mrs. Chubb's mince pies. Once she's caught up in the suppertime rush, she won't have time to cater to you."

Northcott opened his mouth, then shut it again and dropped to his knees without a word.

Pleased with herself, Cecily carefully sorted through the socks, handkerchiefs, and starched collars. She was about to close the drawer when she spotted something in the corner. It seemed to be a torn piece of cardboard, with a corrugated padding.

She was turning it over in her hand when she heard the constable grunt as he climbed to his feet.

"Not as young as I used to be," he muttered, brushing dust from his tunic.

Cecily was about to slip the cardboard into the pocket of her skirt when Northcott asked abruptly, "Whatcha got there, then?"

Sighing, she held it up. "Just a piece of cardboard, that's all."

Northcott grunted again. "Too blinking lazy to throw it in the waste paper basket."

Pushing the cardboard into her pocket, she murmured, "Speaking of the waste paper basket, I should take a look in there. The maids won't have had time to clean the room yet." Before the constable could forestall her, she hurried over to the basket and tipped the contents onto the bed. Out fell an assortment of mint wrappers, a torn train ticket, and a crumpled, out-of-date notice of a Christmas bazaar that was held at St. Bartholomew's church three days earlier.

Northcott joined her at the bedside and poked a wary finger at the wrappers. "Nothing much there but rubbish."

Cecily was inclined to agree. She started to replace the contents of the basket, but then another piece of crumpled paper caught her eye. She closed her fingers over it, but the constable had sharp eyes.

"What's that?"

Cecily sighed, and unraveled the paper. Smoothing it out with her fingers, she held it up to the fading light from the window. "It looks like a note of some sort." She read the words out loud. "'Spotsman seen nearby. Already made run. No sign batman. Still looking. Stop.'"

Northcott frowned. "Makes no sense to me. Let me take a look."

Reluctantly, Cecily handed the note over.

Northcott stared at it for several long seconds, then uttered an exclamation. "Got it! It's got something to do with cricket. Look!" He pointed out the words to her. "He must have been in a bloomin' hurry when he wrote this. He spelled sportsman wrong."

"So he did," Cecily murmured.

"Well, when you look at it now, it makes sense." Proud of his achievement, Northcott puffed out his chest. "Look, 'sportsman seen nearby. Already made run.' Cricket's a sport and you have to make runs, right?"

Cecily nodded in agreement.

"Well, then, it says 'no sign of batman.' That's the next chap up to bat. See? Cricket! He must have been involved with a cricket match."

Cecily frowned. "In the middle of winter?"

Northcott blinked. "Well . . . er . . . I s'pose some people play cricket in the winter." He looked back at the paper. "Yes, that's what it is, all right. A cricket match. Now, if I can just find out where it's being played, I might at least find someone who knows where this chap lives."

Cecily plucked the paper from Northcott's hand. "Good idea, Sam. Why don't you get to work on that." She looked around the room. "I really don't see anything else of interest here."

Northcott headed for the door. "All right, Mrs. B. I'll just pop by the kitchen and see if anyone down there knows anything, then I'll be off." He paused, looking back at her.

"You know I'll have to report this to the inspector. We're dealing with a murder, here. He'll want to know about it."

Cecily felt her stomach muscles clench. She considered Inspector Cranshaw a bitter enemy. Having long suspected that illegal card games were being held in secret rooms under the floorboards of the Pennyfoot, he'd sought long and hard to shut down the hotel.

Now that the hotel was a country club, the card games were no longer illegal. The secret rooms had been closed off, and gentlemen played their games in the new card rooms upstairs. That hadn't stopped the inspector from seeking a way to put an end to the Pennyfoot once and for all. Every time they met, the inspector and Cecily conducted a cat and mouse game that invariably played havoc with her nerves. She was mortally afraid that one day the inspector would win, and the Pennyfoot would be lost to everyone.

Staring hard at Sam, she said quietly, "Will you and your wife be taking your usual Christmas holiday in London?"

The constable nodded. "All being well, yes. We'll be off day after tomorrow."

"It might well take a long time to solve this murder."

Northcott looked worried. "I suppose it might."

"If the inspector is here, he will insist on you staying here until it is solved."

Northcott's face took on a look of desperation. "He will, that."

"Perhaps you should wait awhile before informing him. Until you have more evidence to give him. After all, you don't even know where the victim lived."

Relief banished the pained look from the constable's face.

"You're quite right, Mrs. B. We need to find out first where our victim came from." He pulled back his shoulders. "Which I shall h'endeavor to do first thing in the morning. I'm going to find that cricket match and we'll see what we shall see. Thank you, m'm. I bid you good night." With that, he opened the door, stepped out into the dark, and gently closed it behind him.

Cecily let out her breath. Sam Northcott's eyes might be sharp, but his brain had trouble keeping up. At least she had bought some time. The last thing she needed was Inspector Cranshaw badgering her guests over the Christmas holidays.

So far there was nothing to indicate that Gerald Evans's death had any connection to anyone else in the club. She couldn't dismiss Madeline's cryptic words, however, and it was with an uneasy heart that she made her way back to her suite. A good night's sleep would go a long way toward reviving her, she told herself. In the morning all this would seem like nothing more than a bad dream.

Gertie wasn't normally the first one to go out in the courtyard in the morning. Usually one of the maids was sent out to fill the coal scuttles, drag the laundry off the clotheslines, or fetch in the milk urns left on the doorstep by the milkman.

This morning, however, Gertie had been woken up early by her exuberant twins. She'd promised to take them to see Clive's toy shop that afternoon, and they were both too excited to sleep. Gertie had washed and dressed them both, and left them to wait for Daisy, their nanny, to give them breakfast.

Arriving in the kitchen before anyone else, Gertie headed

for the stove. The cold tiles beneath her feet chilled the vast room, and she couldn't wait to get the coals glowing. To her dismay the scuttles were empty and she had no choice but to fill them herself. It was a job she hated, and she wasn't feeling too cheerful as she stepped outside.

White clouds scudded across a pale blue sky, and sparkling diamonds of frost coated the line of sheets swaying in the sea breeze. Some poor bugger would have to pry the clothes-pegs off the line and haul solid frozen sheets into the kitchen to thaw before she could fold them.

Gertie was just glad it wasn't her. Carrying the scuttles, she started across the courtyard, dreading the moment when she'd have to walk into the dark, dusty, smelly bowels of the coal shed.

She had barely taken a dozen steps when she spotted the bundle lying at the very edge of the yard.

Thinking that some of the laundry had blown off the line, she muttered a curse, dropped the scuttles, and hurried forward to pick it up. It would all have to be washed again, she was thinking as she drew closer. Then her heart stopped, and began beating again twice as fast as before.

It wasn't a bundle of clothes at all. It was a young woman lying curled into a ball, her eyes closed in her chalk white face.

Once, not too long ago, Gertie had found a maid murdered in the coal shed. It was the reason she hated going in there. It had taken her weeks to stop seeing in her dreams that awful look on the dead woman's face.

Now, it seemed, she was destined to go through all that again. Quickly she shut her eyes and turned her back on the woman. Last time she'd fainted. This time she had to get help. She took a step toward the kitchen, then halted when she heard a faint moan behind her.

Heart pounding, she turned back. She hadn't imagined it. The woman's eyes were flickering open. She was alive!

Bursting with gratitude, Gertie dropped to her knees beside the still form. "Are you hurt? Can you get up?"

The pale blue eyes stared back at her, full of confusion. "I don't know."

The words were the softest of whispers, and Gertie had to lean down to hear her. "Here, I'll help you." She put her hand under the frail arm and gave it a little tug.

Shivering and teeth chattering, the woman got to her knees, then unsteadily to her feet.

She swayed so much Gertie was afraid the woman would fall. She grabbed both her arms. "Steady on there, luv. What's your name?"

The woman opened her mouth, hesitated, then closed her mouth again, her eyes widening. "I don't know," she whispered again.

It was Gertie's turn to stare. "You don't know your own name?"

The woman gave a quick shake of her head, followed by a moan.

It was no wonder the poor thing was shivering, Gertie thought. All she had on was a thin woolen frock. "Where's your coat? Where did you come from? How did you get here?"

Tears formed in the woman's eyes and dribbled down her cheeks. She opened her mouth to speak, but Gertie said it for her.

"Don't tell me. You don't bloody know." She started for

the kitchen, dragging the other woman by her arm. "Come on, let's get you warmed up before you bleeding freeze to death. You'll be lucky you don't get pneumonia, lying out there in the cold. How long have you been out there, anyway? All right, I know. You don't know."

She shoved open the door and pushed the stranger inside. "Wait there for me. Go and stand by the stove until I get back with the coal."

Hoping no one would come into the kitchen until she got back, Gertie sprinted across the yard, snatching up the scuttles as she tore by.

It took her several minutes to fill the heavy cast iron containers, and she had to watch her feet as she carried them back to the kitchen, for fear she'd slip on the icy ground. Backing into the kitchen with a scuttle in each hand, she called out, "I'm back, so we'll soon get you warm."

"What's going on here, then?"

At the sound of Mrs. Chubb's voice, Gertie spun around.

The housekeeper stood just inside the door, arms crossed, eyes fixed on the cowering, shivering woman by the stove.

Sighing, Gertie dumped the scuttles on the floor, sending a chunk or two of coal skittering across the tiles. "I found her lying out in the courtyard. She's bloody freezing in that thin frock."

Mrs. Chubb stepped forward, a frown wrinkling her forehead. "Are you hurt? What were you doing in the courtyard?"

Through chattering teeth the woman whispered, "I don't know."

"That's all she can say." Gertie picked up one of the scuttles again and carried it over to the stove. Bending over, she pulled open the hatch, grabbed a small shovel, and started feeding coal into the opening.

"What's your name?" Mrs. Chubb demanded.

"She doesn't know." Gertie straightened. "I think she's foreign and doesn't speak English. All she knows how to say is, 'I don't know.'"

As if to contradict her, the woman muttered, "My head hurts."

"Well," Mrs. Chubb said, "it seems she can speak some English." She walked over to the closet and opened it. Reaching inside, she pulled out a thick, blue woolen shawl. "Here." She walked back to the stranger and draped it around her shaking shoulders. "This'll help."

The woman clutched the shawl as if it were a life belt. "Thank you."

"Okay, ducks. Now tell us your name."

Tears welled up in the woman's eyes again. "I don't know. I don't remember anything before I opened my eyes out there." She nodded at the door to the yard. "I woke up and saw that lady and that's all I remember."

Mrs. Chubb's frown intensified. "What lady?"

The woman pointed at Gertie.

Mrs. Chubb rolled her eyes. "That's not a lady. That's Gertie, my chief housemaid."

Gertie pretended to be offended. Tossing her chin she said loudly, "Well, ta ever so."

"Oh, you know what I mean." The housekeeper gave the stranger another intent look. "You don't remember anything?"

The woman shook her head.

"Well, sit down here." Mrs. Chubb pulled out a chair from

the kitchen table. "I'll make us a nice cup of tea and I'll put a drop of brandy in it. Maybe that will shake up your memory."

"Better not let Michel know you're giving away his brandy." Gertie fetched the other scuttle and stood it by the stove. "He'll have a flipping pink fit."

"I decide where the brandy goes. Not Michel." Mrs. Chubb glanced at the clock. "Put the kettle on, Gertie. We'll have time for a cuppa before the rest of them get here. Then you can take Miss Memory up to Madam to ask her what's to be done."

Gertie raised her eyebrows. "Miss Memory?"

"We have to call her something, don't we?" Mrs. Chubb took the woman's arm and guided her into the chair. "Sit down, ducks. You'll feel better after the tea."

Gertie filled the kettle and carried it to the stove. "I could use a cuppa meself."

"Why are you up so early, anyway?" Mrs. Chubb spoke over her shoulder as she reached into a cupboard for some cups. "Who's watching the twins?"

"They're watching themselves." Gertie took the cups from her and waited for the saucers. "Daisy will be down soon, and they'll be good until their nanny gets there. They know what will happen if they're not."

Miss Memory stared at her with alarm in her soft blue eyes.

"I told them Father Christmas won't bring them any toys if they don't behave," Gertie hastened to tell her, just in case the woman thought she was beating her children.

Just then the door swung open and Michel rushed in, shouting at the top of his voice. "*Sacre bleu!* Why eez everyone standing around doing nothing, eh? Why is—" He stopped short and stared at the woman seated at the table. "Who are you? What are you doing in my kitchen?"

Gertie stared at Miss Memory in surprise. Michel was tall, and loud, and could, at times, be a bit overpowering, but she had never seen anyone shrink away from him like he was some terrible, ugly monster. The woman was practically sliding off her chair as if she was trying to get under the table.

Even Michel seemed surprised. He took off his white chef's hat, scratched his head, and looked at Mrs. Chubb. "What eez the matter with her?"

Mrs. Chubb looked just as mystified. "I think she's ill," she said, tapping a knowing finger at her forehead.

"Ah." Michel put his hat back on. It flopped over on one side, giving him the look of a comical clown.

Miss Memory wasn't laughing. She looked terrified.

Michel tiptoed past her, murmuring, "What will you do with her?"

"Give her a cup of tea," Gertie announced, adding gleefully, "with a good dollop of brandy."

Michel stopped short. "*My* brandy? You give her *my brandy*?"

"It's not your brandy," Mrs. Chubb said crossly, "and for goodness' sake, Michel, stop that infernal bellowing. You're scaring the young lady to death."

Catching sight of steam billowing from the kettle's spout, Gertie snatched up a teapot from the dresser. After spooning three spoonfuls of tea leaves into it, she carried it over to the stove and poured boiling water on top of it.

Michel muttered something she couldn't hear and busied

himself at the counter, pulling out various pots and pans and an assortment of cooking utensils.

Gertie could hear Mrs. Chubb murmuring something to the woman at the table, but couldn't make out what she said, either. This whole thing was so strange. What was the woman doing in the courtyard without a warm coat? Her frock looked to be of good quality, as were her boots. So why wasn't she wearing a coat? Why couldn't she remember anything? What had happened to her for her to end up lying unconscious on the icy ground?

This was going to stir things up, all right. Maybe Madam could sort it all out. She was good at doing that. Gertie couldn't wait to find out all the answers. She just hoped she wouldn't have to wait too long. There was so much going on at present, what with Pansy's wedding and Christmas and everything.

She glanced over at the table. It looked as if Mrs. Chubb had calmed the woman down a bit, though she still appeared as if she might bolt any second.

Gertie felt sorry for her. It must be awful to not remember her name or anything else that had happened to her. She just hoped that Madam would be able to help the poor thing. Though how she was going to do that when the woman didn't even know her own name was beyond her.

This was a mystery, all right, and one even Madam might not be able to solve.

CHAPTER
❋ 4 ❋

"So what is Northcott doing about this chap found on the beach?" Baxter spread a generous coating of marmalade onto his buttered toast, and put down the knife.

Cecily sent an anxious glance around the dining room. Several of the guests still sat at the breakfast tables, but no one appeared to have overheard her husband's words. "This isn't something we should be discussing here, my love," she murmured.

Baxter raised his eyebrows. "Why? It has nothing to do with us, does it? I mean, admittedly the poor fellow was staying here, but that doesn't mean . . ." He paused, his eyes narrowing. "Are you telling me—?"

Cecily forestalled him with a quick shake of her head. "I'm not saying anything, Bax. We don't know where he lives, that's all, and Sam is trying to find out so that we can notify the gentleman's family."

Baxter gave her a hard look, then picked up his toast. After munching for a while in silence, he said quietly, "I sincerely hope you won't be drawn into another unfortunate situation."

"I hope so, too." Cecily reached for a silver jug and poured a small amount of cream into her cup. "More tea, dear?"

For answer, Baxter nudged his cup and saucer closer to her. "Thank you."

She eyed him warily. "For what?"

"For the tea, of course. What did you think I meant?"

She shrugged. "I thought maybe you were thanking me for not getting involved in this unfortunate situation."

Baxter's mouth twitched. "That would be a little premature, I fear."

Cecily relaxed her shoulders. "You know me well."

"I do, indeed." Baxter sighed. "You will keep me informed if anything untoward develops?"

"Of course. Don't I always?"

"Usually not until you are in the thick of things. I'd like to be forewarned this time."

She passed him his cup of tea. "I don't like to concern you unless it's really necessary."

"Well, this time it might well be necessary."

Puzzled, she filled her own cup with tea. "How so?"

"Because Samuel isn't here to protect you."

At the sound of her ex–stable manager's name, Cecily felt another twinge of sorrow. She and Samuel had shared so many adventures together. She had relied upon him so often, and he had never let her down. How she missed him. "I hope I won't need protecting."

"Well, just in case you do, remember I'm here."

She smiled. "I never forget that for a moment."

Baxter drained his cup and put it back on its saucer. "I'm afraid, my dear wife, that I have to disagree. There have been many times when you have taken on these perilous pursuits without consulting or even notifying me of your intentions. Now that you have lost your protector, so to speak, I must ask you—no, implore you—to keep me informed and ask for my help if needed."

Cecily leaned back on her chair. She wasn't quite sure how to take that. Baxter had always been solidly against her penchant for solving crimes, more out of fear for her safety than for any other reason. He had barely tolerated her absences when on the trail of a criminal and had, at times, become quite incensed on the rare occasion she had put herself in actual danger.

He had even considered taking a position abroad in an attempt to remove her from all temptation, though he should have known her well enough to realize that even in a foreign country, she might well be tempted to hunt down a killer.

What he failed to realize was that she usually engaged in these somewhat unbecoming exploits in order to protect the integrity and reputation of the Pennyfoot Country Club and more often than not, the inhabitants therein.

The local constabulary, led by the befuddled Sam Northcott, had proven incompetent at best and totally dim-witted at times. She was constantly battling the imminent appearance of Inspector Cranshaw and the possibility that the Pennyfoot would have to close its doors forever. Thus she had felt compelled to do what she could to bring about the capture of whoever threatened the well-being of those under her roof.

The fact that she rather enjoyed the chase was immaterial.

What mattered now was that her husband appeared to have had a change of heart about her quests. She leaned forward. "Are you saying you approve of me chasing after criminals?"

"Good Lord, no! I'll never approve of it. I have, however, realized the futility of hoping you'll give it all up. Therefore I have to be prepared to help in any way I can, if I'm to have any peace of mind at all." He looked deep into her eyes. "I hope you can trust me enough to do that. After all, I remember several occasions before we were married when I was on hand to assist you at such times."

She smiled at the thought. "I remember, too. We made quite a team. Even if you did complain bitterly every time you thought I was taking a risk." She was silent for a moment, turning his proposal over in her mind. She had come a long way since those early days. Her encounters with so many villains had sharpened her wits and taught her a lot about how the minds of criminals work.

Her experiences had strengthened her capabilities, and Samuel had grown along with her. They had become so accustomed to acting together they were able to predict the actions of each other without a word being spoken.

Baxter had had no such schooling, and much as she loved and trusted her husband, she feared that in the face of danger, he might do something foolish in his eagerness to protect her.

On the other hand, who else could she trust with her well-being, if not the man who loved her?

"I think," she said at last, "that if the occasion should arise, and I hope and pray it doesn't, but if it does, I can't think of anyone I'd rather have by my side."

He gave her his rare smile that could always make her heart flutter. "Then it's settled." He held out his hand. "Partners?"

Gravely she grasped his fingers. "Partners it is."

She was still debating if she'd done the right thing as they parted at the stairs—Baxter to settle down with the morning newspaper while she departed to her office to catch up on some paperwork.

She had barely seated herself at her desk before a light tapping on the door announced her first distraction. Calling out, "Come in!" she leaned back in her chair to wait for whatever new challenge was on the horizon.

The door opened to reveal Gertie, and a young woman she didn't recognize. The poor girl looked about to drop to the floor at any moment. Her face lacked any color, and she clasped her shawl to her throat, as if afraid someone would snatch it from her.

"This is Miss Memory, m'm," Gertie began, "and I found her lying in the courtyard and I thought she was dead only she wasn't but she can't remember her name or where she come from so Mrs. Chubb called her Miss Memory and that's what her name is for now."

Gertie paused for breath, giving Cecily some time to digest what she'd just heard. Looking at the girl she asked gently, "You've lost your memory?"

The girl nodded, her lips pinched together.

"She don't know how she got in the courtyard or what happened to her," Gertie said helpfully.

"Thank you, Gertie." Cecily smiled at the housemaid. "You may go. Leave Miss . . . ah . . . Memory with me."

"Yes, m'm." Gertie gave the young woman a nudge with her elbow. "You'll be all right, you'll see. Madam will take care of you. She's a bloody good sort." With that, she barged out the door, slamming it shut behind her.

The girl jumped at the sound and gripped her shawl tighter.

Cecily waved a hand at a chair. "Please, sit down. Have you had anything to eat?"

Miss Memory shook her head and sat down on the very edge of the chair.

"Are you hurt? In pain?"

The girl moved her free hand to her head.

"You have a headache?"

Miss Memory nodded again.

"Can you speak?"

The young woman lowered her chin and stared at the floor. "Yes, m'm."

"You have no idea where you live? Where your parents are?"

Another sad shake of the head.

Cecily stared thoughtfully at the ledger in front of her. Two lost souls in two days. At least this one was alive. Barely, by the look of it. Making up her mind, she said briskly, "Well, the first thing we must do is get some food inside of you."

"I had tea and brandy," Miss Memory said.

"Well, that's a start, but good food will make you feel much better. I can't have you wandering around the streets, not knowing who you are or where you're going, so you may stay here for the time being. There's a spare bed in Pansy and Lilly's room. You can sleep there. In the meantime I'll have Dr. Prestwick take a look at you and see if he can help you."

At the sound of the doctor's name, the girl shrank back in her chair, violently shaking her head. "No, no, no."

Cecily frowned. "It's all right, child. He's a doctor and a good man. He won't hurt you."

Miss Memory started up from her chair, still shaking her head. "No, no. No doctor. I just need to get some sleep and I'll be quite all right. Please, no doctor."

Seeing that the young woman was quite distressed, Cecily softened her tone. "Very well. I'll ring for a maid and she can take you back to the kitchen. After you've eaten something you can get some sleep in Pansy's room. Then we'll talk again, all right?"

Miss Memory just looked back at her, eyes wide with fear.

Sighing, Cecily tugged on the bell rope. Minutes passed, during which the girl sat in tense silence, and then Pansy arrived at the door.

Cecily got up from her desk and walked over to the girl's chair. "Take Miss . . . er . . . Memory down to the kitchen and see that she eats a hearty breakfast, Pansy. I've told her she can sleep in your room with you and Lilly until we decide what to do about her."

Pansy's eyes brightened at the news. "That will be lovely. Maybe we can help her get back her memory."

"Yes, well, don't dwell on that too much. I'm sure all this is terribly confusing for the poor child."

"Yes, m'm." Pansy curtsied, then took the girl's arm. "Come along, Miss Memory. Wait until you taste Michel's cooking. I bet you never had such scrumptious food."

Miss Memory allowed Pansy to lead her out the door, and Cecily breathed a sigh of relief. That was one crisis resolved. At least for now. She could only hope that the death of Gerald Evans would be as easily settled.

With any luck at all, P.C. Northcott would find out that whoever had killed him had nothing to do with the Pennyfoot and, for once, they could escape the Christmas curse. She tried to hang on to that as she settled down once more with the ledger. Yet Madeline's words still persisted in the back of her mind, and something told her that her involvement in Mr. Evans's death was far from over.

"Maybe she can have a job here," Gertie suggested, upon hearing that Miss Memory was to stay for the time being. She carefully lowered a meat platter into the hot water in the sink. "We could use the extra help."

"We don't have time to train anyone else." Mrs. Chubb dusted her floury hands on her apron. "I've already had to turn down two applications for a maid's job. It's hard enough to train Lilly while we're trying to get everything done in time for Christmas. I just can't take on another new maid."

"Maybe she already knows enough so we wouldn't have to train her."

Mrs. Chubb snorted. "Have you taken a good look at her? She's no maid. She comes from money. That frock must have cost a month's wages."

"Yeah, I noticed." Gertie swished the platter around in the soapy suds. "Her flipping boots, too." She'd taken a fancy to those boots, but she wasn't about to admit it. She'd learned long ago that it was pointless to waste her energy pining after what she couldn't afford. Be thankful for what you have, was her motto. Right now she had everything she needed. Her twins were well and happy, and now that she and Clive had established a more meaningful relationship, they were drawing closer every day.

"Someone out there is missing a daughter, I reckon."

At the sound of Mrs. Chubb's voice, Gertie dragged her mind back to the conversation. "I wonder where she came from. Her family must be looking all over for her."

"Well, I'm sure Madam will be able to find out where she came from. If anyone can, that is."

"I feel sorry for her." Gertie lifted the platter out of the water and stood it on the draining board. "Not knowing where you come from or what happened to you must be worse than having bad memories of your life."

"I'm sure it is." Mrs. Chubb picked up a knife, placed a saucer upside down on the slab of pastry in front of her, and began cutting around it. "She acts as if she doesn't know if she's coming or going, like she's in Wonderland or something."

Gertie laughed. "We should call her Alice."

"That's a good idea. It's better than calling her Miss Memory all the time."

The door opened just then and Pansy walked in, her face creased in a frown.

Gertie glanced at her. "What's the bleeding matter with you, then?"

Pansy shrugged. "Nothing, really. It's just that it's a bit crowded in our room now that Miss Memory's in there."

"We're calling her Alice," Gertie said, drying her hands on a tea towel. "And you won't be here after this week, so you only have to put up with it a few more days."

"Alice?" Pansy looked at Mrs. Chubb.

"Because I said she looked like she was in Wonderland."

Pansy nodded. "Oh yeah. She does look a bit like Alice."

Gertie laughed. "How do you know what Alice in Wonderland looks like?"

Pansy looked put out. "I read the book, didn't I. There was a picture of her in it. She had curly blond hair and big blue eyes like Miss Memory."

"Well, that's enough about the girl," Mrs. Chubb said, glancing at the clock. "Pansy, go out to the stables and tell Charlie that I'll be needing a carriage this afternoon. I want to finish my Christmas shopping. You've got time before you have to be in the dining room. That's if you don't stand around jabbering all morning."

"I don't jabber." Pansy headed for the door. "Not with Charlie Muggins, anyway. Now, if my Samuel was still here, I might be jabbering all morning." She was grinning as she went out the door.

It swung to behind her, then opened again as Lilly barged into the kitchen. Her cheeks were flushed and her cap had slid to the back of her head. "I can't find the ladles for the soup tureens. I've looked everywhere."

"Everywhere except here." Gertie opened a drawer and pulled out a handful of silver ladles. "Pansy must have forgotten to put them on the tray."

"Her head is full of the wedding, that's why," Mrs. Chubb muttered. "I don't know why she's in such a state. She's getting everything done for her. All she has to do is get dressed and walk down the aisle."

"It isn't every day a woman gets married." Gertie started drying the platter with the tea towel. "Of course her mind is on other things."

"Which reminds me," Lilly said. "Pansy said she had to get Mr. Evans's room ready for a new guest this morning. She wanted me to take some coal up there for the fireplace. Should I do it now or wait until after the midday meal?"

Mrs. Chubb stared at her in surprise. "Mr. Evans is gone? No one said anything to me. When did he leave? I thought he was here until Christmas."

Gertie stopped drying the platter. "That's strange. He told me himself he was looking forward to the carol-singing ceremony."

"Something must have happened to him," Mrs. Chubb said slowly.

Gertie exchanged a significant glance with her. She hoped it didn't mean what she thought it might mean. The last thing they needed on top of everything else was another death in the Pennyfoot.

As if to confirm her fears, a sharp tap on the door turned everyone's heads. Gertie caught her breath as P.C. Northcott strolled into the kitchen.

"Don't suppose you've got any more of them mince pies lying around, just begging to be eaten?" The constable looked around, eyes gleaming with anticipation. "I do love coming in here this time of year. It always smells of sugar and spice." He rubbed his belly and licked his lips, reminding Gertie of the fat tabby cat that invaded the courtyard now and then.

Mrs. Chubb clicked her tongue, but walked over to the large tin box where she kept the mince pies. "I can only spare two," she told him. "I have to make some more this afternoon."

"Two's plenty," Northcott, said, his eyes lighting up. "Hand 'em over, then."

"First you tell us why you're here for the second time in two days."

Gertie gripped the tea towel when she saw Mrs. Chubb's face. She knew by the look on it that the housekeeper thought the same thing she did. She wasn't really surprised when Northcott cleared his throat, then said quietly, "There's been a murder, and I'm h'investigating it. That's all I can say."

"Is it Mr. Evans?"

Gertie hadn't realized she was speaking out loud until she saw everyone looking at her.

Northcott looked up at the ceiling as if sending up a prayer. Then he lowered his chin. "I suppose you'll all find out soon enough. Yes, it's Mr. Gerald Evans. Mrs. Fortescue and the colonel found him on the beach. Stabbed through the 'eart, he was."

Lilly made a choking sound, grabbed her throat, and slowly backed out of the kitchen.

Mrs. Chubb threw up her hands. "Now you've done it. It'll be all over the hotel. Gertie, go after her. Remind her of the Pennyfoot code. Nothing of what she sees and hears here gets past her lips."

"Yes, Mrs. Chubb." Gertie dropped the tea towel, picked up her skirts, and charged out into the hallway.

She was just in time to see Lilly's heels rounding the bend at the top of the stairs. Putting her head down, she chased after her.

"I don't suppose you've heard from Northcott yet?" Baxter asked, when Cecily joined him in the suite. "I was hoping he would have cleared up this mess by now."

"He's probably still trying to find out where the victim lived." Cecily sat down in front of the fire. "We both looked at the register yesterday but Mr. Evans had simply signed his name. He'd given no indication of where his home might be."

"That's odd, if you ask me."

"Oh, I don't know. Quite a few people don't bother putting down an address. Like the gentleman who registered this morning. Mr. Fred Granson. He just signed his name, too."

Baxter raised his eyebrows. "What if this Granson chap simply disappeared at the end of his visit without paying? You'd have no way of recouping that money."

Cecily smiled. "Fortunately, most people are honest. In any case, Mr. Granson paid in advance. Just like Mr. Evans did. So now we have a full house again."

"He was lucky we had a vacancy." Baxter leaned forward to stoke the coals in the fireplace. "It always amazes me how some people come down to the coast on the off chance they'll find a room. Especially at Christmastime."

"It might have been a last minute decision. After all, he's

traveling on his own. Perhaps he decided that he didn't want to spend Christmas alone and simply had an impulse to leave for parts unknown."

"There should be a law that says guests have to write down an address when they book into a hotel."

"Or country club," Cecily said, with a sly grin.

"You know what I mean." Baxter laid down the poker. "If that were so, we would have known where the dead man lived."

"Speaking of knowing where people live . . ." Cecily told him about Miss Memory and her predicament. "I told her she could stay in Pansy's room."

Baxter groaned. "It's becoming an epidemic. How many more lost souls will end up at the Pennyfoot?"

"No more, I hope."

"So what are you going to do with her?"

"I'm not sure. I was hoping Dr. Prestwick might be able to help her, but she refuses to see him."

"There can't be much wrong with her then."

"Physically, no. It's her mental state I'm concerned about."

"Then Prestwick's not the chap to help her. She needs a mental institution."

Aghast at the thought, Cecily shook her head. "I'll not send her to one of those horrible places. I'll think of something." She looked up at the sound of someone tapping. "I hope this isn't more bad news."

She got up to open the door, and was surprised to see the housekeeper standing there. "Mrs. Chubb! I hope nothing's wrong?"

"No, m'm. I came to tell you, P.C. Northcott is downstairs. He's eating mince pies right now. He told us that the gentleman down the hall, Mr. Evans, was found dead on the beach."

Cecily exchanged a despairing look with Baxter, who had joined her at the door. "Was there anyone else in the kitchen at the time?"

"Gertie was there, m'm. And the new maid, Lilly. I'm afraid it gave her a bad turn. She went running off somewhere. Gertie went after her but neither of them have come back yet. I thought you should know."

"Oh dear." Cecily silently cursed Sam Northcott's loose tongue.

Mrs. Chubb glanced down the hallway. "I told Gertie to remind Lilly not to say anything to anyone, but you know how easily this kind of news gets out."

"Yes, I do." Cecily sighed. "I suppose it was only a matter of time."

"Pardon me for asking, m'm, but we don't have another killer amongst us, do we?"

Baxter grunted. "There is absolutely no reason to think that, Mrs. Chubb, and if anyone else should voice such a thought, we'd appreciate it if you would quell the suggestion as quickly and firmly as possible."

Cecily gave her husband a grateful smile. She couldn't have said it better herself.

Mrs. Chubb raised her chin. "Of course, sir. Rest assured, I will see that no one mentions one word about it."

"Thank you, Mrs. Chubb. Would you please ask the constable to meet me in the library? I'll be down shortly."

"Of course, m'm."

Cecily closed the door behind the housekeeper. "I'd better go down and see why Sam is here," she said, as Baxter returned to his chair. "I sincerely hope it's to tell us he's found out where that poor man lived and has contacted his family."

"He could have told you that much on the telephone." Baxter picked up his newspaper. "He's here to gobble down more of Mrs. Chubb's Christmas baking. He'd find any excuse to come here this time of year. If he had anything seriously important to report, he would have spoken to you first, before filling his belly with mince pies."

"I hope you are right." She looked back at him on her way out of the door. "You could come with me, if you like."

He peered at her over the top of the newspaper. "I'm sure you'll tell me what he had to say. You know Northcott and I have never seen eye to eye. I'd just be a distraction."

She was still smiling as she made her way downstairs. A long time ago, her husband and Sam Northcott had been rivals for the hand of a young woman. Sam had won, though he had parted company with the woman soon after, and Baxter had never forgiven him. He barely tolerated the constable, and while in his company never passed up the opportunity to make caustic remarks about the lack of common sense and intelligence in the constabulary.

Nevertheless, P.C. Northcott represented the law in Badgers End, and right now he was waiting for her in the library with, she hoped, the good news that he had solved the crime and the guests of the Pennyfoot Country Club could enjoy their Christmas visit in peace.

CHAPTER
❋ 5 ❋

Pansy was halfway across the courtyard when she heard Charlie's voice echoing in the rafters of the stables. He sounded angry, and she slowed her steps as she reached the doors, straining to hear what he said.

He had to be talking to the new assistant, and Pansy felt sorry for that young man as the torrent of words blasted her ears.

"How many bloody times do I have to tell you? You have to get in the stall with the horse. He's not going to eat you, you bloody twit. He's only interested in his feed. Why won't you listen to me? You act as if you're afraid of the horses. Why would you take a job in the stables if you're afraid of horses?"

Henry's high-pitched voice answered him, too quiet for Pansy to make out the words.

Charlie spoke again, softer this time. "Well, all right then. Get in that stall and give Champion his feed before he starts stamping his feet with hunger. He's waited far too long as it is. What? No, he's not going to trample you, silly bugger. I was joking. Can't you take a bloody joke?"

Pansy decided it was time to intervene. She called out as she walked through the doors, "Morning, everyone! What's going on here, then?"

Henry stood at the entrance to Champion's stall, a bucket in one hand and a broom in the other. His face was completely white, except for a bright red spot in each cheek. He stared at Pansy as she approached, as if he were pleading with her to rescue him.

Charlie turned at the sound of her voice and gave her a grin. "Well, here comes a pretty lady to brighten up the place."

Pansy tossed her head, though secretly she was flattered. Charlie was a good-looking young man and knew how to make a woman feel good about herself. Much as she adored Samuel, there were times when she wished he were as generous as Charlie Muggins with the compliments.

"None of your sauce, Charlie," she said, and sent poor Henry a smile. "I'm getting married in three days and that's no way to talk to a married lady."

"You're not married yet, luv. I have to make hay while the sun shines." Charlie moved closer. "So what brings you into our humble abode?"

"Mrs. Chubb sent me to tell you she'll need a carriage this afternoon to take her into town for some Christmas shopping." She looked around. "Where's Tess?"

"Jacob took her out for a walk." Charlie leaned against

the stall door and leered at her. "I wish you'd pay as much attention to me as you do to your dog, the lucky bugger."

Pansy frowned. "I wish Jacob had asked me first before taking her out. She doesn't know him all that well. He might lose her."

Charlie laughed. "Why would he do that?"

"I dunno. She could run off and not listen to him when he called her. I don't want her going out with Jacob. I don't trust him."

"Why not?"

Pansy shrugged. "I dunno," she said again. "There's just something about him. I wish Clive was still here. I could trust him with my life."

"How about me?" Charlie draped an arm around her shoulders. "You trust me, don't you?"

"About as far as I can throw you." She moved out of his reach. "How long ago did Jacob take Tess?"

"Not long. He was just going to take her for a run across the lawns. He'll be back any minute."

"Well, I hope so." Pansy hunched her shoulders against a sharp blast of wind from the ocean. "I'm supposed to be watching after her."

"Well, you can watch after me, instead."

"No blinking thanks." She turned to go. "Don't forget to get that carriage ready."

"All right." Charlie looked at Henry, who still hovered nervously by the stall. "Give me that," he said, holding out his hand. "I'll feed Champion. You go and get a carriage ready for this afternoon. You do remember how to do that, don't you?"

Henry nodded, thrust the bucket and broom at Charlie, and dashed out of the stable.

Charlie shook his head and set the bucket on the ground. "I don't know about that chap. He seems a bit queer to me."

Pansy frowned. "Queer? In what way?"

Charlie grinned. "You know, a poof." He flapped a loose hand at her.

Pansy stared at him. "Whatever are you talking about?"

Charlie cleared his throat. "Er . . . well, never mind, then. So, how about having a drink with me down the pub tonight? Might as well enjoy your last days of freedom, right?"

Pansy pretended to be shocked. Picking up her skirts, she headed for the door. "I don't have time to waste words with you, Charlie Muggins. If you're looking for someone to take out, why don't you ask Lilly? She seems more your type, anyway. She'll probably faint from the excitement if you ask her out, poor bugger."

She marched outside, Charlie's laughter still ringing in her ears.

Across the courtyard she saw Henry struggling to reach the carriage windows with a wet rag. It must be hard for a man to be short, she thought, as she hurried over to him. He wasn't much taller than her, and he didn't look as if he had enough meat on his bones to keep him on his feet all day.

"You need a stepladder for that," she called out as she drew close. "There's one in the coal shed. I'll get it for you."

Henry gave her a smile that completely changed his face. "Thank you. I'm much obliged."

"Not at all. I'll be right back." Pansy hurried over to the

coal shed, dragged out the small ladder, and carried it back to where Henry was polishing the brass on the carriage.

He gave her another dazzling smile as he took the ladder from her. "That's very kind of you," he murmured, in his soft voice.

Pansy hesitated. It was none of her business, of course, but sometimes Charlie could act too big for his britches. She hated to see anyone bullied, and she rather liked Henry. He seemed awfully shy, but she couldn't see anything strange about him, like Charlie said.

"Listen," she said, drawing closer to the young man. "Don't let Charlie boss you around too much. He's only been in that job a couple of months and he thinks he owns the place. He's no better than you, so don't let him talk to you that way. If you stand up to him and give him what for when he shouts at you, he'll soon stand down. You'll see."

Henry looked uncomfortable. "Thank you, Pansy. I'll remember that."

"Good." She gave his bony shoulder a warm pat, then tore across the courtyard back to the kitchen.

Cecily reached the foyer just in time to see Sam Northcott trudging down the hallway toward the library. She was about to follow him when she caught sight of the new guest at the front door. Mindful of Baxter's concerns, she decided to ask the gentleman for his address.

Since they were alone in the foyer, she called out to him as he opened the door. "Mr. Granson! May I please have a word with you?"

To her surprise, he paused in the doorway, paying no attention to her. He appeared to be gazing at something out in the street.

Thinking he must be hard of hearing, she started toward him, raising her voice to carry clearly across the room. "Mr. Granson! I'd like a word with you, if I may?"

Instead of turning his head, he stepped out the door and closed it firmly behind him.

Cecily stood staring at the door in stunned dismay for several seconds. The man had to be deaf. It was odd that she hadn't noticed that when she'd spoken to him earlier. She'd welcomed him to the Pennyfoot and asked him if he had everything he needed. He'd seemed to understand perfectly what she'd said to him.

Shaking her head, she hurried down the hallway to the library. If Mr. Granson was, indeed, unable to hear, he had to be an expert at reading lips. She must remember that next time she talked to him.

When she entered the library, she saw P.C. Northcott in his usual pose in front of the fireplace, his helmet lying on a chair. A quick glance around assured her that none of the guests were in there, and she greeted the constable as she took a seat on her favorite Queen Anne armchair.

She leaned back so that the high wings on either side would keep the draft from her face. "Well, Sam," she said, folding her hands in her lap to warm them, "what news do you have for me today?"

"We've discovered the h'identity of the victim, Mrs. B." Sam scratched the bald spot on his head. "Bit of a puzzle, if you ask me."

Cecily felt a faint stir of anxiety. "A puzzle?"

"Yes, m'm. You see, we found out that Gerald Evans was a private detective."

She frowned. "A detective? I wonder what he was doing in Badgers End."

"Well, m'm, I think it's safe to assume he was either here on holiday, or he was working on a case."

Her anxiety deepened. Evans proclaimed to have switched hotels because he was dissatisfied with his room. Had there been a more significant reason why a private detective, perhaps investigating a crime, had taken a room at the Pennyfoot?

"That brings up another possibility," Northcott was saying. "It's possible that Evans was investigating a case, and got too close to the perpetrators."

The nasty feeling in the pit of Cecily's stomach intensified. "I thought you had established that he was robbed and killed by a vagrant."

"That was before we knew he was a detective. Evans had a partnership in London. I sent a telegram to his partner, a chap called Harry Clements, but I haven't heard anything from him yet. He could be away for the Christmas holiday, of course, in which case, he won't know his partner's dead until the New Year."

"I see." Cecily stared into the flames, trying desperately to think of a way to stall an investigation until after the holidays. "Well, I suppose you will just have to wait to find out what Mr. Evans was working on."

"Yes, m'm. We will." Sam cleared his throat. "I h'investigated the cricket matches in the area. Seems as how there are none.

Haven't been any since September. It looks like that's a dead end. The victim must have written that note to hisself back in the summer and just now got rid of it."

Cecily nodded. "That's entirely possible, Sam."

"Yes, well, seeing as how it could be a week or two before we hear anything from London, there doesn't seem much I can do until I talk to the victim's partner. So I'm going ahead with my plans for the Christmas holiday. In which case, I'm putting in my report that the murder was most likely caused by a vagrant, seeing as how we really don't know that it wasn't. I'll be leaving for London tomorrow, and when I return, I'll take up the case again."

Feeling greatly relieved herself, Cecily rose to her feet. "I hope you and your family have a really nice Christmas, Sam. Thank you so much for coming to tell me all this."

"Yes, m'm." Sam reached for his helmet. "It doesn't seem as how this has anything to do with the Pennyfoot Country Club, but if you should hear something important, I trust you will let me know?"

"Of course, Sam." She walked with him to the door. "Happy Christmas."

"Happy Christmas to you and yours, m'm."

She closed the door behind him and leaned against it for a moment in sheer relief. So far, it seemed, she had avoided a full-scale investigation. But for how long? If the inspector got wind of the murder, and found out the victim was a detective staying at the Pennyfoot, there was no doubt in her mind that he'd arrive at the club with the intention of questioning everyone there, disrupting all her carefully planned events, and ruining everyone's Christmas. Not to mention Pansy's wedding.

There was only one thing she could do, and that was to find out herself who had killed Gerald Evans.

She sat down again and stared once more into the flames. Sam had said something earlier that had rung a bell in the back of her mind. She had learned long ago to pay attention to such instances, since they invariably led her to an important conclusion.

She couldn't imagine why she should attach significance to anything Sam had said. He had assured her that he was satisfied Gerald Evans's death was not connected to the Pennyfoot. Still, if she could find out what crime her guest had been pursuing, she might be able to prove it had nothing to do with the Pennyfoot.

She kept her gaze fixed on the glowing coals in the fireplace. What was it Sam had said that had struck a chord? Something about Gerald Evans's partner. He said he had sent him a telegram and . . .

She sat up straight. Of course. She had received a telegram not so long ago. The way it read had intrigued her. The word *stop* at the end of each sentence. She closed her eyes, seeing again the crumpled note she had found in Gerald Evans's waste paper basket. *Spotsman seen nearby. Already made run. No sign batman. Still looking. Stop.*

That note had convinced Sam it was about a cricket match. She'd thought at the time that there was something really odd about it. Especially the last word. Now she knew why. Gerald Evans had been composing a note for a telegram. Maybe he'd sent more than one.

Excited, she leapt to her feet. She should tell Sam. No, first she needed to make sure there was something to tell.

She had planned to go to the library that afternoon. While in town she would call in at the post office.

Halfway across the room, she paused. This was not her business this time. Baxter would not be at all happy if he knew she was pursuing a case that possibly had no connection to the Pennyfoot. A second later she shrugged. What the eyes couldn't see the heart couldn't grieve over. For her own peace of mind she needed to find answers, and settle this thing once and for all.

She would go to the post office just to see if Mr. Evans had sent any other telegrams and if there was anything in them to help solve his murder. She would then relay the news to Sam and that would be the end of it. Baxter would never have to know.

Pleased with herself, she opened the door and headed down the hallway.

"Where the bloody hell did you get to?" Gertie paused to get her breath, arms folded across her stomach. She'd finally found Lilly in the laundry room, after chasing up and down the hallways looking for her. Now she stood in the doorway, determined not to let the young woman pass until she'd delivered Mrs. Chubb's message.

"I went for a little walk." Lilly's voice sounded strange, as if she was out of breath.

Gertie rolled her eyes. "You're not scared, are you? There's nothing to be frightened of."

Lilly raised her chin. "I'm not frightened."

"You look bloody frightened."

"I'm just shocked, that's all. It's not every day someone ends up dead on the beach."

"Well, as long as it's not you lying down there, you ain't got nothing to worry about, have ya."

Lilly looked as if she were about to be sick. "I gotta go." She shoved past Gertie and tore off down the hallway as if there were a herd of elephants chasing after her.

"Don't say nothing to nobody," Gertie yelled after her, belatedly remembering Mrs. Chubb's directions. She couldn't understand why the maid was in such a stew. It wasn't as if the dead body had been found in the Pennyfoot. Then she'd really have something to worry about.

Stomping down the hallway, she decided she really didn't like the new maid. She couldn't understand why Madam had hired her. It was obvious that Lilly had never worked as a servant before. She knew nothing about the most basic of tasks, and acted as if everything she was asked to do was beneath her.

When Gertie had tried to ask her about her previous employment, she'd been so flustered she'd ended up with the hiccups. Much as Gertie wanted Pansy to be happy, she wished she wasn't getting married and leaving her best friend to put up with the likes of Lilly Green.

Gertie paused at the kitchen door. Thinking about the dead guest had reminded her of something. She needed to talk to Madam, but not right now. She had her chores to finish, so that she could take the twins to Clive's toy shop that afternoon. She'd have to talk to Madam later.

Having made that decision, she pushed the door open and walked in.

Cecily gazed across the table at her husband, who seemed to be a hundred miles away. She had suggested taking the midday meal in the dining room for a change. She loved to dine in there after Madeline had decorated it for Christmas. It looked so festive with all the garlands of holly and fir, the red candles on the tables, the glistening strands of silver woven into the red and green swaths of velvet around the walls.

Madeline had even made centerpieces for the tables—delicate cut glass goblets filled with colored baubles and festooned with red ribbons and a sprig of mistletoe. Right now, however, Cecily's attention was not on the decorations. She frowned as she regarded her husband's somber expression. "Is something wrong?"

He seemed startled when he switched his gaze to her face. "Wrong? No, I don't think so. Is there? I mean, is there something you're not telling me?"

She shifted guiltily on her chair. "Why ever would you think that?"

He shrugged. "Oh, I don't know. Maybe it's the knowledge that someone murdered a private detective just yards from our front door."

A quick glance around assured her they were out of earshot. "That has nothing to do with us, darling. Sam seemed convinced the Pennyfoot wasn't involved."

"And we all know how reliable Northcott's deductions can be."

"I think he's right this time."

Baxter's gray eyes were shrewd as he met her gaze. "You truly believe that?"

"I do. I think this is one time we don't have to worry about the Christmas curse."

"You don't think it odd that Evans picked our country club to stay in while he conducted an investigation?"

"He told Philip he wasn't happy with the hotel he was in and was looking for a better place to spend Christmas." Cecily paused, then added quietly, "I think perhaps he knew whoever killed him had tracked him down to the hotel and he wanted somewhere safe to hide."

"So he picks one of the most prominent establishments on the southeast coast of England."

"Most likely because he felt that whoever was pursuing him wouldn't think of him staying in a place like this."

"Or maybe he picked this place because it was part of his investigation."

Cecily picked up her white linen serviette, dabbed her mouth with it, and placed it by her plate. "I see absolutely no reason to assume such a thing." She kept her gaze down, though she could feel Baxter's scrutiny on her face.

"Very well. Let's both pray you are right. Meanwhile, I must ask you to remember our bargain. Please don't shut me out again."

Surprised, she jerked up her chin. "Shut you out? I've never done that."

His smile was rueful as he leaned forward to take her hand. "My dearest wife, you do it all the time. I'm hoping that the next time you take on one of Northcott's cases, you'll allow me to be at your side as promised."

Warmed by the earnest look in his eyes, she turned her palm up and curled her fingers over his. "I've already agreed to do so," she murmured. "I won't go back on my word." Her visit to the post office didn't count, she assured herself, as they both rose from the table. She was merely doing that to help Sam Northcott solve his case. She had no intention of intruding this time in the constable's investigation.

In fact, had Northcott not announced he was putting everything on hold until after Christmas, she might well have told him about the possible telegram and let him visit the post office. She wasn't about to admit to herself she had doubts about the murder.

Entering the foyer behind Baxter, she saw Gertie over by the front door. The housemaid paused when she saw them, then hurried over to her.

"I've got something to tell you," she said, keeping her voice low.

Baxter had kept going, and was now climbing the stairs, apparently unaware his wife wasn't following.

Cecily decided to catch up with him later. "What is it, Gertie? Not trouble in the kitchen, I trust?"

"No, m'm." Gertie looked anxious and Cecily had the distinct feeling that she wasn't going to like whatever it was the housemaid had to tell her.

CHAPTER

❀ 6 ❀

"Why on earth are we cleaning the lavatories in the middle of the afternoon?" Lilly dumped her bucket and mop in the middle of the bathroom floor. "Why aren't they cleaned in the mornings?"

Pansy shook her head in exasperation. She'd never heard anyone ask as many questions as the new maid did. Most of them were stupid questions. Like this one. "Because," she said, trying to hold on to her patience, "people use the lavatories first thing in the morning. Don't you have to piddle when you first wake up?"

Lilly looked annoyed. "That's none of your business."

"It is when you wake me up at the break of dawn every morning." Pansy pulled a scrubbing brush out of her bucket. "You must drink an awful lot of tea or something."

"I like tea." Lilly glanced at the door. "What if someone wants to use the W.C. while we're in here?"

"There's another one upstairs." Pansy rolled up the sleeves of her blue serge frock. "Besides, most of the guests are resting in their rooms, or playing poker in the card rooms, or taking a stroll along the Esplanade. There's not many of them around here this time in the afternoon."

She walked over to the toilet bowl and lifted the lid. "I'll do this. You can scrub the sink."

Lilly moaned. "That's right, give me the biggest job. Why can't you scrub the sink?"

Pansy rolled her eyes. *Just three more days.* "Suit yourself. I just thought you might be too delicate to clean the toilet."

Lilly picked up her scrubbing brush. "I'm not the one who's delicate around here."

Pansy bit back the smart answer hovering on her lips. Instead, she leaned across the sink and turned on the faucet. To her dismay, instead of water pouring out, a loud burping came from the tap and nothing more.

Frowning, she turned on the other faucet. The same burping erupted from that one. Not a drop of water appeared. "Now what?" she muttered, straightening her back.

Reaching up for the pull chain on the toilet she gave it a tug. Water poured into the bowl, swirled around, and disappeared. Pansy gave the chain another tug. Nothing. The chamber was empty.

Lilly stood with arms folded, a bored look on her face. "Are you finished messing around?"

Pansy threw the scrub brush into the bucket. "Come on.

We've got to get downstairs. Something's wrong with the water pipes. They're not working."

"Oh, this is going to be so much fun," Lilly muttered as she picked up her bucket. "Never a dull moment in this place."

Ignoring her, Pansy dashed out of the bathroom and down the hallway. Lavatories without water meant disaster. That's all they needed with all the Christmas preparations going on. Mrs. Chubb was going to have kittens when she heard, and Pansy wasn't looking forward to breaking the bad news.

Looking at Gertie's worried face, Cecily braced for the worst.

"It's about that Mr. Evans what got killed," Gertie said, lowering her voice to a near whisper.

Instantly on the alert, Cecily glanced over her shoulder. "I do hope there's not any gossip about this. We don't want to alarm the guests without reason."

"No, m'm. Nobody's said nothing."

"Let's keep it that way."

"Yes, m'm. Only I did hear something the other day, and I thought you should know about it."

"What did you hear?"

"It was Lord Bentley, m'm. I heard him shouting at Mr. Evans out by the front steps. I heard him say he would kill him if he touched his daughter again."

Cecily curled her fingers into her palms. *No, not again.* "When was this?"

"The day before yesterday, m'm. I think Mr. Evans was making advances to Miss Essie and she told her father. Lord

Bentley sounded really angry." Gertie looked uncomfortable. "I wouldn't have said nothing, only seeing as how Mr. Evans ended up dead, I thought you should know."

"Thank you, Gertie." Cecily tried to sound unconcerned. "I don't think for one moment that Lord Bentley would have anything to do with this, but I'll pass it along to the constable. Meanwhile I must ask you to keep what you heard to yourself. I—"

She broke off as Pansy burst into the foyer, bucket rattling in her hand.

"You can count on me to keep me mouth shut, m'm," Gertie muttered, then she called out to Pansy, "What the bloody hell are you making all that racket for?"

"The lavatories," Pansy said, between gasps for breath. "There's no water in them."

Cecily stared at her in dismay. "No water?"

"No, m'm. I turned the taps full on and nothing came out. I pulled the chains on the toilets and nothing came out there, neither."

"*All* the bathrooms?" Cecily asked, striving to make sense of Pansy's breathless words.

"Yes, m'm. All of them. I looked in them all to make sure."

"Bloody hell," Gertie muttered.

Cecily was about to head for the nearest telephone when Mrs. Chubb rushed into the foyer, her cheeks red with the exertion of climbing the kitchen stairs. "We can't get any running water." She paused when she caught sight of Cecily. "Oh, there you are, Madam. I was just coming to find you. There's no water in the kitchen."

"Or the lavatories, apparently," Cecily said grimly. "Can

you manage for a little while, Mrs. Chubb? I'll ring for the plumber right away."

"Yes, I think so, m'm." The housekeeper glared at Pansy and Gertie. "What are you two doing standing around here? Ask Philip to write notices saying the lavatories are out of order, then hang them on the lavatory doors. Everyone will have to use the commodes until we get the water running again."

Gertie pulled a face. "That's bloody marvelous. Now we'll be emptying chamber pots all day long."

"It can't be helped. Now get along with you both."

"It's my afternoon off," Gertie protested. "I was just about to take the twins into town."

Mrs. Chubb threw her hands up in the air. "Go on, then. We'll manage without you."

Gertie looked at Cecily for confirmation and she gave the housemaid a nod. "It's all right, Gertie. Take the twins into town. You can't do much about this anyway. I'll ring for the plumber." Without waiting for a response Cecily tore over to the reception desk where Philip was dozing in his chair, his bony chin resting on his chest. Nothing much was left of his white hair except for a few wisps combed across his head, leaving bare skin gleaming in the spaces in between.

Rapping on the counter, Cecily said loudly, "Philip, ring up George Rutter, the plumber. Tell him his services are needed immediately. It's an emergency. If he cannot come, ask him to recommend a plumber. One way or another, we must have one here this afternoon."

Philip blinked, adjusted his spectacles, and sat up. "Yes, m'm. Right away, m'm." He reached for the telephone and held it to his ear, waiting for the operator to come on the line.

"When you have finished talking to George, Pansy needs you to write some notices. She'll tell you what to write." Leaving him to his task, Cecily hurried over to the kitchen stairs. This couldn't have happened at a worse time. A house full of guests, with more expected for the carol-singing ceremony tomorrow evening.

She prayed the plumber would be able to make the repairs in record time. With any luck, they'd have the water running again before too many guests needed to use the lavatories.

Arriving at the kitchen, she stayed long enough to make sure all was well there. Mrs. Chubb seemed to have everything under control. Most of the dishes had been washed and dried before the water had stopped running. The few that were left had been stacked in the sink, and Mrs. Chubb seemed confident they would have enough clean dishes for supper.

"The biggest problem will be cooking the vegetables," she said, pointing to the pile of cauliflowers and carrots lying on the kitchen table. "I don't know how Michel is going to cook them or make soup without water."

"Well, we'll just have to hope George Rutter can get the water running again. He's a very good plumber. I know he'll do his best for us."

"He is, indeed," Mrs. Chubb said, nodding her head. "He's a good lad, that one. I just hope he can get here soon."

"Yes, well, do what you can and we'll all keep our fingers crossed."

Cecily left the kitchen with a knot of anxiety in her stomach. It didn't seem possible that there was no water in the entire building. She'd have to tell Baxter. Not that he could do much to help. Her husband could be quite resourceful when faced with a problem, but a plumbing disaster was a little beyond Baxter's expertise.

Stopping by the reception desk again, she had to rap on the counter to get Philip's attention. She was never quite sure if Philip was actually dozing or if he was either deaf or losing his sight. Perhaps all three.

In any case, he struggled to his feet, one hand smoothing back the imaginary hair that had long disappeared from his scalp. "What can I do for you, Madam?"

"Did you talk to the plumber?"

"Yes, m'm. Mr. Rutter should be along right away."

"Thank you, Philip." Feeling a little better, Cecily began to climb the stairs to her suite. She was not looking forward to telling Baxter about this latest crisis. She could only hope the news that the plumber was on his way would help alleviate some of the concern.

As she turned on the first landing she almost ran into the tall gentleman descending the stairs.

Lord Bentley was an imposing figure, with an abundance of black hair accented by the silver wings at his temples. His luxuriant mustache nestled over full lips, and his dark eyes seemed to penetrate right through Cecily's head.

"Good afternoon, Mrs. Baxter." The gentleman inclined his head in a polite bow. "May I commend you on a well-run establishment. My wife and daughter are enjoying their visit to the seaside."

"Thank you, Lord Bentley. I much appreciate your comments." Cecily smiled up at him, wondering how she could broach the subject of his dispute with Gerald Evans.

She needn't have concerned herself, however. Lord Bentley curled his fingers around his coat lapel and leaned forward. "There is one small thing. I don't like to complain, when everything else is so admirable, but I feel you should know. One of your guests . . . ah . . . accosted my daughter the other day. I had words with the chap and of course, he denied it, but I wanted to warn you that he might not be . . . ah . . . reputable, just in case he attacks someone else."

Cecily raised her eyebrows. "Good heavens, sir. I do hope your daughter was not harmed?"

"Oh no." Lord Bentley straightened. "Just somewhat upset, naturally. If you could perhaps warn the chap to behave, it might prevent another unfortunate incident. I believe his name was Edwards, or Evans. Something like that."

Cecily solemnly nodded. "I know to whom you refer, Your Lordship. I can assure you he will not be bothering anyone again."

Lord Bentley gave her a long, hard stare that made her most uncomfortable, then nodded. "Much obliged, Mrs. Baxter." With that, he jogged down the stairs and out of sight.

Cecily stared after him. Did he really not know Gerald Evans was dead, or was that all an act? She might have given him the benefit of the doubt, had it not been for that scrutinizing stare—as if he were trying to determine whether or not she'd accepted his little charade. Was it at all possible that Lord Bentley had exacted a deadly revenge for the assault on his daughter?

In the next instant, she gave herself a mental shake. She was jumping to conclusions, as usual. There was no indication whatsoever that Mr. Evans was killed by anyone in the Pennyfoot, and the sooner she put the whole event behind her and left Sam to do his work, the better.

She would go to the post office that afternoon just to satisfy her own curiosity. After that, she promised herself, she would spend all her energies on seeing that her guests had the best Christmas possible.

"There's nothing more we can do until the plumber gets here," Mrs. Chubb announced, taking off her apron. She hung it on the hook by the kitchen door and turned to Pansy. "I've got some shopping that has to be done today, so you'll have to wait for George. Just tell him we've got no water. He'll know what to do."

Pansy mumbled a reply. She'd been hoping to have a few moments to visit Tess. Samuel had had to leave her behind when he'd left the Pennyfoot. He was living with his new business partner, Gilbert Tubbs, until after the wedding, when he'd move into the flat over the repair shop with his new bride.

Pansy had to smile at the thought. There was a small yard at the back of the shop, big enough for Tess to play in, and since she'd be a housewife, she'd have the extra time to take the dog walking up on Putney Downs, where she'd have plenty of room to run.

Meanwhile, Tess was living in the stables, and not too happy about it, according to Charlie Muggins. The dog missed her master, and Pansy couldn't blame her. She'd missed Samuel herself since he'd been gone. What with her hours at the country club and him being so busy starting up his business, they'd hardly seen each other these past few weeks.

She jumped when Mrs. Chubb's voice penetrated her thoughts. "Are you going to stand there all day dreaming or are you going to find Lilly for me?"

"Oh, sorry." Pansy grinned at the housekeeper. "What did you want me to tell Lilly?"

Mrs. Chubb rolled her eyes. "I want her to go to the stables and tell Charlie I need a carriage at the front door in five minutes."

"Oh, I'll go to the stables!" Before the housekeeper could snatch away her chance to see Tess, Pansy darted across the kitchen and out the door. She took off at a run across the yard, expecting any minute to hear Mrs. Chubb screaming after her.

She arrived at the stables out of breath and thanking her lucky stars the housekeeper hadn't yelled at her after all.

Just as she reached the door, Henry appeared in front of her, his thin face creased in a frown.

Pansy gasped out her message. "Mrs. Chubb wants a carriage at the front door in five minutes." She took a closer look at Henry's face. He looked as if he was in pain. "What's the matter with you?"

"I have to go to the lavatory," Henry muttered, edging past her.

"You can't use the lavatory. There's no water in there."

Henry stared at her as if she'd slapped him. "No water? Why?"

Pansy shrugged. "How do I know? The whole plumbing system's gone off. We haven't got no water in the kitchen, neither."

Henry looked around, his face drawn with panic. "What am I going to do?"

His voice went really high on a whine and Pansy punched him on the arm. "Shhh! If Charlie hears you making a noise like that he'll think you've gone barmy."

"But I have to go!"

"Then go behind the coal shed. That's where all the lads go when they're in a hurry."

Henry stared at her for a long moment, his eyes wide. Then, with a sound like he was choking, he rushed off toward the coal shed.

Pansy shook her head. No wonder Charlie got annoyed with Henry. He really was a bit of a baby. She soon forgot about Henry, however, when Tess came bounding toward her. Dropping to her knees, she wrapped her arms around the dog's neck. "It won't be long now, Tess," she whispered.

The dog licked her nose as if she understood. Pansy hugged her tighter. Soon she'd be Mrs. Samuel Whitfield, sharing her home with the man she loved and the dog she adored. There couldn't be anyone in the world as happy as she felt right now.

"No water?" Baxter's face grew red. "In the entire building? What in blazes are we going to do now?"

"Don't worry, dear." Cecily crossed the room to the

window. "I've sent an urgent message to George Rutter. He should be here any minute."

"George who?"

"Rutter." She turned to smile at her bewildered husband. "He's the plumber, remember?"

"Oh, the red-headed chap. Whatever happened to Tom Blakely?"

"He died, darling. He had a heart attack. George bought the business from his widow."

Baxter shook his head. "So, is this George going to get the water running again?"

"I sincerely hope so." She looked out the window. The woods looked so stark and bare and the bowling greens were covered with dead leaves. Frowning, she made a mental note to talk to the new maintenance man about that. Clive would have had the lawns cleaned up weeks ago.

How she missed the big, jovial man, with his quiet voice and competent hands. She'd rarely had to give him a task. He'd kept everything in order and had dealt with problems before she'd even been aware there were any.

Jacob Pinstone seemed adequate enough for the job, but he didn't have the initiative or enthusiasm that Clive had, and she couldn't get past the thought that Jacob was hiding a troubling past. He'd been evasive about his time in the merchant navy, and his reason for leaving. She had been in too much need of help to probe too deeply, but she often wondered lately if she'd made a mistake in hiring him.

"What about the other problem?" Baxter asked, interrupting her thoughts.

She swung around. "Which problem is that, dear?"

"The woman without a memory. What are you going to do about her?"

"Goodness." Cecily moved closer to the fire and held out her hands to the blaze. "With everything else going on I'd completely forgotten about her. I suppose we shall have to come to some decision sooner or later. I can't just turn her out into the street. I don't think Mrs. Chubb can take on any more staff. We turned down an application just the other day."

"Well, she can't stay here as a free guest indefinitely. Besides, she must have a family looking for her."

"Yes, you're quite right." Cecily stared at the glowing coals. "I think the best thing is for her to stay at the orphanage. They are always looking for help there. She can help them out until we can find out who she is and where her family might be. Right after Christmas I'll talk to Sam Northcott. Maybe he can help."

Baxter grunted with more than a hint of derision. "I suppose the lavatories are out-of-bounds until we get the water running again."

"I'm sorry, dear. I hope it won't be for too long."

"So do I," her husband said grimly, "or else we'll be facing far more serious problems than a woman who's lost her memory."

"I'd better go down and talk to Miss Memory, I suppose, and tell her what we've decided."

"Don't expect her to jump with joy."

"I know. I hate to do this right before Christmas, but I honestly don't know what else to do with the girl."

On her way down the stairs, Cecily tried to think of a good way to break the news to Miss Memory. She didn't want to seem heartless, but a busy hotel at Christmastime wasn't the best place for a young woman struggling with a lost memory. The orphanage had a medical staff who could do a much better job of helping her than anyone at the Pennyfoot.

Having assured herself she was doing the right thing, Cecily headed for the kitchen stairs. Just as she reached them, a short, stocky man with fading red hair and a droopy mustache appeared in front of her.

"Oh, there you are, Jacob!" Cecily stepped aside to allow the new maintenance man to enter the foyer. "I was hoping to have a word with you."

Jacob's gaze darted everywhere but at her face. "Is something wrong, m'm?"

"Not exactly. I was just wondering when you were going to clean up the lawns. Those dead leaves make the bowling greens look most bedraggled."

Jacob hunched his shoulders. "I didn't think I needed to do much out there, m'm, seeing as how nobody plays bowls in the middle of winter."

Cecily took a minute before answering. It had been on the tip of her tongue to give the man a piece of her mind. The last thing she needed, however, was for her maintenance man to walk out now. "Our guests may not be playing bowls," she said carefully, "but many of the windows overlook the greens, and grubby lawns give the impression that we are not taking care of the premises the way that we should. I'd greatly appreciate it if you would clean them up for me."

Jacob shrugged with a trace of insolence that set Cecily's teeth on edge. "Very well."

"There's one more thing," she said, striving to calm her voice. "Mrs. Fortescue should be in the ballroom by now, holding a rehearsal for the pantomime. This might be a good time to talk to her about the stage set. Have you finished it yet?"

Jacob swung his gaze up at the ceiling. "Not quite, m'm."

Cecily felt like hitting him. Then again, Phoebe would very likely do it for her when she found out her precious stage set hadn't been completed yet. "When can you have it finished, then? The pantomime is in two days. We need that set on the stage by tomorrow morning at the very latest."

Jacob nodded with remarkable indifference. "Not a worry, Mrs. Baxter. I'll have it there first thing in the morning."

"Well, do make sure you talk to Mrs. Fortescue before she leaves."

Jacob touched his forehead with his fingers for an answer and trudged across the foyer to the hallway.

Shaking her head, Cecily hurried down the steps and along the hallway to the maids' quarters. Reaching Pansy's door, she knocked and then opened it.

Miss Memory was lying on the bed reading a magazine. She dropped it when she saw Cecily, and with a look of guilt, swung her feet to the floor. "I was just resting, m'm," she said, getting up to bend her knees in a curtsey.

"That's quite all right." Cecily closed the door and crossed the room to her. "Sit down, Miss Memory. I'd like to talk to you about something."

Looking nervous now, the girl sat on the bed. "They're calling me Alice, m'm," she said, staring at the floor.

"Alice? That's a nice name." Cecily studied her for a

moment. "You still remember nothing about your past? Not even your real name?"

"No, m'm. Nothing." Alice kept her gaze glued to the floor.

Cecily sat down on the edge of the bed next to her. "Look . . . ah . . . Alice, we've been trying to think about what is best for you. This is a very busy hotel—I mean, country club—this time of year and we really don't have the time to look after you properly, so—"

Alice shot up her chin. "You don't have to, m'm. I can take care of myself."

"Yes, I know, but you have a medical problem that needs proper supervision and—"

"No, I don't! I just can't remember who I am or where I came from. It doesn't make me an invalid. I'm perfectly well, otherwise."

Cecily took a deep breath. "I'm making arrangements for you to go to the orphanage. They have people who can take care of you, and while you are there you can help them in return. They'll be most happy to have you and—"

"But I don't want to go to the orphanage. I want to stay here." Alice turned her big blue eyes on Cecily's face. "Please don't make me leave!"

Feeling like an ogre, Cecily got to her feet. "I'm sorry, Alice. I have to do what I think is best for you, and although you might not want to believe it now, eventually you'll find out I was right. I hope you soon recover your memory and then you can return to your own home. You can stay tonight and I'll have Charlie take you to the orphanage tomorrow morning."

She left the girl sitting miserably on the side of the bed,

and tried her best to convince herself she'd done the right thing as she made her way up the stairs again. It might be best for the girl, she thought, as she entered the foyer once more, but right then all she could think about was the misery in that young woman's face. This was not the way to spread the Christmas spirit.

CHAPTER

❀ 7 ❀

Pansy arrived back in the kitchen to find Mrs. Chubb waiting for her. The housekeeper wore her coat and hat, and the minute she laid eyes on Pansy she headed for the door. "Where have you been? I've been waiting here almost half an hour."

"I'm sorry, Mrs. Chubb." Pansy glanced at the clock. "I saw Tess out there and I had to get her back in the stables so she didn't wander off."

"Well, I hope someone's got my carriage ready. I've only got an hour and a half to do my shopping and get back here in time for the supper. I hope—"

She broke off as the door opened behind Pansy and a strange man with fair hair and twinkling blue eyes poked his head around it. "Is this where you need a plumber?"

Mrs. Chubb stared at the stranger. "Yes, it is. Who are you? Where's George Rutter?"

The man walked into the kitchen, a big grin plastered across his face. "I'm Bernard Bingham, the plumber. Just call me Bernie. George twisted his ankle and he's laid up. He sent me instead."

Mrs. Chubb sniffed and peered down her nose at the young man. "Well, I hope you can fix the water pipes. This is a busy place and we need the water back on right away. I have to go, but Pansy will show you where everything is." She stared hard at Pansy, then swept through the door and disappeared.

Pansy gave the plumber a weak smile. "The sink's over there." She nodded her head at it. "We haven't got no water anywhere. Not even in the lavs."

Bernie's eyebrows shot up and he opened his mouth in a round O, making him look a little like the picture of a clown she'd seen in one of the magazines. "Blimey, luv, we can't have that, now, can we. Let's see what we can do, then."

He walked over to the sink and dumped the large leather bag he was carrying on the ground. After turning on both taps, he shook his head, muttered something to himself, and opened the door to the cupboard beneath the sink.

Pansy hesitated, then said quickly, "I've got to go, so I'll leave you to it. All right?"

Bernie looked over his shoulder at her. "Oh, I thought you were going to stay and keep me company."

There was something in the bold way he looked at her that made her uncomfortable. Pansy edged toward the door. "I have to get the dining room ready for the evening meal."

"Well, it can wait awhile, can't it? It isn't every day I get the chance to talk to such a pretty girl. Come over here and tell me all about yourself."

Pansy crossed her arms. "The only thing I'll tell you about meself is that I'm getting married Christmas Eve, so I'm going now."

"Well, you tell your bloke from me he's a lucky lad." Bernie gave her an audacious wink that made her blush.

Her knees felt stiff as she opened the door, conscious of the plumber's eyes on her back. Safely outside in the hallway, she made a face at the kitchen door. *Cheeky bugger.* She should set Gertie on him. That'd soon take that saucy look out of his eyes. Thinking of Gertie, her frown disappeared. Right now her friend was visiting Clive in his toy shop. It had taken months of effort on Pansy's part to get those two together. Gertie had fought hard against falling in love with the big man. Pansy smiled at the memory. Now that her friend had finally listened to her heart instead of her head, Pansy couldn't be happier for her. All she hoped now was that Clive would ask Gertie to marry him and that would make this Christmas perfect for everyone.

Down at the toy shop, Gertie was having a hard time keeping her twins' hands off the merchandise. "Look at them," she said to Clive, as they stood behind the counter, which was piled high with smiling china dolls and stern-faced toy soldiers. "I told them not to bloody touch anything and they still can't keep their blinking hands off the toys."

Clive grinned at her. "They're children, Gertie. Of course they want to play with the toys."

"Well, they're not going to play with things that don't belong to them." She pulled in a long breath and let it out again in a bellow. "James! Lillian! Put that down and come here at once, or I'll tell Father Christmas to put flipping stones in your pillowcase instead of toys."

An elegant customer in a green fur-trimmed coat and enormous hat decorated with red ribbons turned to look at her.

Gertie resisted the urge to thumb her nose at her. Instead she concentrated on the twins, who were slinking up to her with mutiny on their faces. "Now, what did I tell you about touching things that don't belong to you?"

James stared down at his boots while Lillian said meekly, "Sorry, Mama, but the dolls are so lovely."

"I know they are." Gertie sent a wistful look at the fashionably dressed dolls lining the shelves. "But you know what I told you about Father Christmas not being able to bring everything you want. There are lots of children who don't get anything from him, so you have to be thankful for what he does bring."

"Why don't they get anything?" James demanded. "I thought Father Christmas came to every boy and girl."

"Not if they're naughty. Then all they get is stones."

Clive cleared his throat. "Perhaps it's time to change the subject," he said, reaching for the jar of lollipops on the counter. "Is it all right if they have one of these?"

Gertie rolled her eyes, but the twins were eagerly holding out their hands. "Oh, all right, but you'd better eat your supper tonight or—"

"We know," James said, and dropped his voice to a dreary moan. "Father Christmas will bring you stones instead of toys."

Clive burst out laughing, and covered Gertie's hand with his. "How are things at the Pennyfoot?"

"We miss you." She looked up at him. "*I* miss you. That bloody twerp Madam hired to take your place is no blinking good at all. He doesn't take care of the gardens, and he's never around when we need him."

Clive frowned. "I'm sorry to hear that. Perhaps Mrs. Baxter should find someone else."

"I think she only took him on because she couldn't find no one else." Gertie picked up the wrapper Lillian had dropped on the floor and crushed it in her hand.

"Here. I'll take that." Clive took the wrapper from her and dropped it in a basket.

She smiled up at him. It wasn't many men that were taller than her. Then again, Clive wasn't just tall, he was bulky, too. A big man in both size and heart, with the softest brown eyes that seemed to smile all the time he was looking at her. Like right now. "Are you coming to the carol singing tomorrow night?"

"Wouldn't miss it." He nodded at the twins. "Are they coming, too?"

"Nah. They need their sleep."

"Good. There's something we need to talk about."

Something in the way he said it started a niggling worry in the back of her mind. She tried to dismiss it, lowering her voice as the twins wandered off again. "Did you hear about the bloke that was found dead on the beach?"

Clive looked worried. "I did. I hope it wasn't anyone you know."

"He was a guest at the Pennyfoot."

Clive's frown intensified. "Do the police know who killed him?"

Gertie shook her head. "Daffy old P.C. Northcott wouldn't recognize a killer if one came up and introduced himself. I told Madam I thought it might be Lord Bentley. I heard him threatening the dead bloke. When he was still alive, I mean."

"What did she say to that?"

"She said she didn't think it could be him."

Clive nodded. "That's probably right. I'm sure there isn't anything to worry about."

He didn't look sure, though, and Gertie couldn't help feeling uneasy as she walked with the twins back to the country club. It gave her a nasty feeling to know that there could be a killer lurking about in the Pennyfoot. It wasn't the first time that had happened, and when it did, the biggest thing she worried about was her children.

Looking down at them skipping along by her side, she tried to shake off her disquiet. There was something else worrying her, she realized. Clive wanted to talk to her about something and he'd looked really serious when he'd said it. Whatever it was, she had a feeling she wasn't going to like it.

In the next instant, she decided she was imagining things. It was Christmas, and she wasn't about to let anything spoil it for her twins. Clive wouldn't say or do anything to hurt her. She had to believe that. As for Lord Bentley, well, he didn't seem like a killer. The murder couldn't have anything to do with the Pennyfoot. This year the Christmas curse would have to find somewhere else to go.

Having told Baxter she was visiting the library to exchange her book, Cecily ordered a carriage at the front door. It wasn't totally a lie, she assured herself, as she rode along the Esplanade listening to the clattering of the horses' hooves. She had planned to go to the library, just not today.

A chill wind found its way through a crack in the door, and she wrapped her fur tightly around her shoulders. Her toes felt numb, in spite of her warm boots, and she wriggled them to get the circulation back into them.

As the carriage entered the High Street, the horse slowed to a walk, hampered by shoppers crossing the road, people on bicycles, and the occasional motorcar. Cecily was not fond of the noisy machines that were fast taking over from the horse and carriage.

They were always popping and banging, startling the horses and causing more than one to rear up or even bolt down the street with a carriage bouncing behind it. She was quite thankful when the footman pulled up outside the library.

When he jumped down to help her down from her seat, she was surprised to recognize Henry, the new stable assistant. She'd been so wrapped up in her thoughts she hadn't taken notice of him when she'd boarded the carriage.

He seemed nervous as he clutched her gloved hand, keeping his gaze firmly on the ground.

Feeling sorry for him, she gently withdrew her hand. "I didn't expect to see you in the driver's seat, Henry. The footmen must be busy."

"Yes, m'm. Charlie asked me to take over."

Something was bothering him, Cecily thought, as she studied the young man. He seemed determined not to look her in the face. "How are things in the stables? I hope you are happy working for the Pennyfoot Hotel." Baxter's voice corrected her in her mind. *Country Club.* She ignored it. "Is Charlie treating you well?"

"Very well, m'm. Thank you."

"I'm pleased to hear it." She gathered up her skirt. "I shan't be long. You can wait inside the carriage if you like, out of this wind. It's quite biting this afternoon."

"Yes, m'm. Thank you, m'm."

She glanced over her shoulder as she went inside the library. Henry still stood by the carriage as if turned to stone.

Shaking her head, she dropped her book into the return box and headed for the shelves. The library had been built just a year or so earlier, and she still found it overwhelming to be in the midst of so many books with so many choices. Normally she would have spent an hour or so browsing the shelves, but today time was precious and fleeting. She grabbed the first book that looked interesting and carried it to the front desk.

The librarian, a young woman with inquisitive blue eyes and red hair wound into a tight knot, greeted her. "Mrs. Baxter! What a pleasure to see you!"

"Likewise, Caroline." Cecily smiled. "I don't see many people in here today."

"It's the Christmas season. People don't have time to read." She peered at the title on the book. "You will enjoy this, I'm sure." She opened the cover and took out the card. "Isn't it dreadful about that poor man found dead on the beach?"

Cecily took a moment to compose her voice. "Yes, it is. Quite a shock to all of us."

Caroline leaned across the counter. "He was in here, you know. Just a week ago. He spent hours poring over copies of old newspapers. I thought there was something strange about him. Then, when I heard he'd been killed, well, it just about made me ill. I kept thinking about him sitting there, never knowing he was going to die so soon."

"How awful." Cecily shuddered herself. She was glad when another customer approached the desk and she could make her escape.

Handing the book to Henry outside, she told him, "I have to run into the post office. I'll be back in a minute."

Henry nodded, mumbling, "Yes, m'm."

Hurrying into the post office, Cecily saw one other customer ahead of her—an elderly gentleman with a shock of white hair and a monocle. He nodded at her as he left, and she smiled in return, then turned her attention to the postmaster.

He was a robust man with red-stained cheeks and a nose that could be attributed to a fondness for the excellent ale served at the Fox and Hounds. He seemed astonished to see her, as well he might. She could count on one hand the number of times she had visited the post office in the last few years. In fact, she was rather surprised he recognized her.

"Good morning, Mrs. Baxter. This is a pleasant surprise.

How are things at the Pennyfoot Hotel? Business booming, I hope?"

"Very much so, thank you, Mr. Thompson." She opened the black-beaded pouch she carried and withdrew the note. "I have a favor to ask of you," she said, laying the note in front of him. "I have reason to believe that one of our guests sent this as a telegram. I was wondering if you could possibly tell me to whom it was sent, and if there were any others sent to the same person?"

Thompson puffed out his chest. "Well, now, Mrs. Baxter, I don't think I can do that without the gentleman's permission. I don't suppose you have a signed statement from him giving you permission?"

Cecily leaned forward and lowered her voice. "The gentleman in question is dead, Mr. Thompson. Otherwise I would have asked him myself about the telegram."

Thompson coughed, cleared his throat, and stretched his neck. "Ah, I see. I'm assuming we are referring to the dead man found on the beach yesterday?"

Cecily sighed. It was naïve of her to think that the news wouldn't have spread throughout the village. "Oh, so you've heard about that," she murmured.

"Yes, m'm." He leaned toward her. "I heard that Northcott was on the case."

"Well, yes, he is, but—"

"Say no more, m'm. We all know who really solves these cases." He reached for the note and read it. "My telegraph operator isn't in today, but I should be able to find it in the files." He turned to take down a large box file from a shelf and laid it on the counter. After sorting through its contents for a moment or two, he pounced on a sheet of paper and held it up. "Ah, here it is." He handed her the paper. "Is this what you were looking for?"

Cecily took the page and studied it. It was addressed to Mr. Harold Clements, at an address in Finsbury Park, London. It read exactly as the note she'd found. "Yes, it is. Did he send any others to this address?"

"Let me look." Thompson riffled through the papers again. "That's strange. I seem to remember . . . Ah! Here it is." He studied it for a second or two. "Sent on the day he died, by the look of it."

Pulse quickening, Cecily took the form from him. The words seemed to jump out at her.

> STAYING AT THE PENNYFOOT STOP
> CERTAIN OUR SEARCH ENDS THERE STOP
> JOIN ME AT FOX AND HOUNDS
> IMMEDIATELY STOP

Cecily stared at the words for several seconds, her mind racing. All the suspicions she'd done her best to ignore rushed to the forefront of her mind. Whatever crime Gerald Evans had been investigating had something to do with the Pennyfoot. That's why he'd booked a room there. And that was most likely why he was killed. So it would seem that once more the Pennyfoot was playing host to a killer.

She had one more stop to make before she could go home.

"I need to pay a visit to the Fox and Hounds," she told Henry, when she returned to the carriage.

His eyes opened wide. He started to speak, swallowed, then managed a hoarse, "Yes, m'm."

Rolling her eyes, Cecily climbed up into the carriage. Even Samuel, who had been by her side through so many hair-raising adventures, had always acted shocked at the thought of her visiting a public house. This in spite of the fact that she had done so many times, and so far had suffered no consequences.

The ride out of town was quite pleasant, in spite of the cold. The quiet country lanes, lined with bushy green hedges and leafless trees, seemed tranquil after the bustling streets of the town, and by the time they reached the Fox and Hounds she was feeling a little more relaxed.

Barry Collins, the jovial publican, greeted her with a hearty welcome. "You're alone?" Barry looked past her to where Henry stood dutifully by the horse's head. "Where's Samuel?"

Again the twinge. Cecily took a deep breath. "Samuel is no longer with us. He has his own business now. I'm surprised you didn't know that."

Barry grinned. "I did. It just seems strange not to see him hovering behind you." He nodded at Henry. "He's not coming in?"

"Not this time. I shan't be long." She stepped inside, out of the wind, but refused Barry's offer to be seated in the private lounge. "I have no more than a moment," she said. "I was wondering if you knew the gentleman who was found dead on the beach yesterday."

As she'd expected, Barry nodded his head. "Mr. Evans. I was surprised to read about it in the newspaper. He was staying here, you know, right up until four days ago. He'd booked for two weeks, right through Christmas, but he was only halfway through the first week when he said he had to return home."

"Did he say why?"

"Family emergency."

"I see." Gerald Evans had said he was dissatisfied with his hotel. He hadn't mentioned the public house. Obviously his decision to move to the Pennyfoot had been a sudden one. She wondered what he'd discovered to send him posthaste to the country club. "Did he talk to anyone in particular while he was here?"

Barry shrugged. "Not that I know of. He seemed a bit of a loner. Went off quite a bit on his own. He wasn't one to enjoy a chat, if you know what I mean."

"Well, thank you, Barry. I appreciate you taking the time to talk to me."

"Sure you don't want to stay for a nice drop of your favorite sherry? It's been a long time."

It was tempting, but again she refused. Bidding him a happy Christmas, she left the warmth of the Fox and Hounds and braved the cold, damp seat of the carriage once more.

On the ride back she went over in her mind what she had learned. Gerald Evans had done some extensive research at the library. Had there been something he'd found in those old newspapers that had led him to the Pennyfoot?

Whoever had killed him must have discovered his whereabouts and what he was up to, despite all the care he had taken. He had sent that final telegram the morning he'd died—the telegram that stated his belief that his search ended at the Pennyfoot. It was up to her now to find out exactly what he meant by those cryptic words.

CHAPTER

❀ 8 ❀

"I cannot believe you would hire someone so utterly incompetent and downright offensive." Phoebe's frail frame shook with anger as she waved a hand at the ballroom door. "That . . . that *ruffian* had the nerve to tell me he had more important things to do than mess around with my stage set." She glared at Cecily. "Where on earth did you find him? Does he have *any* idea who I am and what I do? Does he even know how to make a stage set?"

Cecily tried to ignore the throbbing pain in the back of her head. It had been a very long day and all she wanted was to go up to her suite, put her feet up on a hassock, and close her eyes. She had waited until the entire dance troupe had left before seeking out Phoebe in the ballroom, and she wasn't in any mood to deal with her friend's histrionics. "Jacob assured me he would have your set ready by tomorrow morning," she said, trying to keep the irritation out of her voice.

"Well, I should hope so." Phoebe straightened her hat, which had tilted forward in her indignation. "Did he give you references when you hired him? His manner is most uncouth. He most likely got sacked from his last employment."

"Actually Jacob was in the merchant navy before coming here. He seemed to know a great deal about making repairs and general custodial work." Not that it was any of Phoebe's business, she told herself, with just a hint of resentment.

Phoebe opened her eyes wide. "In the navy? No wonder the man is so coarse. Why did he leave?"

"I didn't ask. Janitors are hard to come by in these parts."

She must have spoken more sharply than she intended. Phoebe had the kind of look on her face she always got when her dance troupe misbehaved—which was practically all the time. "Well, I certainly hope he keeps his word. Though, if you ask me, a man with that kind of attitude rarely keeps his word about anything. I just hope we don't have to do the entire pantomime without a set or props." Her expression suggested that the consequences would be entirely on Cecily's shoulders.

Too tired to argue further, Cecily walked to the door. "I'm quite sure we can come up with a solution that will work for you, Phoebe. Now, if you will excuse me, I have to take care of something."

"Does anybody know who killed that man on the beach yet?"

Cecily paused, one hand on the door. "I imagine P.C. Northcott will let us know when he has some news about that."

"Oh, I thought you might be looking into it." Phoebe joined her at the door. "After all, everyone knows you do most of the investigating when something like this happens."

Cecily looked her squarely in the eye. "I'm much too busy with everything going on here to chase after murderers."

Phoebe actually looked disappointed. "Ah, well, that's one murder that will probably never be solved, then. Good night, Cecily. I do hope you are in a more congenial frame of mind by tomorrow." She swept out the door, leaving Cecily feeling guilty for apparently upsetting her friend.

On her way up the stairs, she passed Lord Bentley and Lady Elizabeth, together with their daughter, Essie. Both women nodded and murmured a greeting, but Lord Bentley passed by her without acknowledging her presence.

It would seem that Jacob Pinstone wasn't the only gentleman without manners, she thought wryly as she mounted the rest of the stairs. They made her husband seem positively merry by comparison. Smiling, she quickened her pace. Baxter would be waiting for her, and right now she could ask for nothing more than that.

"I want everyone upstairs," Mrs. Chubb announced the following morning, when the last of the breakfast dishes had been put away. "Although we've got water in the kitchen, Bernie is still working on the plumbing in the upstairs lavatories. The downstairs lavatory is working, but until they're all working again, we'll have our hands full emptying chamber pots."

A chorus of groans answered her and she folded her arms across her bosom. "I don't want any cheek from any of you.

You're all lucky to be working in a hotel that has indoor lavatories. When I started out the lavatory was a shed outside with a toilet bowl under the seat and nothing to flush it all away. It had to be emptied and cleaned out every day."

"Was that when you worked on Noah's Ark?" Lilly asked, prompting shouts of laughter from the other maids.

"None of your cheek, Lilly Green." Mrs. Chubb wagged a finger at her. "For that you can start on the top floor. You'll have to bring down the chamber pots one at a time and empty them in the maid's lavatory."

Lilly opened her mouth to answer, then at the sight of Mrs. Chubb's fierce scowl, apparently thought better of it. Without another word, she stomped out of the kitchen.

Standing at the sink, Gertie nudged Pansy in the ribs. "Serves her bloody well right," she murmured, just loud enough for her friend to hear. "Who does she think she is, anyway? She acts like a bleeding duchess instead of a maid."

Pansy smiled. "I don't think she's used to working in a hotel. Maybe she was a lady's maid before this. They don't have to work as hard as we do."

Gertie sniffed. "Pampered, that's what they are. They don't know what hard work is, that's for blinking sure."

"Well, Lilly will learn. She's still getting used to everything."

Gertie wiped her hands on a tea towel. "I'm going to miss you," she said, suddenly realizing how much. "It won't be the same around here without you."

Pansy's bottom lip quivered just a bit. "I'm going to miss you, too. I'll try to come and visit as often as I can. You can come and visit me in my new home."

"I'd like that." Gertie hung the tea towel over the sink. "Can I bring the twins?"

"'Course you can! You know I always love to see them. They can play with Tess."

"They'd love it." She opened a drawer and started taking out a handful of silverware. "I wonder if P.C. Northcott has found out who killed Mr. Evans yet."

Pansy's smile vanished. "What made you think of that?"

"Dunno. Thinking about the twins, I suppose." Gertie pulled a tray toward her and laid out the knives, forks, and spoons. "I think Lord Bentley had something to do with it. I heard him shouting at Mr. Evans for messing about with his daughter."

"Well, if you ask me, the bloke deserved it."

Gertie stared at her in surprise. "Whatcha mean?"

Pansy's cheeks turned red, and she kept her gaze firmly on the warming plate she was cleaning. "I mean that Mr. Evans couldn't keep his hands to himself. I had to squeeze by him once in the dining room 'cos his big, fat belly was in the way. As I went by him he put his hands where he shouldn't."

Gertie gasped. "Did you tell Mrs. Chubb?"

Pansy shook her head. "I was too upset to say anything to anyone. I just made sure I kept out of his way after that."

Gertie gritted her teeth. If there was one thing she couldn't stand, it was a man who took advantage of a woman. She was feeling a lot less sorry for Gerald Evans now.

"I wasn't the only one," Pansy added, just as Gertie was about to head for the dumbwaiter.

Gertie paused, the heavy tray in her hands. "Who else, then?"

"Lilly." Pansy glanced over her shoulder. "I saw Mr. Evans

113

and her in the hallway. He had her backed up against the wall. She looked scared to death. I called out to her and he walked away from her in a hurry." Pansy laid the warming plate down on the counter. "She didn't even thank me for rescuing her. She just ran off down the hallway."

"Bloody sod. Good job he didn't try anything with me."

Pansy managed a wobbly smile. "He was probably afraid you'd box his ears."

"I'd have done a lot more than that." Seething with anger against the dead man, she stared down at the tray. No wonder someone had stuck a knife in him. If that filthy bugger had tried anything with her she might have done it herself.

"He was always talking smarmy," Pansy said, shuddering. "Not like Charlie, or that new plumber. They're just being cheeky, and they never put their hands where they shouldn't."

Gertie raised her eyebrows. "The new plumber? He was cheeky to you?"

Pansy shrugged. "Yeah, but he didn't make me cringe the way Mr. Evans did."

"Why are you two standing around blabbering when there's work to be done?"

Mrs. Chubb's irritated voice made Gertie jump. "We're just getting ready to go up to the dining room." She hurried over to the dumbwaiter, laid the tray on the platform, and started pulling on the rope.

"Well, get a move on. We haven't got all day." The housekeeper spun around and headed for the pantry.

Gertie made a face. "What's got her bleeding knickers in a twist today?"

Pansy shrugged. "I dunno. But we'd better do as she says or she'll be——"

She broke off as the door flew open so hard it banged against the wall. Lilly appeared in the doorway, her cap half off her head and her eyes wide in her white face. "There's been an accident," she said, her voice high with anxiety.

Mrs. Chubb burst out of the pantry holding a milk jug and a plate of butter. "Accident? Where? Who's hurt?"

Lilly's voice broke on a sob and Gertie got a sick feeling in her stomach. *Please, not another murder.* She stared at Lilly, waiting with thumping heart for the bad news.

Pansy edged close to Gertie, one hand over her mouth. "Oh, Gawd, what now?" she mumbled.

"One of the maids . . . Charlotte . . . she's hurt!" Lilly got out, then promptly burst into tears.

"Here. Sit down." Mrs. Chubb dragged out a chair and unceremoniously shoved Lilly down on it. "Now, take a deep breath and tell us what happened."

Lilly gulped, swallowed, and managed to take in a lungful of air. "She tripped coming down the stairs and fell all the way to the bottom."

"Bloody hell," Gertie muttered. "Was she carrying a full chamber pot? I bet that made a bloody mess."

Mrs. Chubb gave her a withering look. "How bad is she hurt? Is someone with her?"

"Philip sent for Mrs. Baxter. He said to come and tell you."

"I'd better get up there and see what's going on." Mrs. Chubb untied her apron and threw it at the hook on the wall. It missed and fell to the ground, but the housekeeper ignored it. "Get that silverware up to the dining room," she said, as the door closed behind her.

Gertie stared at the door for several seconds, then Lilly moaned, grabbing her attention. "I hope she's not dead. Two dead bodies in one week is more than enough for me. This place is cursed, just like I was told."

Gertie crossed her arms. "Who bloody told you that?"

"Lots of people. They all said that the Pennyfoot is cursed around Christmastime."

"Well, they're flipping wrong." Gertie nudged Pansy again. "Tell her they're wrong."

"They're wrong," Pansy said obediently.

Lilly sniffed. "Then why is one of the guests dead and probably a maid, as well?"

"It could happen anywhere." Gertie walked over to her and bent down so she could look her in the face. "We don't talk about no curses here. Not to anyone. We never mention the word. Understand?"

Lilly nodded and fished in her apron pocket for a handkerchief.

"Good. Now, did all the chamber pots get emptied?"

"I dunno." She gasped. "Oh, crumbs. I left one sitting by the stairs. I had to jump out of the way when Charlotte came tumbling down and I put it down on the floor. In all the commotion I forgot it."

Gertie rolled her eyes. "Well, you'd better get back up there and fetch it. If Mrs. Baxter sees that she'll have a pink fit."

Without another word Lilly shot off her chair and rushed from the kitchen.

Pansy stood by the sink, hugging herself as if she were cold. "Do you think Mr. Evans's killer pushed Charlotte downstairs?"

"No, I don't." Gertie's voice was sharp with apprehension and she made an effort to soften it. She didn't want to believe there was another killer on the loose in the Pennyfoot, yet Lilly's mention of the curse had filled her with dread. "I think it was an accident, and poor Charlotte tripped on the stairs. She's always been a bit clumsy. I just hope she's all right."

Pansy looked ready to cry. "So do I. Why is all this happening now? I should be happy and excited, looking forward to my wedding, not shaking inside with fear."

A surge of sympathy for her friend prompted Gertie to put an arm around Pansy's thin shoulders. "Don't worry, luv. We're not going to let nothing spoil your wedding, and that's a promise."

Pansy turned soulful eyes up at her. "I hope you're right. I've been waiting for this day all my life."

"And it's going to be the best day of your life, you wait and see." Gertie forced a grin and tried not to listen to the voice in her head reminding her of the chaos the curse could create. She sent up a silent prayer instead, asking that Pansy's wedding be everything her friend had dreamed about. Killer or not.

After receiving the bad news from a teary-eyed maid, Cecily had raced down the stairs fast enough to put herself in danger of falling. Now kneeling beside the still figure of Charlotte, she prayed the child wasn't seriously hurt. At least she was still breathing, though her face was the color of Mrs. Chubb's bleached sheets. "Ring for Dr. Prestwick," she told Philip, who hovered above her like an anxious bee. "Tell him to come at once. He should be in his surgery at this hour."

Charlotte moaned and to Cecily's relief opened her eyes. She started to speak then cried out in pain, clutching her arm.

"She's probably broken it," Mrs. Chubb said, having just arrived. She sounded out of breath and held her hand at her throat. "Poor little lamb."

Cecily laid a hand on Charlotte's shoulder. "Lie still, child. I'm hoping the doctor will be here soon." She looked up as Philip appeared at her side.

"Dr. Prestwick says he'll be here just as soon as he can. He said not to move her, unless she can get up by herself."

Cecily looked at the tears rolling down Charlotte's cheeks. "I don't think she's getting up by herself." She looked up at Mrs. Chubb. "We'll have to make her as comfortable as possible here. A pillow, blanket, and fetch me a powder and a glass of water."

"Right away, m'm." The housekeeper frowned at the dark stains on the stair carpet and the remains of the smashed chamber pot scattered across the floor. "It looks like we've got some cleaning up to do, as well. I'll get someone up here with hot water and vinegar. Thank heavens we've got water in the kitchen again." She stared anxiously at the fallen maid. "I do hope she will be all right."

"If it's no more than a broken bone, that will mend." Cecily smiled down at Charlotte. "The doctor will take care of you and you will soon be right as rain. Gertie's son broke his arm one Christmas and by the spring he was doing hand-stands on the lawn."

Charlotte managed a weak smile, making Cecily feel a good deal easier. Mrs. Chubb had vanished, no doubt on her way to fetch the items Cecily had requested. All that was left now was to try and keep Charlotte comfortable until Kevin Prestwick arrived.

A minute or so later Gertie appeared with the pillow and blanket under one arm and carrying a glass of water. Lilly trudged behind her hauling a bucket of water and rags. While she got to work on the carpet, Gertie helped Cecily prop the pillow behind Charlotte's head and covered her with the blanket. The young maid seemed to be in a good deal of pain, and Cecily hurriedly shook the powder into the water and instructed Charlotte to drink it all down.

She had just swallowed the last drop when the door opened and Dr. Prestwick strode in carrying a large black bag.

"I'm so happy to see you," Cecily declared as he crouched down beside the maid. "Charlotte fell a full flight of stairs. I think her arm may be broken."

The doctor gently ran his fingers over Charlotte's arm, causing another moan from her. "Bear with me just a moment," he murmured, and ran his hands over her other arm and legs, all the while asking if that hurt and getting a shake of the head in answer. Finally he seemed satisfied and reached for his bag. "You're right, Cecily. The arm is broken. I'll strap it up here and then take her to my surgery, where I can put it in a cast." He smiled at the tearful maid. "Looks like you'll be out of action for a while, young lady. It could have been a lot worse."

Cecily shivered. "That corner of the staircase is too shadowed on these dark winter days. The light from the gas lamps doesn't reach there. We usually have an oil lamp sitting on the corner table. I don't know why it isn't there now, but I'll make sure it's there in future."

"Good idea." Prestwick took bandages from his bag and began carefully strapping the maid's arm.

Cecily watched anxiously until the doctor was finished. She was relieved when he assured her that Charlotte's injury was a simple break and would heal in a few weeks. She watched them leave, and was about to go upstairs to inform Baxter of the latest calamity when Alice appeared across the foyer at the top of the kitchen stairs.

She wore a hat and warm coat, no doubt given her by one of the staff. Cecily felt a glow of pride at the thought. She had the best people in the world working for her.

Walking toward the girl, she was impressed by the way Alice held herself, with a straight back and head held high. Obviously she had come from a good home, and some good people must be worrying themselves sick wondering what had happened to her.

If only Gerald Evans hadn't died, he might have been able to find her parents. Then again, no one in the country club had known that he was a private investigator, so that would have been a moot point. Though Cecily liked to think she would have guessed as much, had she had the chance to talk to him.

Reaching Alice, she gave the young woman a warm smile. "Ready to go? I expect Charlie will be here any minute with the carriage."

Alice didn't return the smile. "I heard about the maid falling down the stairs," she said, looking up at Cecily with sad eyes. "I hope she isn't badly hurt?"

"A broken arm, I'm afraid."

"Oh, I'm so very sorry. I suppose that means she won't be able to work for a while."

Cecily sighed. "Yes, that certainly seems to be the case."

Alice took a small step toward her, hope creeping across her face. "I was wondering if you need someone to take her place? Just to get through the Christmas rush, I mean. I'll be glad to help out if you like."

Cecily hesitated. Alice didn't look robust enough to take on the work of a maid in a place as busy as the Pennyfoot. Then again, she'd had young girls working for her before who had seemed just as frail. It was more the girl's demeanor—*delicate* was the word. Alice didn't look as if she'd lifted a finger her entire life.

"I'll work really hard for you," Alice said, practically going on her knees in her effort to convince Cecily. "Please, Mrs. Baxter. I really don't want to spend Christmas in the orphanage."

It was those last words that broke down Cecily's reservations. "Very well, then. Someone will have to show you what to do, and that's going to take time away from whoever does that, so I'll expect you to put in an extra effort."

Alice nodded the whole time Cecily was talking, her face glowing with relief. "Oh, I will, Mrs. Baxter. I promise."

"Then go down to the kitchen and tell Mrs. Chubb that I hired you. Just until after the Christmas holidays. Is that clear?"

"Oh yes, Mrs. Baxter. Thanks ever so much!"

"And please tell Mrs. Chubb that I would like to speak to the plumber. I would like to know when he expects to get the upstairs lavatories working again."

"Yes, Mrs. Baxter, I'll tell her."

Baxter's voice spoke from behind Cecily, startling both women. "Is this the young lady who lost her memory?"

Alice's expression changed so swiftly Cecily was shocked. With a look of terror on her face, she bent her knees in a curtsey and spun around so fast she almost lost her balance. Flinging one hand out to steady herself, she leapt down the stairs and disappeared.

Cecily turned to see astonishment on her husband's face. "Good Lord, whatever did I say to cause that?"

"I have no idea, darling, but I'm sure it wasn't anything you said." She slipped her hand under his arm. "Come, let us go upstairs."

"But I've just come down. I was going to take a stroll outside before the midday meal."

Cecily gave his arm a tug. "I'm afraid I have some unsettling news and it's best that I tell you all of it in the privacy of our suite."

"All of it?" His eyes opened wider in alarm. "Not another dead body, I hope?"

"No, dear. At least it's not that bad." She led him to the stairs, nodding at a couple of guests as they passed by. He wasn't going to be too happy with her news, she thought, as she climbed the stairs. It was bad enough that she had to tell him about Charlotte's unfortunate accident. The news that Gerald Evans had been investigating a crime involving the

Pennyfoot would really upset her husband. A promise was a promise, however, and if she intended to find out what was going on, she had no choice but to include him in her investigation. That was something she looked forward to with a certain amount of trepidation.

CHAPTER

❊ 9 ❊

Mrs. Chubb stood in the middle of the kitchen, arms folded and a fierce scowl on her face. "Are you telling me," she said, "that Madam hired you as a maid to work here throughout Christmas?"

Alice meekly nodded. "Yes, Mrs. Chubb."

"Have you done any maid's work before?"

Alice stared up at her. "I don't know," she said at last.

Feeling sorry for the girl, Gertie spoke up. "How could she know that?" she demanded. "She ain't got no bloody memory, remember?"

Mrs. Chubb pinched her lips together. "Well," she said at last, "I don't know how much good you'll be. You'll just have to do your best and not get in anybody's way. We don't have the time to teach you anything. Not in the middle of the Christmas season and with a wedding and all. We're rushed off our feet as it is."

"I'll teach her," Gertie said, drying her hands on her apron. "Lilly's doing all right now. She can help. Between us we'll get through Christmas. As well as the wedding."

"All right, then." Mrs. Chubb rubbed a floury hand across her forehead, leaving a white streak behind. "I just keep wondering what else can happen to make things more difficult for us."

"Oh, and Mrs. Baxter said to tell you she wants to speak with the plumber," Alice said, after giving Gertie a grateful smile. "She wants to know when the lavatories will be working again."

"So do I," the housekeeper said, looking grim. "Gawd knows what he's doing up there. George would have had it all done by now."

The door swung open as she spoke and Michel barged into the kitchen, his white chef's hat bobbing on his head. "Why eez everyone standing around twiddling their thumbs, eh?" He pointed a bony finger at Alice. "You again? Why does she keep coming in my kitchen?"

To everyone's surprise, Alice shrieked and dived behind Mrs. Chubb's plump body.

Michel took a step back. "*Sacre bleu!* What is the matter with the child?"

"She's not a child," Mrs. Chubb said, putting a hand behind her to hold Alice's arm. "Gertie, take Alice up to the dining room and show her how to lay a table." She glanced at the clock that hung over the stove. "You'll have to get a move on. It's almost time for the midday meal."

"Yes, Mrs. Chubb." Gertie headed for the door. "Come on, Alice. Let's get started on the blinking tables before the hungry mob gets there." She waited for Alice to dart into the hallway ahead of her, and exchanged a mystified look with the housekeeper before letting the door swing shut behind her.

Alice was already halfway up the stairs when Gertie caught up with her. "What's your bloomin' hurry?" she muttered as she reached Alice's side.

"I thought we were in a hurry to get the tables laid."

Gertie rolled her eyes as Alice sped across the foyer and into the hallway. It was almost as if the girl was afraid to be seen. She followed more slowly, determined not to be rushed more than she had to be. Alice would just have to learn to take the proper time to do things. Shaking her head, she headed for the dining room.

"Charlotte *what*?"

Cecily winced at the desperation in her husband's voice. "She broke her arm. Kevin assured me she will be just fine in a few weeks. Meanwhile I—"

"A few weeks?" Baxter sank onto a chair, rubbing at his brow with two fingers. "We shall have to find someone to replace her."

"I already have, darling." Cecily seated herself on the other side of the fireplace. "Alice asked if she could fill in for the Christmas season. It was fortunate she was here. She might not know much about working in a hotel—country club . . . but I'm sure she'll work out just fine. She seems quite bright."

"That's apart from the fact that she has no idea who she is or where she came from."

"Yes, there's that." Cecily stared into the embers smoldering in the fireplace. "I have to admit, I did have reservations, but Alice seemed confident she could manage the work, so I suppose we shall just have to wait and see."

Baxter leaned back in his chair. "I wish Pansy had waited to get married until after Christmas."

"But Christmas is such a lovely time to have a wedding, with all the decorations and excitement of the season. The reception should be lovely. I'm looking forward to it."

Baxter glanced at the window. "Well, let's hope we don't have a snowstorm to complicate matters. Things get so messy when it's snowing out there."

Cecily drew a deep breath. "There's something else you should know." She told him about her visit to the post office. "It would appear that the crime Gerald Evans was investigating somehow involves the Pennyfoot."

She saw his expression change and quickly added, "I know I should have told you last night, but I was so tired, I just couldn't face discussing it all."

She expected an outburst from her husband, and was surprised when, after a short pause, he murmured, "You didn't really expect anything else, did you?"

Flustered, she locked her fingers in her lap. "I suppose I was hoping it had nothing to do with us, though I have to admit, I've had an uneasy feeling about the whole thing since Mr. Evans's body was found."

"Well, it wouldn't be Christmas at the Pennyfoot if we didn't have at least one dead body turning up." Baxter stretched out his legs and stared gloomily at his feet. "I suppose you'll have to inform Northcott, and then we'll have him poking around all over the place."

"As a matter of fact," Cecily said carefully, "I do believe he's due to leave for his annual visit to his wife's relatives in London."

Baxter eyed her with a furrowed brow. "Does that mean what I think it means?"

Cecily fidgeted with her feet. "It means I shall have to look into this myself."

She waited for an explosion that never came.

Baxter stared at her for several long seconds, then uttered a lengthy sigh. "All right then. Where do we start?"

She leaned forward. "You really want to help?"

"Of course I do. I've told you that already."

She reached out for his hand. "Thank you, dear. Though right at this moment, I really don't have much to go on." Something clicked in her memory, and she got up from her chair. "Just a moment. I do have something."

Hurrying into the boudoir, she tried to decide if she was happy or apprehensive about her husband's assistance with the investigation. Not that it made much difference at this point, she reminded herself. The deal was already struck and she was stuck with it—good or bad.

She opened the wardrobe and dived into the pocket of her blue serge skirt. Her fingers found the slab of cardboard she'd found in Gerald Evans's room. Carrying it back to the fireplace, she handed it to Baxter. "What do you make of that?"

Baxter turned it over in his hands. "It looks like some kind of protective packaging."

"That's what I thought."

"Where did you get it?"

"I found it in a dresser drawer when Sam and I searched Mr. Evans's room." She sat down again. "I was going to throw it away, but forgot about it until now. I can't imagine why it would be important, yet now that I think about it, since it was carefully tucked into the drawer, it must be significant in some way. I think Mr. Evans was keeping it for a reason."

"It doesn't look like anything we'd use here at the club."

"I know. I just wish I could tell where it came from."

Baxter held the cardboard up to the light from the gas lamp on the wall. "I can't see any lettering anywhere."

"There is none."

"So how is this going to help us?"

"I don't know." She paused, then added slowly, "I just know somewhere in the back of my mind there's a connection between this and something else I've seen. Or maybe heard. I'm not sure. I just have to remember what that is."

Baxter looked intrigued. "I never could understand how you do that."

She smiled. "I haven't done anything yet. But it's there, and sooner or later I'll make that connection. Whether or not it will tell us what Gerald Evans was doing here remains to be seen."

Baxter nodded. "I have not a single doubt, my dear wife, that you will untangle all the knots and solve this puzzle as you have done so often in the past. And this time, I will be here to help you."

He got up and walked over to a cabinet, where he took out a bottle of sherry and two glasses. "It's a little early in the day, but this calls for a toast." He walked back to her and stood the glasses on the table at her side.

She watched him pour the dark brown liquid into the glasses and took the one he handed her.

"To a new partnership," he said, and touched her glass with his. "May we be successful in finding out what the late private detective was doing in Badgers End, and who killed him."

"Amen to that." She sipped the sweet cream sherry, and prayed that no matter what awaited her and her new partner in crime, they would both emerge unscathed.

Pansy slipped the large bone into her apron pocket, hoping it wouldn't stain too much. The laundry maids were always complaining about her greasy pockets, thanks to her habit of smuggling treats for Tess out of the kitchen.

Glancing at the clock above the stove she decided she had maybe fifteen minutes before Mrs. Chubb would be hollering for her. Lilly was up in the dining room laying tables with Gertie and the new maid, giving Pansy a few minutes' respite before the midday meal was served.

She waited until Mrs. Chubb went into the pantry. A quick glance at Michel assured her he was too busy with his boiling, bubbling pans to worry about what she was doing. Quietly, she opened the kitchen door and stepped outside.

The icy contrast from the heat in the kitchen took her breath away, and she wished she'd grabbed her shawl before venturing outside in the gale blowing off the sea. She'd taken no more than a few steps across the yard before she heard her name called.

Turning, she was surprised to see the plumber heading toward her, the collar of his jacket turned up against the wind. Anxiously she waited for him to reach her. "Is something wrong?" she called out, when he was close enough to hear her.

Laughing, he shook his head. "You women are always expecting trouble. I just wanted to say good morning, that's all."

"Oh." Now she felt foolish. "Well, good morning, then."

She started to pass him, but he held out his arm. "Wait a minute. What's yer hurry? Haven't you got a minute to chat with a friend?"

She felt her cheeks burning as she backed away from him. He was entirely too cheeky, though she could see why some women might like him. He wasn't bad looking, and his cheerful grin made her want to grin back at him. Maybe if she wasn't so in love with Samuel, she might have welcomed his attention, but right now, all she wanted was to give Tess her bone and get a hug in return.

"Sorry," she called out as she sped by him. "Gotta run." She could almost feel his gaze on her back all the way across the courtyard.

As she rounded the corner she saw a sight that halted her in surprise. Tess stood outside the stables, with Henry kneeling beside her, his hands ruffling the fur on her neck.

Pansy watched in amazement for several seconds, intrigued that the young lad had won the dog over. Tess usually avoided all men, and even with Samuel she was skittish at times, though she was a different dog when she was around women. She adored Pansy, who loved her just as much in return.

Samuel had found Tess wandering in the woods. He'd

told Pansy later that he thought Tess had been ill-treated by a man, and that's why she wouldn't have anything to do with any of them. She was afraid of them.

Watching Henry playing with the dog, Pansy was struck by another thought. Maybe that was why Alice was so afraid of men. She'd been hurt by a man. Someone who'd ill-treated her. She wouldn't remember that, of course, since she didn't have any memory, but her instincts would warn her not to get close to a man again.

Excited at the revelation, Pansy couldn't wait until she got back to the kitchen to share her thoughts with Gertie and Mrs. Chubb. Right now, though, there was a little matter of a bone and a big, lanky, adorable dog.

Approaching the two of them, Pansy was startled when Henry jumped to his feet, shooting her a guilty look as if he'd been doing something wrong. At the sight of Pansy, Tess trotted over her to and pushed her cold, wet nose into Pansy's hand.

"She likes you," Pansy said, smiling at the stable lad, who was backing away from her. "She doesn't usually like men."

"I'm really good with dogs," Henry muttered, then touched his cap with his fingers and fled back to the stables.

Shrugging, Pansy knelt by Tess's side and wrapped her arms around the big dog's neck. "How's my baby doing, then? Do you miss me?"

For answer the dog started sniffing at her apron pocket, wagging her tail so furiously Pansy could feel the draft. Laughing, she pulled the bone from her pocket. "Here you are, then. Chew on that for a while."

Tess took the bone in between her teeth and lowered her haunches. She looked so funny sitting there with the bone sticking out each end of her jaws, Pansy burst out laughing. Standing, she patted the dog on the head. "I've got to get back," she said, leaning down to drop a kiss on Tess's soft head. "Don't worry, Tess. Soon we'll be together all the time. You, me, and Samuel."

Excitement surged through her at the thought and she straightened, feeling like flinging out her arms and doing a dance. It was just as well she didn't, because just then she caught sight of Bernie, the plumber. He was standing at the corner of the stables, watching her.

As their gazes met, he waved an arm at her, and reluctantly, she waved back. He was a nice, friendly chap, she thought, as she hurried back to the kitchen, but she wished he wouldn't keep bothering her. She'd already told him she was getting married. That should have been enough to put him off.

At the thought of her wedding, as always, all other matters vanished from her mind. By Christmas Eve she'd be Mrs. Samuel Whitfield. Giddy at the thought, she skipped the rest of the way to the kitchen door.

Opening it, she was dismayed to see Mrs. Chubb waiting for her, arms folded, which meant the housekeeper was getting ready to yell at her. "I'm sorry," she said hastily, as she draped her shawl over the hook on the wall. "I just stepped out for a minute."

"Taking one of my soup bones for ze mangy mutt," Michel called out from the stove. He waved a wooden spoon at her. "How am I supposed to make soup for all ze guests when you steal ze bones, eh?"

"It was just a little bone. I didn't think you'd miss it."
Pansy slipped past Mrs. Chubb. "I'd better get upstairs to
the dining room."

"Yes, you'd better," Mrs. Chubb said, looking stern. "The
guests are on their way there now. Get a move on and get a
clean apron before you go up there. You've got grease all over
that one."

Pansy looked down at her stained apron. "Yes, Mrs. Chubb.
Sorry, Mrs. Chubb." She flew out the door before the housekeeper could say anything else. Relieved that she'd escaped so
lightly, she headed for the laundry room.

One of the laundry maids grinned at her as she threw the
soiled apron into a basket. "Been feeding that dog again,
have yer?"

Pansy nodded. "It's Christmas, isn't it. Dogs like a Christmas treat just like humans."

"They do that." The maid gave her a sly look as she handed
her a clean apron. "All ready for the wedding, are yer?"

"Almost. I haven't got the dresses yet but they should be
here by this afternoon."

"Must be lovely, knowing you're getting married Christmas Eve."

"It is." Aware of the time ticking away, Pansy pulled on
the apron and turned to the door.

"What about that new plumber bloke then?"

Pansy paused, looking back over her shoulder. "What
about him?"

"Bit of a saucy lad, he is."

Pansy opened her eyes wide. "Is he? I wouldn't know."

"Word is he's making eyes at all the women here." She giggled. "He caught up with me out there in the corridor and told me I was the prettiest girl in the club."

Pansy nodded. "Sounds like something he would say." She opened the door. "I gotta go. Thanks for the clean apron." She was out the door before the other woman had time to answer.

Gertie was just inside the door of the dining room when Pansy reached it. "Where the bloody hell have you been?" she demanded. "I've been waiting for you to get here so as I can go and look in on my twins. I couldn't leave Dopey and Dozey alone up here. One doesn't know what she's doing and the other one doesn't bleeding care."

Pansy followed Gertie's gaze to the other side of the room, where Lilly and Alice appeared to be arguing over who should ladle the soup. "I'll go and sort them out," she told Gertie. "You go and look after your twins."

"Thanks." Gertie grinned at her. "Bloody good luck with those two."

Sighing, Pansy made her way across the dining room, being careful to skirt the tables, which were filling up with guests. Reaching the two young girls, she had to raise her voice to get their attention. "What's going on here, then?"

Lilly turned a flushed face in Pansy's direction. "I'm trying to show her how to pour the soup into the bowls but she doesn't want to listen. She keeps staring at the guests, instead."

"I know how to pour soup," Alice said, giving Lilly a nasty look. "It's not that difficult."

Lilly raised her chin. "I thought you didn't remember nothing."

136

Alice's face turned red now. "I don't remember my name or where I came from. I do remember other things."

"All right." Lilly shoved the ladle at her. "Take four bowls of soup to the table over there." She nodded at a table by the window.

Alice took one look and shuddered. "There's men at the table."

"Of course there's men. They're at every table." Lilly looked at Pansy in disgust. "What's the matter with her?"

Pansy quickly stepped in. "All right. Alice, you can stand here and ladle the soup. Lilly and I will serve it."

Lilly stared at her. "But—"

"Never mind." Pansy gave her a sharp nudge in the arm. "Just do what I say."

Obviously annoyed, Lilly shrugged. She waited, tapping an impatient toe, while Alice spooned soup into the bowls and placed them on a tray. Then, with an air of being put-upon, Lilly picked up the tray and carried it over to the window table.

"Thank you," Alice whispered, as she ladled more soup into bowls.

"It's all right." Pansy picked up a tray. "I understand." She'd have a word with Lilly afterward, she decided. Maybe she could get her to be more sympathetic.

She got her chance after the entire meal had been served. Gertie had returned and taken Alice off to help her load the dumbwaiter, while Lilly stayed behind with Pansy to finish clearing the tables.

"You should be nicer to Alice," Pansy said, as the two of

them collected the dirty dishes. "She must have had a terrible time to lose her memory like that."

Lilly scowled. "I do feel sorry for her, but she's so slow, and she acts silly whenever a man comes near her."

"I think she's afraid of them."

Lilly looked as if someone had slapped her.

Shocked by the stricken look on the face of the maid, Pansy said hurriedly, "It's just an idea, that's all. But Alice acts the same way Tess does around men. Samuel said it was because Tess had been ill-treated by a man and now she's afraid of all men. I think that's why Alice is afraid of them."

"I'm sorry," Lilly stammered. "I didn't know."

"She probably doesn't even know about it." Pansy picked up a plate and stacked it on the pile next to her. "What with her lost memory and all. Don't say nothing to her. It would only upset her and besides, I don't really know if it's true."

Lilly gathered up the crumpled serviettes and shoved them in the basket. "Well, I pity her if it is," she muttered. "Some men are filthy pigs. They should all be strung up to burn in hell."

The venom in Lilly's voice unsettled Pansy, and she quickly changed the subject. But the look on the maid's face stayed with her throughout the rest of the day.

CHAPTER

❋ 10 ❋

Cecily had just reached the bottom of the stairs on her way to her office when she saw Miss Essie Bentley entering through the front door. Seizing the chance to speak with the young woman, Cecily hurried over to her.

Essie gave her a shy nod and would have brushed past her had Cecily not stepped in front of her to bar her way.

"I do hope you are enjoying your stay with us," she said, noting the way the young girl kept her gaze on the floor. "If there's anything we can do to make your visit more pleasurable, do be sure to let us know."

Essie murmured something too low for Cecily to understand. Taking that to mean all was well, Cecily added quietly, "A member of my staff informed me that one of our guests has been annoying you. Mr. Gerald Evans, I believe. I just wanted to assure you that he is no longer in the Pennyfoot, so he won't be bothering you again."

Essie raised her chin, and looked directly into Cecily's eyes. "Then it's good riddance to bad rubbish."

Taken aback, Cecily watched her hurry over to the stairs. It would seem that Miss Essie Bentley had more gumption than anyone realized.

Following more slowly, she reached the stairs just in time to see Fred Granson turn the curve and start down toward her.

She waited for him to arrive at the bottom, then tapped his arm as he passed her.

He turned his head, seeming startled by the contact. Giving her a slight bow, he murmured, "Mrs. Baxter? Can I help you with something?"

She made sure to exaggerate every word when she answered him, forming each word carefully so that he could read her lips. "Mr. Granson, I trust you are comfortable in your room?"

Wrinkles appeared in his forehead as he stared at her. "Very comfortable, I assure you."

"I was wondering if I may ask that you include your address in the hotel register." She smiled in an effort to put him at ease. "It's just a formality, of course. We ask that all our guests leave their address. It helps us to return any items that are left in the room."

The brow grew more furrowed. "Items?"

She opened her mouth a little wider. "Things you may forget to take with you when you leave."

Anxious to make sure he understood her, she had unknowingly raised her voice. A couple of guests crossing the foyer gave her a curious stare, and she hastily stepped out of their way so they could use the stairs.

Mr. Granson stood where he was, an odd expression on his face. Just then Philip came up to him and handed him a folded newspaper. "I found a copy of our local news rag, sir," he said, holding it out to him.

Mr. Granson took it and unfolded it. He was still studying it when Philip said softly, "I trust it's the one you were looking for, sir?"

"Yes, yes," Granson said, folding it up again. "Thank you. I appreciate you finding it for me."

"Not at all, sir."

Philip glided away, leaving Cecily feeling extremely foolish. "You're not deaf," she said, wishing she were anywhere but in the foyer.

Granson raised his eyebrows. "Deaf? No, I'm not. What made you think I was?"

Confused and embarrassed, she shook her head. "I have no idea. I'm so sorry. It was a stupid mistake. I do hope you are enjoying your stay with us?"

"Yes, thank you. I am."

She wanted to leave, but it seemed churlish after she had made such an ass of herself. She struggled to find the right thing to say. "You're from London? What brings you down to our quiet little town for Christmas?"

Granson looked past her as if longing to escape. "I just needed a break from all the celebrating going on in the city. It can be rather overwhelming when one has to spend Christmas alone."

Feeling sorry for him, she nodded in sympathy. "Oh, you have no family?"

"No."

That was a bit abrupt. She tried again. "So what do you do in London, Mr. Granson?"

He stared at her, as if not understanding the question. For a brief instant she wondered if he really was deaf and was just trying not to let her know that, but then he answered, "I'm a shoe salesman."

She pounced on that immediately. "Oh my, I just adore shoes. Especially those new-fashioned ones with the skinny heels. Though I'd never be able to balance on them. I'm afraid I'm stuck with the Louis heels, which have served me well enough." She smiled up at him. "I suppose you sell a lot of those new heels in London. I can't think what they call them. Spindle, or something like that?"

She waited, expecting him to give her the answer, but instead he threw a desperate glance at the grandfather clock in the corner. "I'm so sorry, Mrs. Baxter, but I have an urgent appointment I simply must keep. Perhaps later?"

"Of course." Frowning, she watched him rush to the front door and disappear through it, almost crashing into the gentleman who had just entered.

The young man approached her, doffing his cap. "Mrs. Baxter? I'm Bernard Bingham, the plumber, though everyone calls me Bernie. I heard you were looking for me?"

Cecily studied the man in front of her. She could tell at once, by the gleam in his eye, that he wasn't one to stand on ceremony.

She wasn't wrong. He gave her an audacious wink,

murmuring, "It's always a pleasure when a charming lady such as yourself seeks my company."

Deciding not to respond to that, Cecily said crisply, "I hear that the upstairs lavatories are still out of order. Is there a problem I should know about?"

Bernie's expression turned wary. "Problem? Other than the tanks not filling with water, you mean?"

"I mean, it seems to be taking an inordinate amount of time to get them working again. I was wondering if you needed some extra help."

His face cleared. "Oh no, Mrs. Baxter, thank you. It's just that upstairs plumbing can be tricky. The water has to flow upwards, you see, and that's not natural for water, is it. I'm sorry it's taking so long, but I still have to find exactly where the problem is to take care of it. Most likely a leak somewhere, I'd say. If that's so, we have to be really careful we don't aggravate things, so to speak, or we could end up with a flood somewhere, and I'm sure you won't want that."

"No, of course not. I——" Cecily paused as Bernie's cheerful expression turned sour. He was staring at something behind her, and she turned her head just in time to see Jacob Pinstone disappearing down the kitchen steps.

"What's *he* doing here?"

Surprised by the disgust in the plumber's voice, she said mildly, "Jacob is my janitor. Do you know him?"

"I know of him." Bernie shoved his hands in his pockets. "I heard he got chucked out of the navy. Killed someone in a knife fight. I'd be careful around that one, if I were you."

Shocked, Cecily struggled to control her voice. "I'll take that into account, Mr. Bingham. Now, about the lavatories.

I trust you will do your best to correct the problem with as much speed as possible."

Bernie gave her another wink. "You can bet your dainty boots on that, Mrs. Baxter. And may I say it's a great pleasure to meet you. I've heard some very nice things about you from the downstairs crew. You're quite a lady."

Unsure whether she should be flattered by the praise or offended by the familiarity of a repairman, Cecily murmured her thanks and hurried off. As she turned the bend of the stairs, she glanced back. The plumber was standing where she'd left him, watching her.

She shook off her uneasiness as she climbed the rest of the stairs. All she could hope was that the plumber finished the job by the end of the day. Something about that man put her teeth on edge. As for Jacob, just as soon as Christmas was over, she'd start looking for a new janitor.

"Gertie hates coming down here," Pansy said, unlocking the door to the wine cellar.

Lilly eyed the darkened steps and shuddered. "It does look blinking creepy down there."

Pansy handed her the wine basket and reached for the oil lamp that hung on the wall. "It's not too bad once you get down there. It smells a bit, and it's cold and damp, but it only takes a few minutes to find the wine and then you're out of there."

"Why does Gertie hate it so much, then?"

Pansy started leading the way down the narrow steps. The lamp swung in her hand, and the women's long, skinny shadows danced down the walls ahead of them. "She was caught down here once by a murderer, and almost got killed. Ever since then she's hated it down here."

"I don't blame her." Lilly's shaky voice sounded right behind Pansy.

Reaching the cellar floor, Pansy raised the lamp so that Lilly could see the long racks of wine. "You have to read the list that Mrs. Chubb gave you and find the bottles she wants. They're grouped together by the vineyards, which are in alphabetical order, so they're not too hard to find. After a while you'll remember where most of them are on the shelves."

Lilly shivered and rubbed her upper arms. "It smells like cat's piss down here."

"I know." Pansy held the list up to the lamp. "It smelled a lot worse before Madam had the wall built."

Lilly looked around. "What wall?"

Pansy nodded at the far end of the cellar. "That wall. There used to be a passageway there, leading to the card rooms." She started down one of the aisles, searching for the bottle of burgundy that was first on the list.

Lilly followed, keeping as close as she could without actually running into her. "Card rooms? But I thought the card rooms were upstairs, next to the library."

"They're the ones they use now. Before the Pennyfoot was a country club, it was a hotel, and gambling's not allowed in hotels. So the toffs used to come down here and play in secret card rooms where no one could see them and the bobbies never knew anything about it."

"The toffs came down here?" Lilly said, sounding incredulous.

"Well, they didn't come down this way. There was a trap-door leading down from the hallway outside the ballroom, and they'd go down that way. When Madam took over the country club, she had the trapdoor boarded up and a new floor put in. But you could still get to the secret card rooms from the cellar."

"So she put the wall up here, too?"

"Well, this summer I saw some big rats running about down here. Scared me half to death. When Madam heard how frightened I was, she sent Clive down here to get rid of the rats and put a wall up so no more could come in from the passageways."

"Clive?"

"He was our handyman before Jacob. He owns a toy shop in the High Street now, and that's why Madam hired Jacob." Pansy sighed. "I really miss Clive. He was so nice and friendly. Not at all like Jacob."

Lilly stared at the wall. "The toffs must have been really fond of gambling if they came down a trapdoor to play."

Pansy pounced on the bottle of burgundy and laid it in Lilly's basket. "Yeah, well, that's not the only trapdoor. There's another one in one of the secret card rooms that leads down to a tunnel underneath here."

Lilly's eyes widened. "Tunnel?"

"It leads all the way out to the ocean. The Pennyfoot used to be the country home of the Earl of Saltchester, and every-one thought he'd had the tunnel built so his family could get to the private beach without anyone seeing them in their bathing clothes. Then a while ago someone wrote in the newspaper that it was really smugglers what built it. They used the tunnel to store contraband they brought in from France."

"Go on!" Pansy looked up to see Lilly's gaze fixed on her face, her eyes wide with excitement. "All that was going on underneath the Pennyfoot and nobody knew about it?"

"Well, it wasn't the Pennyfoot then, was it." Pansy took the list from Lilly and studied it. "Here, you go and get the bottle of Chianti. It's got its own little basket so you should find it without any trouble."

Lilly glanced at the list, then at the dark shadowy aisles. "I'll need the lamp."

"I'll put it up here." Pansy stood the lamp on a high shelf. "You should be able to see down there."

Lilly moved off reluctantly, and Pansy turned back to the racks, looking for the bottle of Riesling next on the list. Moments later she heard a yelp, followed by a crash, then Lilly's wail echoed throughout the cellar.

Grabbing the lamp, Pansy headed down the aisle. As she reached the far end she saw Lilly sitting on the ground, holding her ankle, and wailing like a hungry baby. Beside her lay shattered glass and a spreading pool of dark red liquid.

"Crikey, that will come out of your wages," Pansy said, eyeing the mess in dismay.

Lilly's voice was high-pitched with pain when she answered. "Never mind the blinking wine. I think I broke my ankle."

"Oh no!" Pansy dropped to her side, mindless of her apron dipping into the red wine. "You can't do that! You're supposed to take over for me when I leave."

"Well, I can't take over if I broke my ankle, can I."

Pansy stared at her, visions of a cancelled wedding

torturing her mind. "See if you can stand on it. Maybe it's just bruised. How did you fall down, anyway?"

"I tripped over that." Lilly pointed at a brick lying next to her.

Pansy frowned. "Where on earth did that come from?" She got up and moved closer to the wall, swinging the lamp higher so she could see. Her eyes widened when she saw a gaping hole in the brickwork.

Behind her, Lilly gasped. "Blimey," she said, "they must be bloody great big rats to do all that."

"I don't know what to make of that new plumber," Cecily said, as she joined her husband in front of the fireplace.

Baxter looked up in surprise from the ledger he was studying. "I thought you had some work to do in the office."

"I did." She sat down. "I do. I got distracted and decided to come up here instead."

Baxter peered at her over the top of his glasses. He had only recently taken to wearing reading glasses, and spent more time looking over them than through them. "Is there something bothering you?"

"Well, now that you mention it, yes, there is." She settled herself more comfortably. "It's Jacob." She told him what the plumber had told her. "I knew there was something fishy about him," she added, when she was done. "I'd like to get rid of him now, but it's too late to hire anyone else and we can't manage without a janitor." She shook her head. "That reminds me. I should see if Jacob put up the set for Phoebe and I have to talk to Madeline about the floral arrangements for the wedding and—"

"Whoa, there!" Baxter held up his hand, a smile playing around his lips. "You're making me tired just listening to you. Why don't you let me do something to help out?"

She nodded at the ledger on his lap. "You're working."

"No, I'm simply passing time with work until my wife can join me. From what you're saying, it doesn't sound as if that will happen until the New Year."

She gave him a tired smile. "You could be right."

"Then let me help."

"I don't think you want to talk to Madeline about floral arrangements, and I'm quite sure you don't want to tackle Phoebe and all her problems."

He winced. "You're right. I'd rather not. There must be something else I can do."

She leaned back in her chair, her smile widening. "Well, this is a new Baxter. I must say I quite like it."

He shrugged, looking a little embarrassed. "It occurred to me some time ago that I've been far too wrapped up in my own affairs for much too long. It's time I pulled my weight around here."

"But we agreed when we took over the Pennyfoot again that I would take care of the country club while you took care of your business."

"That was before I knew you would go back to your old sleuthing ways."

She sighed. "I never intended to do so."

"I know. Nevertheless, here we are, faced with yet another

murder, and a hotel full of guests expecting to be fed and entertained for Christmas, not to mention a wedding."

"Well, I don't seem to be progressing too well with the murder investigation." She stretched out her feet and studied her shoes. "I have to admit, the news that Jacob was involved in a man's stabbing death is a little too close for comfort. I'm wondering if it was Jacob whom Mr. Evans was investigating, and he killed the detective."

Baxter pursed his lips. "It certainly doesn't make me comfortable knowing he was involved in a man's death. Then again, if he was at fault, wouldn't he be in prison?"

"I would think so." Cecily frowned. "Which makes me wonder how the new plumber knew about it."

"Perhaps he made up the story about Jacob for some reason. Maybe he doesn't like the chap and wanted him to lose his job."

Cecily shook her head. "I don't know. Mr. Bingham is irritating, but he seems a perfectly pleasant young man. Though I must say, he doesn't know his place. He walked into the foyer through the front door instead of using the tradesman's entrance. His manner is a bit too familiar for my liking. He was quite audacious."

Baxter's brows drew together. "In what way? He didn't insult you, did he? If so, I'll have a word with the rascal."

"No, no, it's not that." She thought about it. "It's almost as if he doesn't know how to behave in front of a superior."

"That doesn't surprise me. In spite of the great strides the women's movement has managed to bring about, there are still a vast majority of men who will never consider a woman their superior, no matter what their station."

"Maybe not," Cecily said, folding her hands, "but they do know how to address a woman according to protocol. Mr. Bingham is sadly lacking in such matters."

"So he's merely rude then?"

"Yes, I suppose that's it." She leapt to her feet. "Goodness, look at the time. I have to find Madeline and ask her about the wedding arrangements."

"And you're sure there's nothing I can do?"

She hesitated. "There are several invoices that need attention in my office."

He rose at once, laying down his ledger on the seat behind him. "I will take care of them for you." He placed a gentle hand on her shoulder. "When I proposed a toast to our new partnership, I fully intended that in every aspect of our lives. Not just a murder investigation."

She looked up at him, tears prickling her eyelids. "Bax, my love, I don't think I've ever loved you more."

He dropped a swift kiss on her forehead. "Nor I, you. Now let's go and take care of our duties. In the meantime, I'll have a word with your Mr. Pinstone and see if I can find out the truth about his reason for leaving the navy."

"Oh, would you? That would be such a load off my mind."

"Of course!" He led her to the door, then stood back to allow her to step out into the hallway. "I meant what I said. Partners in every way."

The warm feeling those words gave her promised to stay with her for the rest of the Christmas season.

CHAPTER
❋ 11 ❋

"Whatever happened to you!" Mrs. Chubb stared in dismay as Lilly limped into the kitchen, supported by Pansy.

"She tripped over a brick in the cellar," Pansy said, struggling to get her breath back as Lilly plopped onto a chair. "She's hurt her ankle."

"I think it's broken," Lilly said, holding up her knee.

Pansy felt like crying. "I won't be able to get married if she can't take over for me."

"Nonsense." Mrs. Chubb bustled over to Lilly, her ring of keys clinking on her belt. Leaning over the young woman, she took the ankle in her hands. "You're getting married, Pansy, even if everyone in this country club comes down with an ailment. Nothing is going to stop that wedding."

Pansy swallowed hard. "I hope so," she muttered. "So far

things are not exactly going smoothly here. I've got the feeling that the fates are trying to stop me getting married."

Mrs. Chubb looked up so sharply Lilly's foot jerked in her hands, causing the girl to utter a yelp of pain. "Don't say that, Pansy. Don't ever say that. I tell you, your wedding will go on and you will be married on Christmas Eve, if I have to fight the devil to see it done."

Tears spurted from Pansy's eyes and she dashed at her cheeks with the back of her hand.

"Don't say nothing else," Lilly pleaded. "Not while she's got hold of my foot."

"Sorry." The housekeeper carefully tilted Lilly's foot up and down. Though the maid winced, she didn't yell out again. "It's not broken. Probably a sprain." Mrs. Chubb lowered the foot and let go. "I'll strap it up and you'll have to stay off it for a day or so, but you should be able to get around on it by Christmas Day." She folded her arms and looked from one girl to the other. "What were you two doing to get her in this state?" she demanded, staring at Pansy.

"Nothing, Mrs. Chubb. Honest!" Pansy drew a cross on her chest. "Lilly was getting a bottle of wine," she said, swallowing, "which she dropped when she tripped over the brick."

The housekeeper rolled her eyes. "Did you clean up the mess?"

"Not yet. I had to get Lilly back here. She was hurting really bad."

"Then you'll have to go back down and clean it up."

"Yes, Mrs. Chubb." Sighing, Pansy headed for the door.

"Where did that brick come from anyway?" Mrs. Chubb asked, as Pansy reached the door.

She paused and looked back at the housekeeper. "It looked like it fell out of the wall. There was more than one of them."

Mrs. Chubb frowned. "Very well, run along. Don't worry about Lilly. She's going to be all right."

"Yes, Mrs. Chubb." Pansy let the door swing to behind her and headed down the hallway to the laundry room. She was not looking forward to going back down to the wine cellar. That place was creepy, just like Lilly said. Especially now there was a hole in the wall. She shuddered when she remembered what Lilly had said. She just hoped that the next time she went down there she wouldn't come face-to-face with a giant rat.

The first place that Cecily intended to look for Madeline was the library. Since the carol-singing ceremony was to be held in there, Cecily was hoping she'd find her friend putting finishing touches to the decorations. Madeline always managed to come up with something spectacular, both in the library and the ballroom.

Since Phoebe was at this very minute holding a dress rehearsal in the ballroom, Cecily was reasonably confident that Madeline would not be in there.

Opening the door to the library, she was pleased to see her friend in front of the fireplace, laying garlands of spruce and holly along the mantelpiece.

"White candles," Madeline said, as Cecily approached. "I think they will look very nice in their brass candlesticks."

Cecily shivered. Every time someone mentioned candles in the library, she was reminded of the time the candles on the Christmas tree caught fire. The library was partially destroyed, and it was only the quick thinking of her husband that had saved her life.

Madeline must have caught the reflex, as she turned at once. "Oh, I'm so sorry, Cecily. So thoughtless of me. I won't light them, of course."

Cecily shook her head. "It's quite all right, Madeline. It's not as if they are on the tree, and you are quite right. White candles are just what that display needs."

Madeline studied her with a critical eye. "Something is worrying you. Is it Baxter?"

Cecily looked at her in surprise. "Baxter? No, he's the least of my worries. Why would you think I was concerned about him?"

"Oh, nothing. Please forget I said anything."

Madeline turned back to the mantelpiece, but something in the way she held herself made Cecily uneasy. "Are you not telling me something I should know?"

The other woman seemed to hesitate for a long time before answering. "I'm sure it's nothing to worry about. It's just that I had a . . . premonition."

A cold stab of apprehension caught Cecily under the ribs. "Premonition? About Baxter?"

"Yes, but it was so very vague. You know how sometimes these things mean nothing at all."

"I know that when you have a premonition about something there's usually some truth in it." Cecily moved closer to her friend. "Tell me, Madeline. What was it?"

"I don't really know." Madeline laid a hand on Cecily's

arm. "It was just a faint warning that Baxter needs to tread carefully. I'm not sure why."

"But if you were you would tell me, wouldn't you?"

Madeline smiled. "Of course. It's probably no more than him catching a cold, or losing something he values, something simple like that. I shouldn't have mentioned it."

Not entirely convinced, Cecily decided to change the subject. "Well, I was wondering how the church floral arrangements were coming along for the wedding."

Madeline brightened at once. "Oh, the wedding! I'm so looking forward to it. I've ordered the flowers. They will arrive from Covent Garden around eight o'clock in the morning. That will give me all day to have everything ready by the five o'clock ceremony."

"Well, if you need any help, let me know and I'll send along a maid. I'd send two but one of our maids has broken her arm, so that will leave us a little understaffed for the Christmas rush."

Madeline gave her a sharp look. "An accident?"

Cecily raised her eyebrows. "I beg your pardon?"

"I'm sorry. Take no notice of me. Christmastime always plays havoc with my senses."

Cecily was about to answer when a polite tap on the door interrupted her and Mrs. Chubb appeared in the doorway.

"I'm sorry to disturb you, m'm. May I have a word with you?"

"Of course." Cecily beckoned to her housekeeper to come closer.

"I'll leave you alone," Madeline said, reaching down to

retrieve the basket at her feet. "I need to add some more greenery to the staircase anyway."

"There's no need . . ." Cecily began, but Madeline had already vanished out the door.

Mrs. Chubb stood rubbing her hands together—a sign that she was agitated.

The cold feeling Madeline's words had given Cecily spread across her back. "Is something wrong, Mrs. Chubb?"

"Yes, Madam. Well, not really. It's just that Lilly has sprained her ankle. I'm afraid she won't be on it for a day or two."

"Oh dear. Is she all right?"

"Yes m'm. I sent her to her room to rest it. I'm hoping she'll be better in time for the Christmas festivities."

"I hope so, too, Mrs. Chubb. Not only for our sake but hers, too. It's so painful to be hobbling around on a sprained ankle. How did it happen?"

Mrs. Chubb fidgeted her feet. "Well, that's what I wanted to tell you, m'm. She tripped over a brick in the wine cellar."

"A brick?"

"Yes, m'm. Pansy said it had fallen out of the wall. It wasn't the only one, neither."

Cecily had trouble digesting this latest calamity. "Bricks are falling out of the wall in the wine cellar?"

"Yes, m'm. Lilly said as how it must be rats. I told Jacob about it and he . . ." She paused, then added quickly, "He didn't seem too concerned about it, m'm. I thought maybe you should have a word with him about it."

"Oh, I will, Mrs. Chubb. Thank you."

The housekeeper looked relieved. "Thank you, m'm. We

don't want rats running around the wine cellar again, like they were in the summer."

"No, indeed. Don't worry. I'll have Jacob seal up the wall again."

"Yes, m'm."

The housekeeper started for the door, pausing when Cecily asked, "How is the new girl, Alice, getting along?"

"She seems eager to please. I think she'll work out just fine. We're lucky to have her, now that Lilly won't be able to work."

"We are, indeed." Cecily followed the housekeeper to the door. "Please let me know how Lilly is doing and make sure she has everything she needs."

"I will, m'm. Thank you."

Mrs. Chubb toddled off down the hallway, while Cecily headed in the other direction. She wasn't looking forward to her meeting with Phoebe. Much as she loved her friend, Phoebe could be quite impossible when conducting the final rehearsal for her pantomime.

She could hear the commotion from the ballroom as she drew close to the doors. Phoebe's shrill tones were raised above what sounded like a squabble going on amongst the dance troupe, which was nothing new. Phoebe's dancers seemed to find it impossible to get along in rehearsals—one of the reasons Cecily did her best to avoid them.

She pushed open the doors to the ballroom, wincing as the volume of voices threatened to shatter her eardrums.

The pianist Phoebe had hired sat slumped behind the grand piano. Another fellow leaned against his double bass, staring into space, while two saxophone players sat close together apparently exchanging a joke, since they were both laughing uproariously. Only the drummer seemed concerned with what was going on onstage. In fact, judging from the worried look on his face, he was aghast at the whole fiasco.

Phoebe stood on the stage, gesturing and shouting at someone wearing a furry cat costume and whiskers painted on her face. Another dancer in tights and a leather tunic was also shouting at the cat, who seemed to be ignoring both of them.

Deciding that perhaps this wasn't the best time to talk to Phoebe, Cecily hastily retreated from the ballroom. Just as she turned the corner of the hallway, Jacob appeared at the end of the corridor, walking toward her.

As he drew closer, she called out, "Jacob! I'd like a word with you, please."

He halted at once, waiting for her to reach him. He seemed ill at ease, fidgeting with his cap as she approached.

"Mrs. Chubb told me there's a problem with the wall in the wine cellar. I'd like you to inspect it and let me know what's happening down there."

He stared at her as if she were speaking a foreign language. "What's happening?"

"We put up a new wall down there this past summer, and the maids tell me the bricks are falling out of it. We need to repair it."

His frown cleared. "Oh, that's all right, m'm. I went down and looked at the wall. It's just a little dust down there, that's all."

Surprised, she stared at him. "Dust? Then why did the maids tell me the bricks were falling out?"

"It were just one brick, m'm. You know how these young

girls exaggerate. I put it right back in." He frowned. "But you're right. Perhaps it does need a thorough inspection. It might be better if the maids don't go down there until I've had a chance to look at it properly."

"They have to go down there to fetch the wine. So please see to it as quickly as possible."

"Yes, m'm. I just have to take care of something in the ballroom first." Jacob touched his forehead with his fingers and continued on his way toward the ballroom.

Cecily headed for the foyer, hoping that Jacob's task didn't involve Phoebe. If so, he was in for a difficult time. Now she needed to look in on Lilly and make sure the girl was not in need of Kevin Prestwick's ministrations.

On her way down the kitchen stairs, heavenly spicy aromas floated toward her. Michel must be boiling the Christmas puddings. She would have to find an excuse to stop in there on the way back.

She reached Pansy's room, tapped on the door, and opened it.

Lilly sat up on the bed, a magazine spread over her knees. She seemed startled, and made a move to slide off the bed, but Cecily stopped her with a raised hand.

"Stay where you are," she said, closing the door behind her. "We don't want to do more damage to that ankle."

Lilly subsided against the wall. "Yes, m'm. Thank you, m'm." She nodded at her ankle. "I'm sorry about this, m'm. I know it's putting everyone out, especially with the wedding coming up and all."

"It's not your fault, Lilly. I'm sure you didn't do it on purpose."

"No, m'm, I didn't." Lilly looked worried. "I think it must be rats that put that hole in the wall."

Cecily smiled. "I've never heard of rats chewing through bricks before. I think it's more likely a bad mixture of cement. It happens sometimes. Anyway, Jacob will take care of it."

At the mention of the handyman, Lilly's expression changed. "Well, I hope he doesn't make it worse."

Cecily pursed her lips. "You don't like Jacob?"

Lilly scowled at her bandaged ankle. "No, I don't."

Cecily was about to say something, then thought better of it. "Are you in a lot of pain?" she asked instead.

"Only when I stand on it."

"I can have Dr. Prestwick give you something for the pain, if you like."

Lilly looked up at her. "Thank you, m'm, but I'll be all right. I hope it will be better in a day or two. I'd like to be back on my feet by Christmas."

"Well, I'll have a word with the doctor in any case. There must be something we can do to hasten the healing."

"Thank you, m'm."

It was the first time Cecily had seen the girl smile. It completely changed her face.

Lilly should smile more often, Cecily thought, as she closed the door and hurried down the hallway. That girl walked around as if she had the troubles of the world upon her shoulders.

As Cecily stepped inside the kitchen, the familiar warmth seemed to wrap around her. Michel stood at the stove, poking inside bubbling pots with a wooden spoon. Mrs. Chubb hovered over the huge scrubbed table, holding a bag of royal icing. Three white iced cakes in different sizes sat in front of her.

Over at the counter, Gertie was placing miniature mince pies into square biscuit tins. Alice stood next to her, tying thin red ribbon around large slices of shortbread.

Mrs. Chubb dropped the icing bag when she caught sight of Cecily. "What can we do for you, m'm?"

Michel turned around, nodding so hard his tall white chef's hat slipped sideways. He pushed it back with an impatient hand and went back to his boiling puddings.

Gertie looked over her shoulder, while Alice sent one scared glance at Cecily and hunched over her task again.

Cecily stood for a moment, breathing in the sweet fragrance of baking shortbread and cinnamon. "I just had a word with Lilly," she announced, "and I hope you will all be able to manage without her for a day or two."

"We will, m'm," Gertie called out cheerfully. She gave Alice a nudge that almost sent her off her feet. "Won't we, Alice?"

Alice gave her a frightened nod.

"If you don't," Michel said, pointing his spoon at Alice, "I beat you with this."

Alice uttered a shriek that made them all jump.

"*Sacre bleu!*" Michel staggered backward as if someone had pushed him. "I was joking. You not take a joke, *non?*"

Gertie glared at him. "There are some things you don't joke about, you big twerp."

"Who do you call a twerp?" Michel's face turned even redder, and he advanced on Gertie, spoon raised.

Alice screamed, and Mrs. Chubb rushed over to her and

stood in front of her. "Michel! Get back to your stove. Can't you see you're scaring the girl to death?"

Michel dropped the spoon and turned back to the stove, muttering, "Nobody knows how to take a joke anymore. I keep my mouth shut from now on. No more jokes."

"Thank Gawd for that," Gertie said, fanning her face with a tin lid.

Alice stood trembling, the ribbon floating from her fingers to the floor.

Mrs. Chubb tutted and bent down to pick it up. "Look at that. Now I'll have to get more ribbon. You can't use this on the shortbread."

Alice promptly burst into tears.

Cecily decided it was time to leave. She crept unnoticed to the door and let herself out into the hallway.

As the door closed behind her, someone moved in front of her, making her heart skip. At first she didn't recognize the man standing in the shadows between the gaslights. Surprise rippled through her when she realized who stood there. "Mr. Granson! Whatever are you doing down here?"

The man raised a hand to his tie, and she noticed at once that grime clung to his fingers, as if he'd been digging in soil. "Mrs. Baxter! I'm so sorry if I startled you. I was looking for a maid. There's no water in the lavatories, and I was wondering if I might have a jug of hot water in my room."

"I'll see that one is sent up there," Cecily said, uncertain as to whether or not she believed him. It occurred to her that he might have been lurking about, perhaps listening to the argument going on in the kitchen. And what had he been doing to get so much dirt on his hands?

The more she saw of this man, the less she liked him. Had P.C. Northcott not left for London, she would have had him investigate the man. First there was Granson's reluctance to leave an address in the guest ledger, then the odd way he'd ignored her when she'd called his name, and now this.

Realizing the man's intense gaze was probing her face, she managed a smile. "Is there anything else we can do for you, Mr. Granson?"

"No, no, thank you." He continued to stare at her for a moment longer, then abruptly turned tail and marched down the hallway to the stairs.

Cecily waited a moment to gather her composure. Granson's penetrating gaze had unsettled her again. It was as if he were trying to read her mind. Perhaps gauging how well she had received his excuse of needing hot water?

Just as soon as she had the opportunity, she decided, she would search the man's room. If there was anything incriminating about him, she might well find something useful there. Having made that decision, she hastened to return to her office, where pressing tasks awaited her.

CHAPTER

❋ 12 ❋

Pansy's feet dragged as she crossed the courtyard. The day was only half over and already she was worn out. She'd covered a plate of mince pies, sausage rolls, and cheese sticks with cheesecloth to protect the food from the elements as she carried it over to the stables. Right now the wind was cutting through the heavy wool shawl she wore, and she gripped the plate with one hand while the other held on to the shawl.

How she wished she was going to visit Samuel instead of Charlie Muggins. She felt a tug of nostalgia every time she walked into the stables and Samuel wasn't there. She could still see him leaning against the stalls, broom in hand, grinning at her as she ran toward him.

But Samuel was working day and night in his repair shop, and she hadn't seen much of him at all the past three months.

Sighing, Pansy walked into the flickering shadows of the stables. The dim glow of oil lamps made it difficult to see, but as she stepped inside a voice called out to her from the back of the vast building.

"Hey there! You're a sight for sore eyes!" Charlie strolled toward her, hands in pockets, a cheeky grin plastered on his face.

"Hey yourself." She thrust the plate at him. "Mrs. Chubb sent you some grub."

Charlie took the plate from her and lifted a corner of the cheesecloth to peer underneath. "Blimey! What did I do to deserve this?"

Pansy shrugged. "She said it was for taking her shopping. You're supposed to share it with Henry, since he got the carriage ready for her."

Charlie pulled a face. "All right, if I have to, I will."

Pansy looked around. The horses were quiet, with only the occasional shuffling of their hooves on the straw to break their silence. "Where's Tess?"

"Sleeping." Charlie whistled, and a bark answered him. A moment later Tess bounded into view, tail wagging furiously.

Pansy squatted down to hug the dog, and received her usual wet kiss from the dog in return. "Is Henry here?" She wanted to be sure the young lad got his fair share of the food.

"He's out with a carriage, picking up guests from a Christmas party."

She gave Tess a final pat on the head and stood. "Well, all right. Just make sure you give him some of that." She nodded at the plate in his hand.

"I will, I will." He started walking with her back to the

doors. "He's a strange one, that Henry. He knows quite a bit about motorcars, but not a lot about horses. It's almost as if he's afraid of them."

"I'm sure he's not."

"Well, he acts funny when he's around them."

She paused, looking up at him. "You don't like him much, do you?"

Charlie shrugged. "He's all right, I suppose. It's just hard to get along with him. He doesn't laugh at my jokes."

"That's because they're not funny."

Charlie poked her in the arm with his knuckles. "He's such a baby in some ways, but he's got a temper on him. I remember when that bloke who died, Mr. Evans, yelled at Henry for not tightening the girth on his horse. He came stamping back in here swearing he was going to get even."

Pansy felt as if the wind had frozen her bones. Staring at Charlie, she whispered, "Do you think he did?"

Charlie frowned. "Did what?"

"Get even. Do you think he killed Mr. Evans?"

Charlie uttered a shout of laughter. "Henry? Are you daft? That lad doesn't have the nerve to kill a goose, much less stick a knife in a man's gut."

Pansy shivered. "Well, all I can say is, you never know." She pulled her shawl tighter around her shoulders. "Don't forget to give Henry his fair share." With that she fled across the courtyard to the warmth and safety of the kitchen.

Seated in the dining room, Cecily hastily swallowed the last of her egg and cress sandwich and washed it down with a mouthful of hot tea. She gave Baxter what she hoped was a winning smile and murmured, "I'm sorry, darling, but I have to take care of an urgent matter. Would you mind awfully if I leave?"

Baxter finished chewing and swallowed. "Yes, actually. I would mind. I don't see enough of you as it is." He frowned. "What is so terribly urgent that you can't take care of it a little later?"

Remembering their partnership pact, Cecily felt a stab of guilt. "I . . . ah . . . have to search someone's room."

"Ah! I suspected as much." He swallowed the last of his tea and replaced the cup in the saucer with a loud clatter. "And you were intending to sneak off and snoop without me."

She had to grin. "Snoop?"

He shrugged. "What else would you call it?"

"Investigate."

"Hmmph. Just another fancy word for snooping."

She leaned forward. "I have to do it now, darling. Mr. Granson will be returning to his room shortly. I don't want him to find me there."

Baxter's eyebrows shot up. "Granson? The new guest?"

"Shshh!" She glanced around. "I don't want anyone to hear us talking about him."

"What makes you think he's got anything to hide?"

She laid her fingers on his hand. "Can I explain later? As I said, this is urgent."

His expression softened. "When you look at me like that, my love, I can deny you nothing."

She pulled her hand back. "Have you been drinking?"

"Only tea. Why?"

"It's just that . . ." She paused, uncertain how to finish, then said in a rush, "It's been quite a while since you spoke to me that way."

"Has it really? Then shame on me. I must endeavor to do better. Now, let us go upstairs and take care of your urgent matter."

Her heart gave a little skip. "You're coming with me?"

"Of course." He stood, and offered her his hand. "I'm your partner, remember? Shame on you for forgetting that."

"I didn't forget." She stood, too, and stepped ahead of him. "You always objected so loudly whenever I had to . . . ah . . . investigate someone's room. I thought it prudent not to cause an outburst."

"Well, there'll be no more objections from now on. Unless you venture into danger without me."

He'd whispered this last in her ear as they exited the dining room. She smiled up at him. "No more, my love. I promise."

Looking well satisfied, he accompanied her down the hallway and up the stairs to the second floor.

Reaching Granson's room, she looked back at him. "Do you want to keep watch outside while I search?"

"No. I'll come in with you. I just hope the chap doesn't get back here and catch us in the act."

"We'll make up some excuse."

"Such as?"

She opened the door with her master key and stepped inside. "Such as, the fireplace needs attention of some sort."

He smiled. "It has been a long time since we did something like this together. I had forgotten how resourceful you can be."

"And I had forgotten how much more fun this is with you by my side." She took a long look around the room. The heavy drapes had been drawn back, and weak sunlight filtered through the net curtains at the windows.

The maids had already made up the bed and cleaned the room. Everything looked neat and tidy. Cecily crossed the carpet and opened up each dresser drawer. Careful not to dis-arrange anything, she slid her fingers beneath socks and under-garments, finding nothing of interest.

"What do you need me to search?" Baxter asked. "The wardrobe?"

"Yes, please." She crossed to the bedside table and opened the drawer. It was empty. Frowning, she reached for the waste paper basket. It, too, held nothing but a tiny scrap of paper that seemed to have been torn from a bill of some sort.

She looked up at the sound of the wardrobe door closing. "Anything?"

Baxter shook his head. "Nothing. Just a couple of suits, shirts, and a pair of slippers." He looked at his fingers. "The maids need to do a better job of cleaning wardrobes." He dug into his pocket with the other hand and drew out his handkerchief.

"Wait!" Cecily hurried over to him. "Let me see."

He held out his fingers. The tips were covered in a reddish dust.

Cecily peered closer. "That's not ordinary dust." She drew a quick breath. "It looks like dust from bricks."

"Bricks?" Baxter stared at her. "Why would Granson have bricks in his wardrobe?"

"I don't think he did," Cecily said, remembering the grime

on the guest's fingers. "But I think I know where this dust comes from." Quickly she told him about Lilly's accident with the fallen brick. "I think," she added at the end, "that perhaps we should go down to the wine cellar and take a look at the wall. If I'm right, something down there seems to be of great interest to our newest guest."

"But how would he get in there? Doesn't Mrs. Chubb keep the door locked?"

"That," Cecily said grimly, "is a very good question. And one I intend to ask Mr. Granson just as soon as I set eyes on him."

Gertie stomped up the kitchen steps, her brow furrowed in a deep frown. She'd been waiting over half an hour for Alice to get down to the kitchen from the dining room. The girl was supposed to have finished clearing the tables ages ago. Annoyed at having to go all the way up to the dining room to find her, Gertie charged around the corner of the hallway, and then came to an abrupt halt.

There was Alice at the other end of the corridor. With the plumber, Bernie Bingham. Gertie rolled her eyes. Pansy kept saying as how Alice was afraid of all men. Well, there was one she wasn't afraid of, judging by the attentive look on her face.

Gertie had to give Bernie credit where it was due. The man seemed to be able to charm every woman he came across. Even Mrs. Chubb acted barmy when he spoke to her. But Alice was something quite different. Bernie must have been blessed with a special appeal that was too potent to ignore. Except for her, she hastily reminded herself as Bernie turned his head and caught sight of her.

He left Alice's side immediately and came strolling toward Gertie, the cheeky grin playing across his face. "Hello, gorgeous," he murmured, as he sauntered past her. "How about taking a stroll along the Esplanade with me later? I could show you a good time."

"Yeah," Gertie answered, feeling flattered in spite of herself, "I just bet you would, and all."

"Is that a yes?"

She laughed. "Sorry, mate. My boyfriend wouldn't like it."

He paused and looked back at her. "He wouldn't have to know."

Shaking her head at the man's audacity, Gertie turned her back on him and headed for Alice, who seemed to be hanging back in the shadows. "Here," she called out. "Whatcha doing up here? You're supposed to be helping me in the kitchen."

Alice shuffled toward her, head down. "Sorry," she mumbled.

"You'll be sorry if Mrs. Chubb gets on to you. Come on." Beckoning to the girl, Gertie spun around. Bernie had disappeared. Feeling somewhat relieved, Gertie led the way back to the kitchen with Alice trailing along behind her.

"I haven't been down here in ages," Cecily said, as she followed Baxter down the steps to the wine cellar. "I'd forgotten how musty and unpleasant it smells."

Baxter held up the oil lamp, letting the glow swing to and fro across the dark shelves. "It amazes me that the wine can taste so good after being buried in this putrid environment."

"Apparently it's good for the wine, just not the nose."

"It didn't seem to bother you in the old days."

She laughed. "I was usually worrying about far more important things than the smell. We were running illegal card rooms. There was much to worry about."

Baxter stepped down onto the floor and held the lamp even higher for her. "I lived in fear that we would be found out and you would end up in prison."

"It was worth the risk. The card rooms were a great way to satisfy all those aristocrats craving excitement. We filled the guest rooms every single week. It was their money that helped pay off the Pennyfoot's debts."

"That and your cousin's offer to buy the place and turn it into a country club."

"Yes, well, if I'd known that gambling was legal in a country club I'd have turned the Pennyfoot into one years ago." Cecily reached the floor with a sigh of relief. The steps were narrow and creaked ominously with every step. She really should have them replaced, she thought, as she led the way down one of the aisles to the far end of the cellar.

As Baxter's flare of light fell across the wall, she gasped. A sizable hole had appeared in the middle of the wall, and what seemed to be the missing bricks were neatly stacked at one end.

With a muttered exclamation, Baxter strode past her, his lamp held high. "What the—" He looked back at her. "What's going on here?"

Cecily pursed her lips. "I'd say that someone is methodically taking down the wall. I have no doubt it is Mr. Granson. I saw dirt all over his fingers yesterday, and then there's the brick dust you found in his wardrobe."

"It certainly does seem like it." Baxter looked back at the wall. "But why on earth would he want to do that?"

Cecily stared at the wall. In her mind's eye she saw again the cryptic words of a telegram. "I think I might have an idea," she murmured. "There's something else, however, that interests me. Jacob told me there was only one brick missing, which he replaced. Either he lied, or Mr. Granson has been remarkably industrious in such a short time."

Baxter frowned. "You think our new maintenance man is working with Granson?"

"I think there are a few questions I'd like to ask both of them." Cecily started walking toward the stairs. "Come along, Bax. I think we've spent entirely too much time down here already. I have to get ready for the carol-singing ceremony shortly."

"Suspects," Baxter mumbled, as he led the way up the stairs. "Now I remember why I worried about you chasing after criminals."

"It's all right, dear." Cecily stepped out into daylight and drew in a deep breath of the damp sea air. "Now that I have you to protect me, I'm quite sure I shall be perfectly safe." She trotted off across the courtyard, well aware of her husband's suspicious gaze on her back.

Poor Bax. He never quite knew when she was being facetious. Her smile faded as she thought about the hole in the wall. Jacob had some explaining to do. As for Fred Granson, she would have to tread a great deal more carefully with him. But first, she needed a visit to the library, which she would do this very afternoon. There were certain things she wanted to research. If she was right, then some of the answers she sought would fall neatly into place.

Pansy stood at the sink, up to her elbows in hot, soapy water. Searching around in the suds, she found a meat platter and swished it back and forth before lifting it up to inspect it. A few spots of gravy remained stubbornly on the rim, and she rubbed at them with a dishcloth until they disappeared.

Alice stood at her side, waiting to be handed the dish. "It's heavy," Pansy told her as she held it out. "So don't drop it."

Alice took the platter and laid it carefully on the draining board. "It's big enough to hold a cow." She started wiping it with a tea towel. "It must be so heavy when it's loaded with meat."

"It is." Pansy pulled a face. "Good job we've all got muscles." She glanced at Alice. "Except you and Lilly. You're both as skinny as straws. Just wait until you've worked here a few months. You'll have muscles as big as a dustman's."

"I won't be here that long," Alice muttered, giving the platter a fierce swipe, making it spin around.

"Here, watch it!" Pansy shot out a hand to steady the dish. "If you break this, Mrs. Chubb will dock your pay."

Alice shrugged. "So what?"

Pansy heaved a sigh. "Alice, if you do a good job and work hard, Madam might keep you on after Lilly comes back. Mrs. Chubb is always saying as how she needs an extra hand. Especially in the summer when all the toffs are down here."

Alice didn't answer, but kept her head down as she finished drying the platter.

Pansy stared at her, confused. One minute the girl was begging for a job, the next she acted as if she couldn't care less about working at the Pennyfoot. What happened, Pansy wondered, to change Alice's mind so suddenly?

At that moment the back door opened, and a familiar voice rang out from the doorway. "Happy Christmas, everybody!"

"Samuel!" Abandoning the soapy dishes, Pansy rushed over to the young man and threw her arms around his neck. "I'm so happy to see you! What are you doing here?"

"Came to see you, didn't I." Samuel looked around the kitchen. "Where is everybody?"

"Mrs. Chubb is taking a short rest in her room, and Michel went into town to buy some more spices. Gertie and the rest of the maids are upstairs, getting the dining room ready for supper." Pansy drew back, laughing as Samuel wiped wet suds from his cheek. "Sorry, luv. I forgot my arms were wet."

"That's all right." Samuel let out a big sigh. "Much as I love being my own boss, I really miss this place. I miss everyone."

"We miss you, too." His sad expression worried Pansy, and she laid a hand on his arm. "You don't regret leaving, do you?"

"No, of course not." He glanced around again. "It's just that the memories keep coming back. After all, this is where I met you."

"Yeah." Her sigh matched his. "I still remember the first day I set eyes on you."

"Me, too." He was grinning now, his melancholy apparently banished. "I saw Charlie's new assistant when I came in. How's he coming along?"

Pansy shrugged. "I dunno. Charlie gets impatient with him. Says he's afraid of horses."

Samuel let out a shout of laughter. "Afraid? How can anyone be afraid of a horse?"

Pansy felt uncomfortable. She liked Henry, in spite of his shyness and lack of confidence. Or maybe because of it. In any case, she didn't like Samuel making fun of him. "Maybe he got hurt by one once."

"Yeah, well, I'll tell you something. It doesn't surprise me that he's a cry baby. He walks like a girl."

Pansy frowned. It was time to change the subject. The last thing she wanted was to argue with Samuel right before the wedding. "I can't believe we're getting married the day after tomorrow."

Samuel put his arm around her and drew her close. "Looking forward to it, are you?"

"'Course I am." Her annoyance forgotten, she beamed up at him. Excitement bubbled up inside her at the thought of marrying this man. "My wedding dress should arrive this afternoon. Madam's dressmaker is bringing it for me to try on."

"Well, then, I'd better not stick around too long." He let her go. "It's supposed to be bad luck for the groom to see the bride in her wedding dress before the wedding."

Her excitement dwindled a little bit. "You're not leaving again so soon?"

"Have to, luv. I was just passing by. That's why I dropped in, just to say hello. I'm on me way back to the shop. I want to get all the orders caught up before I walk down that aisle with my lovely bride."

Blushing, she dropped her gaze. "Go on with you. Well, at least you can meet Alice before you go." She turned around and stared at the empty space in front of the sink. "Where'd she go?"

"I saw someone slipping out the door as I came in," Samuel said. "Was that her?"

Pansy shook her head. "She's a strange one."

"I don't remember seeing her here before."

Pansy filled him in on Alice's story. "I can't make her out. She begged Madam for a job here, yet she acts as if she can't wait to get out of here."

Samuel dug his hands in his pockets. "Well, I suppose it's hard on her, not remembering anything about her past and all."

"Yeah, I suppose so. I think she's afraid of all men. That's probably why she left when you came in. She doesn't want nothing to do with any of them. Not even when they're as nice as you."

"That's sad." He reached her and drew her close. "I'm really glad you're not afraid of me."

Pansy giggled. "I'd be a sorry sort of wife if I was."

Samuel grinned. "My wife. It sounds strange. I suppose I'll get used to it."

"You'd better." Pansy pulled away from him as the door opened.

"Samuel!" Mrs. Chubb bustled in, hands outstretched. "Let me look at you." She took him by the shoulders and looked into his face. "Are you taking care of yourself properly?"

"'Course I am, Mrs. Chubb. I gotta look good for the wedding, don't I."

"You do, indeed." She glanced up at the clock. "What are you doing here? You've not closed the shop this early?"

"Nah. I had to go fetch some spare parts." Samuel blew a kiss at Pansy. "I'd best be off. See you at the church!"

Pansy's stomach seemed to flip over. "I'll be there!" *With bells on*, she silently added, hugging herself.

CHAPTER
❋ 13 ❋

Alone in the library, Cecily searched along the shelves for the book she needed. One of these days, she told herself, she'd have someone come in and organize the books. Once upon a time the shelves had been neatly arranged, with fiction at eye level, history and classics above, and the rest below. Now there were Dickens and Sherlock Holmes mixed in with *The History of the British Empire* and *The Ladies' Compendium of Good Manners*.

Shaking her head, Cecily ran her gaze along a row of history books, finally pouncing on the title she'd been seeking. Taking the book over to the fireplace, she sank onto the green brocade chair and flipped open the pages.

Before long she found exactly what she needed to know. With a satisfied sigh, she slapped the book closed. At least she had an idea what Gerald Evans was investigating, and why it concerned the Pennyfoot. The next step was to find out exactly who was involved. Once she was certain of that, she could ring the authorities in Wellercombe to take care of things.

Feeling pleased with herself, she left the library and headed down the hallway to the ballroom. She could no longer put off talking to Phoebe. The pantomime was to be presented tomorrow night, and Phoebe was at that moment conducting the final dress rehearsal. There wasn't much Cecily could do to prevent at the best a slip-up, or at the worst, utter chaos, as was more often the case, but at least she could perhaps ward off a tragedy by overseeing the rehearsal.

She pushed open the doors and as usual, pandemonium reigned on the stage. Standing front and center, Phoebe and Jacob faced off, both red in the face, both shouting above the din going on behind them.

The dance troupe had apparently been ordered to rehearse one of the musical numbers. A determined-looking pianist pounded away on the piano, while a discord of wind instruments and an enthusiastic drummer accompanied him. The women onstage gamely sang along, mostly off-key, which was nothing new, and with complete disregard for timing or rhythm.

Wincing, Cecily closed the door behind her and advanced into the room. Spotting Madeline at the other end, she headed over to her friend, putting off the inevitable for just a few moments longer.

Working on a display of holly and pine, Madeline lifted her head as Cecily approached. Instead of her usual smile, however, her face looked drawn, her eyes heavy lidded with dark circles beneath them.

"Madeline!" Cecily halted by her side. "Are you ill? It's not Angelina, I hope?"

Madeline worked at a smile. "No, the little one is just fine, thank you."

"Then what's wrong? I can tell something is bothering you."

Madeline looked back at the display. "It's nothing. I haven't been sleeping well, that's all."

Seriously concerned now, Cecily leaned closer. "Tell me, Madeline. What is it?"

Her friend seemed to be fighting with indecision, then shuddered. "I feel death in the air. Very close."

Cold fingers clutched at Cecily's heart. She couldn't forget Madeline's ominous words earlier. *It was just a faint warning that Baxter needs to tread carefully.* She couldn't bring herself to ask her friend if the death omen was for her husband. No matter what Madeline answered, it wouldn't be enough to soothe her fears.

"Don't mind me," Madeline said, grasping Cecily's hand. "It could mean anything. It doesn't necessarily mean someone is going to die. It could just be the end of something."

That didn't help at all. Cecily tried to look unconcerned. "I know. I have to go and sort out whatever is going on with Phoebe now, so I'll leave you to your task."

Madeline looked worried. "Please try not to concern yourself too much. I shouldn't have said anything."

"It's all right," Cecily assured her, knowing it was anything but all right. She would worry now, every moment she was apart from her husband. She felt as if a heavy weight sat on her shoulders as she walked back to the stage.

Mercifully, the song had ended, and the musicians were busy sorting through their music. Phoebe still stood on the stage, shouting and gesturing at her dancers, but there was no sign of Jacob. Cecily was thankful, however, to see the backdrop and set were in place. At least the man had done something right.

She headed for the door that led to the wings. She would join Phoebe onstage and find out how the rehearsal was going, though judging from what she'd seen so far, it didn't look too promising.

Just as she reached the door, Jacob rushed through it, seemingly in a great hurry. "Sorry, m'm," he muttered, as he brushed past her.

She called out to his hastily retreating back. "Just a moment, Jacob!"

It seemed as if he would ignore her and keep going, but after a few steps he halted, turned, and trudged slowly back to her. "Yes, m'm?"

"My husband and I went down to inspect the wall in the wine cellar," she said, watching his face closely.

Alarm flashed in his eyes, and his voice rose a notch. "Yes, m'm?"

"There were a good many more bricks out of that wall than you led me to believe," Cecily said quietly.

Jacob stretched his neck as if his collar was too tight. "Yes, m'm."

"Would you care to tell me why you lied?"

He cleared his throat. "I didn't want to worry you, m'm.

You being so busy with Christmas and the wedding and all. I thought I'd just take care of it and put all the bricks back where they belong."

"So it was you who stacked the bricks up like that?"

"Yes, m'm. They were all over the place, so I tidied them up until I could get down there to replace them."

"What I'd like to know is how they fell out in the first place."

Jacob looked a little strained. "I imagine it were rats, m'm. Some of those things can be as big as a cat. Saw plenty of them in the navy, I did. They could put a hole in a wall big enough to fit an elephant."

Cecily stared at him. "Rats."

"Yes, m'm."

"Mrs. Chubb gives you the key to the cellar when you go down there?"

"Yes, m'm."

"And you give it straight back to her?"

Jacob looked confused. "Yes, m'm. I put it in her hand the minute I get back to the kitchen."

"Every time?"

"Yes, m'm. Every time."

There were three keys to the wine cellar. Mrs. Chubb kept one hanging on the key ring on her belt. Cecily had another on her key ring. The third was in the safe with the extra set of master keys. It seemed unlikely anyone else could have found his way into the wine cellar. Deciding there wasn't much else she could ask him right then, Cecily gave him a brief nod. "Thank you, Jacob."

"Yes, m'm." Looking relieved, Jacob touched his forehead,

spun around, and charged across the floor as if the rats he'd mentioned were chasing after him.

Cecily stared for a long time at the doors after they'd closed behind him. Did Jacob truly believe the bricks had been pushed out by rats, or was he involved in something a lot shadier than hungry rodents?

"Cecily! Thank goodness you are here!" Phoebe's shrill voice penetrated the sound of the orchestra, which had started up again with another strident number.

Cecily acknowledged her greeting with a wave of her hand, then hurried through the door to the backstage area. As she turned the corner, she heard a scuffling of feet and muffled giggling. One of the dancers was just disappearing around the corner, with a footman in hot pursuit. Shaking her head, Cecily followed them out into the wings.

Phoebe caught sight of her and furiously beckoned to her to come out onstage. Obeying the signal, Cecily joined the dancers, resisting the urge to cover her ears at their robust bellowing.

Phoebe said something that was immediately lost in the blast of tuneless noise.

Cecily cupped her ear and Phoebe screamed louder. "Jacob Pinstone is an idiot!"

Cecily shook her head and lifted her hands in a gesture of defeat.

Phoebe turned to the dancers and flapped her hands at them. "Enough!" She had to shout it three times before the awful cacophony gradually subsided. Apparently the orchestra hadn't noticed Phoebe's commands, and it played on, blissfully unaware of the show's producer practically leaping up and down in an attempt to silence them.

Finally, one by one, the instruments trailed off, leaving only the drummer pounding away until the conductor hit him on the arm with his baton.

Phoebe clutched her hat with both hands and yelled, "Thank you!"

Cecily sighed. This was the first time in many years that she'd agreed to hire an orchestra for one of Phoebe's presentations. Until now they'd made do with only a pianist, due to the fact that Phoebe alienated every musician she came across with her misguided stage directions. It was far simpler, and considerably less expensive, to replace one pianist than an entire orchestra.

This year, however, since Pansy's wedding reception was to be held at the Pennyfoot, the orchestra Cecily had hired for the wedding had offered to also play for the pantomime at a greatly reduced price. Cecily had made the grave mistake of mentioning that fact to Phoebe, who assumed Cecily had agreed to the offer and spread the word around the village.

By the time Cecily found out about her friend's loose tongue, it would have seemed churlish to back out, and so here they were, all thirty-two musicians, under Phoebe's baleful eye.

Taking advantage of the sudden and blessed peace, Phoebe grasped Cecily's arm. "Look at that!"

Cecily followed her friend's shaking hand pointed at the rear of the stage.

"That backdrop is supposed to be the grand hall of a

palace. It looks more like the inside of a prison. The only thing missing are the convicts."

Cecily studied the backdrop. She had to admit, the dreary colors and strange black stripes didn't exactly portray a palace's grand hall. "Perhaps if we added a few splashes of color?" she ventured.

Phoebe leaned toward her, her voice a low hiss. "The show goes on tomorrow night."

Cecily resisted the urge to roll her eyes. "Let me talk to Jacob. I'll see what we can do before then."

"No!" Phoebe straightened her back and settled her hat more firmly on her head. "I do not trust that man to touch any more of the set. Perhaps the footmen can do what is necessary to brighten things up."

Cecily took another good look at the offending backdrop. In front of it sat an armchair on a low platform. "Is that supposed to be a throne?"

"Yes." Phoebe's voice dripped with disgust. "That's the best that Jacob could do. Does that man have any idea what he's doing? Oh, how I wish Clive were here. He created magic for me. This Jacob person creates nothing but . . ." She sought for a word, then apparently giving up on finding a fitting description, finished lamely, ". . . rubbish."

"Well," Cecily said, "we happen to have a pile of gold velvet curtains that we took down from the library when it was renovated after the fire. They are a little stained from the smoke and water, but that won't be noticed from the audience. We could drape them over the armchair and hang some of them up behind it. I'll see if Madeline has time to add a few of her touches. Don't worry, Phoebe. I'm sure it will all look wonderful."

Phoebe looked a little less frazzled. "Well, thank you, Cecily. I'm sure we'll all be grateful for any help you can give us." She smoothed the skirt of her green silk tea gown with her fingers. "If I were you, I'd give that man the sack."

Cecily fully intended to do that, just as soon as the Christmas season was over, but in view of Phoebe's penchant for gossiping, she would be the last person to know that. "I'll tell one of the maids to bring the curtains up here, and I'll tell two footmen to give you whatever help you need. You won't have to deal with Jacob again."

Now Phoebe was actually smiling. "Thank you. You are a good friend. I feel better already." Her smile vanished as she turned back to her dancers, who were standing around talking together in whispers. "Why are you dawdling about? Take your places! We have work to do!" She signaled to the conductor, who picked up his baton. "Another chorus of 'Turn again, Whittington,' please."

The conductor raised his baton, and Cecily left the ballroom to the strains of the tune now being belted out again by the enthusiastic dancers.

"We need three bottles of burgundy and two of port," Mrs. Chubb said. "Bring up three bottles of champagne as well." She handed the basket to Pansy. "The list is in there. And take Alice with you."

Pansy made a face. "Do I have to? She's so scared of everything, she'll probably wet her knickers down there."

Mrs. Chubb raised her chin. "Pansy Watson! What a way to talk. And you soon to be a respectable married lady. Don't

191

you let Samuel hear you talk like that. He might change his mind about marrying you."

Pansy grinned. "Who do you think taught me to talk like that?"

Mrs. Chubb gasped and clutched her throat. "Well, I never did."

Sobering, Pansy thrust her arm through the handle of the basket. "So where's the key?"

"Jacob's got it. He's working on the wall down there. The door should be unlocked. If not, just bang on it. He'll come up and open it for you."

"Why don't I just go on my own? I've gone down there plenty of times before without anyone holding my hand."

"I want Alice to go down there with you. Madam might decide to keep her on, and she needs to know where everything is in the wine cellar, in case I have to send her down there on her own."

"All right. But don't blame me if she comes back with wet drawers." Pansy escaped from the kitchen before the housekeeper could chastise her again.

She found Alice in the laundry room, sorting out the linens. On the other side of the room, three other maids huddled over an ironing board, apparently ignoring Alice. She didn't seem bothered by it, just stood there with her head down, concentrating on her job.

"Mrs. Chubb wants you to come down to the wine cellar with me," Pansy said, holding up the basket. "We've got some bottles to bring up."

Alice's chin shot up. "Me?"

"Yes, you." Pansy shifted the basket to the other arm.

"But I'm doing this." Alice nodded at the pillowcases she held in her hands.

"Well, leave that for now. You can come back to it later."

"But—"

"I haven't got all day," Pansy said, trying to curb her impatience. "It'll be time to serve supper before long. We have to get the wine now."

Alice looked as if she would argue, but just then the other maids giggled, and throwing them a dark look, she dropped the pillowcases and joined Pansy at the door.

Aware of her companion's sulky silence, Pansy said nothing as they crossed the courtyard and arrived at the door to the cellar.

Once there, she nudged the door open with her foot. "Jacob must have taken the oil lamp down there," she said. "It's usually hanging on this nail on the wall." Turning her head, she realized she was talking to thin air. Alice was already walking gingerly down the steps.

A dim light glowed from the far end of the cellar, but left most of the front end in shadow. Pansy hung on to the railing as she felt her way to the bottom.

Alice waited for her, staring nervously at the dark aisles.

"Here," Pansy said, handing her the list. "We'll have to go to the other end to read this. Everything is in alphabetical order, so we'll just work backward. I should have brought another lamp with me. Come on."

She started down the aisle, hearing Alice's footsteps trailing behind her. As soon as she was close enough to the glow from the lamp, she put the basket down to read the list. Alice still hung back, and Pansy called out to her. "Here, come and read this. You need to recognize some of these names."

Alice shuffled closer. "It smells down here."

"You'd smell, too, if you never saw the light of day." Pansy held up the list. "Vallée Verte Winery, two bottles of Pinot Noir. They should be on the shelf over there." She pointed without looking, and studied the list again.

Alice plodded off, and Pansy started looking for the port wine. It was awfully quiet down there. She paused. If Jacob was fixing the wall, he wasn't making much noise. Tilting her head to one side, she listened. Nothing. She couldn't even hear Alice. What *was* Jacob doing if he wasn't fixing the wall?

Spotting the winery label, she reached for the port. As her fingers touched the bottle, the silence was suddenly ripped apart by a shrill, bone-chilling scream.

Unnerved, Pansy froze, her fingers still resting on the bottle. The scream shattered the air again, this time followed by pounding feet. Alice raced into view, head down, her sobs echoing along the rafters.

She reached Pansy, who was struggling to get her breath. "It's Jacob!" Alice's fingers bit into Pansy's arm. "He's covered in blood, and I think he's dead!"

Cecily had almost finished dressing for the evening when she heard the sharp rapping on the front door of her suite. Something about the urgency of the sound made her uneasy. She decided to remain in her boudoir and let Baxter open the door. Her nerves seemed to be unsettled. Probably by Madeline's gloomy predictions.

She waited, her back tense, as the sound of Baxter's voice drifted back to her. She couldn't hear what he said, and a moment later she heard the door close. When he didn't come in to her right away, she laid down her comb and hurried out into the front room.

One look at her husband's face told her it was bad news. She lifted a hand to her throat and sat down by the fire. "What is it now?"

Baxter's face was drawn, his mouth a thin line. He gave her a long look, then stepped toward her, holding out his hand. "There's been another . . . death."

For a moment, she felt nothing but relief. Madeline's words rang in her head. *I feel death in the air. Very close.* At least it wasn't Baxter who had died. In the next instant, she felt ashamed. "Who is it?" she asked sharply. "Please don't tell me it's one of our people."

"I'm afraid so." Baxter took her hand. "It's Jacob Pinstone."

She looked at him, her mind blank with shock. For some reason Jacob was the last person she would have expected to die. He always seemed so invincible, so capable of taking care of himself. "How?" she asked, when she could find her voice.

"Cecily . . . apparently he was stabbed. Pansy and that new girl found him in the wine cellar. Mrs. Chubb sent a footman down there to take a look after the girls got back to the kitchen. He told me what he saw. There appeared to be a large knife wound in Jacob's chest."

Her bottom lip trembled. "He was murdered?"

Hearing the wobble in her voice, Baxter pulled her to her feet and wrapped his arms around her. "We'll have to call in the constabulary. I'm so sorry, my dear. There couldn't be a worse time for this to happen."

She closed her eyes and laid her head on his shoulder. "Dear heavens, what am I going to do? The pantomime, the wedding, Christmas . . . I can't have constables swarming all over the place, questioning the guests, maybe bringing in Scotland Yard, Inspector Cranshaw. . . ." She fought against the tears. "This can't be happening."

"Calm down." Baxter gently pushed her back onto her chair. "It's a shame Northcott isn't here. We could have bought his silence for a few days."

"We've done that already with Gerald Evans's death. We can't possibly get away with hiding two bodies. As it is I'll probably get both Sam Northcott and Kevin Prestwick into trouble by asking them to delay their investigation this long." Cecily shook her head. "No, we have to tell the authorities."

"All right. With any luck, Cranshaw will be away on holiday and won't be back until after Christmas."

"Poor Jacob." Cecily shook her head. "I didn't like him much but I would never have wished him dead. I don't think there's any doubt that his death is linked to Gerald Evans. I was going to discuss this with you after supper but I might as well tell you now." She paused, weighing her words. "I think I know what Mr. Evans was investigating."

Baxter's eyes widened. "You do? Well, what is it?"

"Just a moment." She got up and rushed into the boudoir. The cardboard and note were still lying in her drawer where she'd left them. Carrying them back to Baxter, she said, "Remember this?" She held up the cardboard.

"Yes, of course. You found it in Gerald Evans's room."

"That's right. I also found this piece of paper with the words to a telegram on it."

"I remember. You said Northcott was going around looking for a cricket match, or something."

"He thought the words referred to a cricket match, yes. But they don't." She glanced down at the paper. "Sam thought that Mr. Evans had spelled the word *sportsman* wrong." She held out the note. "What does that say?"

Baxter took it and studied it. "'Spotsman seen nearby. Already made run. No sign batman. Still looking. Stop.'"

"Yes, 'spotsman.' Not 'sportsman.' It's the name given to a member of a smuggling crew. He's the one responsible for choosing a safe place to land a boat when bringing smuggled goods onshore."

Baxter's eyebrows shot up. "Smugglers?"

"Yes." She pointed at the note. "'Already made run.' That refers to a smuggling expedition. Actually Sam came pretty close to cricket with 'batman.' It actually refers to someone who uses a cricket bat to defend his contraband."

"Good Lord!"

"So the telegram was talking about a smuggling ring." She held up the cardboard. "This is the kind of packing shippers use to transport paintings. Didn't you tell me that some art was stolen in London last week?"

Baxter sat down hard on his chair. "Are you telling me that you think those art thieves killed Gerald Evans?"

"I believe so, yes. I think Mr. Evans was hot on their trail and got too close." She paused, then added quietly, "I also think the thieves might be using the underground tunnel to store the stolen goods."

Baxter's eyes seemed about to pop out of his head. "Good Lord!"

"I think Jacob stumbled upon something incriminating and was killed by the thieves. Just like Gerald Evans."

Baxter took some time to digest what he'd just heard. "But what does that have to do with the bricks missing from the wall?"

"Well, I don't know, of course, but if I were to guess, I'd say that Jacob, after finding the loose bricks, was taking down more of the wall, possibly curious to find out what was behind there. I think the thieves might have heard him working on the wall and attacked him."

"Then why didn't they get rid of the body? As they did with Evans? And what about Granson? Where does he fit into all this?"

Cecily shook her head. "I don't have all the answers. I'm merely guessing, trying to come up with a viable scenario."

"Well, that's the duty of the constables. I think we should inform them and let them work out what happened. If there is stolen artwork down there, they can find it and apprehend the criminals."

"I hope so. Sam is probably on his way to London. Maybe by the time he gets back the constables will have solved the case." Cecily rose to her feet. "Will you ring the constabulary and Kevin Prestwick? I need to talk to Pansy."

"Of course."

"Thank you, dear." Cecily followed him out the door. Now all she could do was wait until the constable arrived and hope that his investigation wouldn't cause too much disruption to what was turning out to be a very stressful Christmas season.

CHAPTER
❋ 14 ❋

Sitting on the hard wooden chair in the kitchen, Pansy did her best to control her tears. Nothing seemed to help. Not Mrs. Chubb's kindly patting on the shoulder. Not Michel's gruff voice as he thrust a glass of brandy into her hand. Not Gertie's loud assurances that nothing was going to spoil her wedding. Not even the fact that her wedding dress had been delivered and was actually hanging in her wardrobe.

There'd been another murder. This time in the Pennyfoot itself. Soon there'd be bobbies all over the place and everything would be in an uproar. How could she walk down the aisle with a smile on her face, while all the time the vision of that bloody body was fresh in her mind?

She couldn't seem to stop shaking. Mrs. Chubb stood over her, her wrinkles deepened by her concern.

"Drink the brandy, lass. It'll help."

Pansy took a sip of the fiery liquid and shuddered. "It burns."

"It is supposed to burn," Michel called out from his usual station at the stove. "That is how it does good, *oui*? It calms the brain so you feel better."

"I won't feel better if my stomach is burned out."

Mrs. Chubb rolled her eyes and took the glass out of Pansy's hand. "All right, now. Take a deep, deep breath and let it out as slowly as you can."

Pansy did as she was told, though her mind still reeled with shock and despair. What good was all this if she couldn't walk down the aisle a happy, smiling bride? There were supposed to be pictures and all. Madam had hired a photographer. Pansy had never in her life had her picture taken. The first picture she'd ever have, and she'd be looking miserable in it. A tear spilled out of her eye and trickled forlornly down her cheek.

The door swung open, and Mrs. Chubb swung around as Madam walked in.

"Ah, there you are, Pansy. Do you feel up to talking to me about what you saw?"

Pansy was all ready to give Madam a violent shake of her head. She caught sight of Mrs. Chubb's eye, however, and it was clear that the housekeeper was silently ordering her to do what Madam asked.

"Yes, m'm," she said meekly, then closed her eyes at the thought of revisiting that horrible sight.

Madam drew a chair over to sit next to her. "Now then, tell me exactly what you saw."

Pansy swallowed. So far all she'd told anyone was that

Jacob Pinstone was lying dead on the floor of the wine cellar. Alice hadn't even managed that much. She'd screamed and cried all the way back to the kitchen, and was making so much noise that Mrs. Chubb had led her to her room to stay with Lilly until she calmed down.

Now, Pansy thought, she would have to tell Madam all the details. She just hoped she wasn't sick all over her in the telling. "It was Alice what saw him first," she muttered, in a last, desperate hope to escape the inevitable. "She could tell you what we saw."

"Alice is in no shape to tell us anything," Mrs. Chubb said quickly. "So be a good girl and tell Madam what you saw."

Pansy looked at the glass in Mrs. Chubb's hand. "P'raps if I had another sip of that stuff?"

The housekeeper glanced at Madam, who nodded. "Let her drink it. It will help soothe her nerves."

Pansy certainly hoped so. She took the glass, gulped it all down, and promptly choked.

"*Sacre bleu*," Michel muttered. "What a bloody waste."

Mrs. Chubb silenced him with a lethal look.

"Now," Madam said, when Pansy had stopped coughing and spluttering. "Just tell me quickly what you remember. Then you can forget it."

Never, Pansy thought, fighting nausea. She was never going to forget that ugly sight. "Jake was lying on his back, near the wall. There was . . ."—she swallowed hard—". . . blood oozing down his side and all over the f-f-floor . . ." She burst into tears.

"Did you see anything else?" Madam covered Pansy's hand with her own. "A knife? Footprints? Anything out of place?"

Pansy shook her head, struggling to control her sobs. "Alice was screaming. I j-just took one look and we ran all the way back to the kitchen." She caught her breath. "I left the basket down there. I didn't get the wine."

"Don't worry," Mrs. Chubb said, patting her shoulder. "Give me back the key and I'll send one of the footmen down for it."

Pansy swallowed. "I haven't got it. Jacob had it, remember?" She shot a worried glance at Madam, who seemed to be thinking about something else and wasn't even looking at her.

"I'm afraid you'll have to do without the wine until after the police have been," Madam said, getting to her feet. "It's a crime scene now and they'll want to take a look at it." She looked down at Pansy. "The door was open when you and Alice got to the wine cellar, wasn't it?"

"Yes, m'm." She shuddered. "That could have been me and Alice lying there."

"Well, it wasn't," Mrs. Chubb said briskly, "so just put that idea right out of your head."

Pansy nodded. She was beginning to feel sleepy, and the kitchen seemed to be swaying like she was on a ship. "I don't feel very well."

"I don't wonder at it," Michel said, "knocking back my best brandy like that. Brandy is supposed to be sipped and savored, not guzzled down like a thirsty cow."

"Perhaps she should go and lie down," Madam said, as she walked over to the door. "She can't serve supper like that."

Mrs. Chubb muttered something under her breath. "We're going to be shorthanded in the dining room now."

"It can't be helped." Madam paused at the door. "I'm sure you'll manage beautifully, Altheda, as you always do. I hope you soon feel better, Pansy. I'm sorry you and Alice had such an unpleasant experience."

"She's worried that all this will ruin the wedding, m'm," Gertie said. "I keep telling her it will be all right."

"I'll make sure everything goes well for your wedding, Pansy." Madam held up her hand. "And that's a promise." The door swung to behind her, and that was the last thing Pansy saw as she slipped off the chair into darkness.

"Stabbed right through the heart," Kevin Prestwick said with relish. "Just like Gerald Evans."

Standing in front of the library fireplace, Cecily let out her breath. "Would you say it was the same weapon used?"

"Hard to say for certain." Kevin held his hands out to the warmth from the coals. "It's certainly possible. Same size wound in the same place. I'd say it's very likely the same person killed them both."

Cecily glanced at the clock on the marble mantelpiece. "The constables are taking a long time with their investigation."

"There's only one. Most of them are on holiday." Kevin rubbed his hands together. "Poor devil will be working alone over Christmas by the looks of it."

Cecily relaxed her shoulders. A single constable would be far easier to handle. She looked up as the library door opened after a brief knock.

The young man who entered didn't look old enough to

be out of school, much less qualified for the police uniform he wore. He seemed ill at ease, fidgeting with his helmet as he paused just inside the door. "Mrs. Baxter? May I have a word with you?"

"Of course." She beckoned to him. "Come over to the fire. You look cold."

"It was a bit chilly down there in that wine cellar," the constable admitted, as he sheepishly crept forward. "P.C. Potter, m'm. At your service."

"Constable Potter. I assume you've already met Dr. Prestwick?"

"Yes, m'm. Down in the cellar." The constable visibly shuddered. "Nasty business that."

"Yes, I imagine it wasn't a pretty sight." Taking pity on the young man, she beckoned him to come closer. "Am I right in thinking this is your first murder?"

"Yes, m'm." The constable shuffled a little closer to the fire. "I only joined the constabulary a few months ago. Nothing much happens in Wellercombe. Mostly shoplifting, runaway horse, or a motorcar accident. Now there's been two murders here."

"I'm sorry." She exchanged a look with Kevin. "I suppose your superiors are on holiday, then?"

"Yes, m'm. I'm the low man on the totem pole, so to speak. I had to take the Christmas shift. I won't be off duty until the New Year." He stared into the flames. "Of course, I can always ring Scotland Yard. They'll send someone down to help me if I need it." He pulled a notebook from his pocket. "P.C. Northcott is working on the first murder. He reported that the victim was possibly robbed and killed by a vagrant."

"So I believe," Cecily said evenly. She could feel Kevin's questioning gaze on her face, but she ignored him. Mercifully he kept quiet as the constable scribbled in his notebook.

Finally the young man lifted his head. "It appears to me to be the same kind of weapon used in this case. Is that also your opinion, Dr. Prestwick?"

Cecily held her breath.

After a short pause, Kevin said quietly, "That is certainly a possibility, yes."

P.C. Potter stared at his notes, then closed the notebook. "Seeing as how there was no evidence, so to speak, I'll release the body to you, Doctor. There isn't much I can do right now, except keep an eye out for a suspicious individual in the area. I don't think it's necessary to call in Scotland Yard at present though it worries me that we have a possible Jack the Ripper in Badgers End. I'll issue a warning for everyone to be on guard, and then P.C. Northcott can take it from there when he returns. He may very well want to contact headquarters at that point."

Cecily's forehead felt warm with relief. "Thank you so much, P.C. Potter. May I wish you and your loved ones a very happy Christmas."

"And the same to you, Mrs. Baxter." He nodded at Kevin. "Doctor."

Kevin raised a hand. "Happy Christmas, Constable."

"Just one thing," Cecily said, as the constable opened the door. "I assume you searched the victim's pockets?"

"Yes, m'm. Standard procedure, that is."

"Quite. Did you happen to find a key in his pocket?"

P.C. Potter frowned. "Not that I recollect. If there is one I'll see that it's returned to you eventually."

"Thank you, Constable."

The door closed behind the young man and Cecily sank onto a chair. "Thank goodness. I was so afraid he was going to launch a full-fledged investigation."

Kevin sat down opposite her, his face a mask of curiosity. "What are you hiding?"

She looked up, trying her best to keep a blank expression on her face. "Hiding? Whatever do you mean?"

"Come on, Cecily." Kevin leaned forward. "I know you well enough to see that you're keeping something to yourself. Something you didn't want the constable to know. Don't worry. I'm not going to chase after him to tell on you."

She had to smile. "You're far too perceptive for comfort, Kevin."

"It comes with the territory. Doctors have to be able to read between the lines."

"Very well, but what I have to say is all conjecture, and I have nothing to support it other than my own speculation."

"I'm listening."

She told him what she suspected about the use of the tunnel below and the motives behind the two murders. "I believe both men died to keep them quiet," she finished. "If I'm right and this is a gang of thieves, they are dangerous and unpredictable."

"In which case you should have told the constable what you suspect."

She might have known he'd say that, and part of her agreed with him. If it hadn't been for the chaos an investigation would have caused, she might have shared her suspicions with P.C. Potter. Though if she had done so, he would undoubtedly have called in Scotland Yard. The chance that she would have to deal with Inspector Cranshaw, her mortal enemy, was just too much to risk at any time, much less with Christmas and a wedding right around the corner.

"I have no proof whatsoever," she said, squarely meeting his gaze. "I could disrupt Christmas for a good many people, for absolutely no reason. I can't take that chance. I'm by no means certain of my suspicions, and until I am, I prefer to wait until P.C. Northcott returns."

"When Christmas and Pansy's wedding are over with," Kevin said dryly.

She dropped her gaze. "You do know me well," she murmured.

Kevin stood, bringing her to her feet also. "How do you propose to find out if your suppositions are correct?"

"I'm not sure." She glanced at the clock. "I'll sleep on it, then decide."

"Be careful, Cecily. You don't exactly have a good track record when it comes to chasing villains."

She felt offended by that. "I've brought many of them to justice, when the efforts of the constabulary have failed."

"Ah, but at great risk to your personal safety. There have been times when we have all feared for your life."

"Well, all life is a risk, dear Kevin, is it not? Otherwise, what is the point? I'm not one to sit embroidering samplers all my life."

He uttered a shout of laughter. "Your escapades are a far cry from any normal activities of a well-bred woman, yet somehow you manage to imbue gentility and decorum. You are one of a kind, my dear Cecily, and your Baxter is a lucky man." He reached for her hand and drew it to his lips. "I shall leave you to your precarious pursuits, but I do beg you to take care. The world would be a miserable place without you."

She had almost forgotten how utterly charming he could be, and how much she adored his compliments. "I have every intention of staying in it just as long as the good Lord allows me to, but I thank you for your concern, and your friendship. It means a lot to me."

His blue eyes crinkled at the corners. "Always, Cecily. I will see you tomorrow night. Madeline and I are looking forward to the pantomime. At least, Madeline is. She takes a perverse pleasure in watching Phoebe make a fool of herself, I'm afraid."

"She doesn't mean it. She would be heartbroken if Phoebe were actually hurt by her calamities. To tell the truth, I do believe Phoebe enjoys the attention, whether it's for a successful presentation, or for a catastrophe onstage. Either way, people applaud her for the enjoyment, and she thrives on it."

"So everyone is happy, no matter what happens."

"Precisely." She smiled. "Good night, Kevin, and thank you."

He paused at the door, looking back at her over his shoulder. "For what?"

"For not telling on me."

He grinned at her. "Anytime. Good night, Cecily."

She stared at the door long after it had closed. Had it not been for Baxter, she might have ended up married to Kevin Prestwick. She tried to imagine what life would have been like as the doctor's wife.

After a while she returned to the fire and held out her hands to the flames. No matter what life would have been like as Mrs. Kevin Prestwick, it could not possibly have been nearly as interesting, exciting, and exhilarating as being Mrs. Hugh Baxter, manager of the Pennyfoot Hot . . . Country Club.

Smiling, she headed for the door. She needed to see her husband. And right now. Tonight was her favorite event of the Christmas season—the carol-singing ceremony. Nothing lifted her spirits more than standing in a crowded library, surrounded by people enjoying themselves, and the beautiful music of the Christmas carols filling the air all around her.

For one evening she intended to forget her troubles and enjoy the occasion with her beloved husband by her side. Gerald Evans's investigation and his killer could wait.

Gertie and the rest of the maids had assembled in the library before the guests arrived for the carol-singing ceremony. In one corner the string quartet sat tuning up, creating a discord of sound that jarred Gertie's ears.

It always amazed her that musicians could sound so bloody awful before the performance and then once they began to play the music was so beautiful it made her want to cry.

Not that she cried much anymore. Tonight, though, she felt strange, like she didn't know whether she wanted to laugh or cry. Usually at Christmastime she'd get a kind of fluttery feeling in her stomach, but this was different. This was more like being afraid and excited all at the same time and she had no idea why she should feel this way.

One thing she did know—she was looking forward to

seeing Clive again. They had seen so little of each other since he'd opened the toy shop. She missed seeing his burly figure striding down the hallway toward her, that big grin lighting up his craggy face.

Across from where she stood, the carol singers were lining up in uneven rows. The women wore red ribbons in their hair and the men sported red bow ties. Gertie loved singing carols. She smiled, remembering when Clive had come to her room one Christmas and they'd sung carols with the twins.

He was a good man, and she was lucky to know him.

The door opened just then, and the guests started wandering in. The women wore elegant tea gowns in soft pastel colors that complimented the dark dress coats of the men. Gertie saw Madam talking to the carolers. She stood out from the rest in a dark blue velvet gown and white lace stole.

Mr. Baxter stood behind her, waiting for her to finish her conversation. They made a handsome pair.

Gertie felt a pang of envy that took her by surprise. She hurried over to the sideboard in an effort to escape her peculiar feelings. She had to be coming down with something, she thought, as she seized a platter of vol-au-vents and started offering them to the guests.

For the next hour or so she divided the time between handing out refreshments and watching the door. The carol singers were halfway through their performance, and still there was no sign of Clive. Even the glorious sound of so many lovely voices raised in harmony failed to soothe her nerves.

She was so anxious her stomach felt like it was tied up in knots, and although the food looked and smelled delicious, she had no desire to sample any of it. Not that they were allowed to taste anything until the ceremony was over and all the guests had departed. Still, usually she was starving by then and couldn't wait to get a sausage roll or treacle tart in her mouth.

Walking back to the sideboard with an empty platter, she tried her best to concentrate on the next carol. It was one of her favorites—"Silent Night." As the beautiful chords echoed throughout the room, she felt a lump in her throat.

Impatient with herself, she turned sharply, and found herself face-to-face with the cause of her chaotic thoughts.

"Happy Christmas, Gertie."

Looking up into Clive's eyes, so full of tenderness, Gertie gulped. "Happy Christmas, yourself."

Clive looked around the room. "How long do you have to stay?"

"I don't really have to be here." She glanced over her shoulder at the carol singers. "I offered to help out the maids because we're shorthanded."

"Can you slip away for a few minutes? There's something I need to talk to you about."

"All right." Now she was worried. He looked serious. Was something wrong at the toy store? Was he going to tell her he was giving up on it? Surely not! There'd been plenty of customers there yesterday afternoon.

With questions racing through her mind, she followed him out into the hallway. A couple of guests strolled toward them, and Clive quickly led her the other way toward the ballroom. Pushing open the doors, he stepped back to let her go ahead of him.

It was dark in there without the gas lamps lit. She stood

hesitating as Clive stepped inside, leaving the doors open so that a faint light from the hallway spilled across the threshold.

"This isn't what I'd planned," he said, his voice sounding deeper than she'd ever heard it before.

He'd changed his mind. He was going to break up with her. That could be the only explanation for the strange sound in his voice. She tried to make light of things, though her heart was hammering out her dread. "What did you have planned, then? A picnic on the beach?"

He laughed, though it sounded strained. "No, though that might have been a good idea."

She couldn't see his face properly because he had his back to the light, but she could tell when the smile left and the serious look returned. *Here it comes*, she thought, and prayed she wouldn't make a fool of herself by crying in front of him.

"Gertie."

He took her hand, and she felt the strength of his warm fingers wrapped around hers. How was she going to survive the next few weeks with the pain of losing him? How could she carry on without him? Bloody hell, she was going to cry after all.

"I think you know how I feel about you. I've had to tread carefully, knowing that you weren't ready to make this decision, but the time has come when I can wait no longer."

To her utter astonishment, he sank to one knee. "I love you, Gertie Brown McBride. I've been waiting to ask you until I was sure I had the means to support you and the twins in the way you all deserve. My shop is doing well, and I feel confident I have a secure future, so I'm asking for your hand in marriage. You and the twins. If you'll have me."

The unfamiliar tears streamed down her face. She saw the ring sparkling in its little box in his hand and convinced herself she wasn't dreaming. As always, she couldn't resist the cheeky remark. "What took you so bleeding long? Of course I'll marry you!"

She threw her arms around his neck, toppling him over and falling with him to the floor.

Laughing, he took hold of her hand again. "Let's get this ring on your finger before you change your mind."

Happily she straightened her fingers so he could slide the lovely ring on. "I ain't never going to change my mind, so you're stuck with me now. Me and the twins." She caught her breath. "They are going to be so bloody happy."

"Do you want to go and tell them now?"

"No." She gently stroked his face. "I want to keep this to ourselves for a bit, so I can enjoy it without having to talk about it to anyone. We'll tell the twins on Christmas morning. It will make a lovely Christmas surprise for them."

"As you wish." He leaned forward. "Can I kiss the bride?"

"You don't have to flipping ask, silly." She closed her eyes. This was the happiest she'd ever felt, and she knew, without a single doubt, that she'd remember the feeling for the rest of her life.

CHAPTER
❀ 15 ❀

"My ankle's better," Lilly declared, sitting up in bed the next morning. "I'm going back to work. I'm sick of being stuck in this room. Especially with her." She nodded at Alice's empty cot. "I'll be glad when she's gone. She keeps me awake at night with all that talking in her sleep."

Pansy swiveled around on her chair, her hairbrush poised over her head. "Alice talks in her sleep?"

Lilly rolled her eyes. "Don't tell me you don't hear her. She goes on and on about somebody called Gwen, and going to Paris."

"Paris?" Pansy burst out laughing. "She must be dreaming."

"Yeah, and they're not pleasant dreams, either. She was going on last night about being caught up in something. She sounded really scared."

Pansy sobered at once. "Oh, poor thing. I know what it's like to have nightmares. I get them meself sometimes. Usually when I've eaten some of Michel's pickled onions." She stared at the bed. "Where is Alice, anyway? I didn't hear her get up."

"She's probably in the lav." Lilly slid off the bed and reached for her dressing gown. "I've got to go myself, so I'll see if she's all right. After the night she's had, she's probably being sick in there."

"Well, let me know if you need help cleaning it up." Pansy shuddered, and turned back to the dressing table mirror. She heard the door close as Lilly left, but was too busy staring at her hair to pay much attention.

Mrs. Chubb had promised to style it for the wedding. Pansy scowled at her image. It looked a mess this morning. Her hair needed washing, but she wanted to wait until the morning of the wedding. If she washed it too often it dried out and looked too wispy.

Tucking a strand behind her ear, she decided she needed more hairpins. She opened her box of accessories and hunted through the barrettes, ribbons, and decorative combs. Everything but hairpins.

Sighing, she closed the box. She was always running out of the flipping things. Her hair was baby fine and silky, and the pins fell out almost as soon as she shoved them in. She looked back in the mirror. If she didn't anchor that strand of hair behind her ear, it was going to fall in the porridge she had to serve very shortly in the dining room.

She leaned back in her chair and prepared to wait for Lilly to come back. Lilly always had plenty of pins.

After a while she became restless. She was already late, and by now Mrs. Chubb was probably getting ready to tell her off the moment she showed her face. After another minute or two, she reached for Lilly's drawer in the dresser. Lilly wouldn't mind, she told herself. They shared lots of things, and it was only hairpins. She'd pay her back the next time she went into town to shop for them.

She pulled open Lilly's drawer. Rows of underwear lay neatly folded side by side. Pansy pulled a face. Her own underwear was always in a tangled pile in her drawer. What was the use of taking all that time to fold it, and stack it neatly, when she'd be pulling it out to wear it again?

Feeling somewhat guilty about probing among something as personal as someone's underwear, she slid her hand beneath the garments to feel for the box of pins she knew Lilly kept in that drawer.

Her fingers collided with something cold and sharp. Drawing her hand back with a gasp, she saw a tiny trickle of blood on her thumb. She stuck it in her mouth and with the other hand, pulled the pile of petticoats aside to see what had nicked her. Staring at the object, she let out a whimper of shock and dismay. Then she quickly drew the petticoats back in place and closed the drawer.

Hairpins were no longer on her mind. Ignoring the strand of hair that swung across her face, she charged out of the room and down the hallway to the kitchen stairs.

Cecily was in her office, sorting through the bills, when Kevin knocked on the door and poked his face around it.

She greeted him with a smile. "Kevin! I wasn't expecting to see you until tonight. What brings you back so soon?"

"I was just passing by." Kevin strolled over to the window and looked out. "You have such a nice view of the bowling greens from here."

"I do. It can be a little distracting in the summertime."

"I can imagine." He turned to look at her. "Walter Pinstone is in Badgers End. He wants to take his brother's body back to London. I had to tell him that the case is unsolved and I can't release the body to him until after the constables have completed their investigation."

Cecily stared at him in dismay. "Goodness. That could be days."

"Unless I can get them to release the body earlier." He walked over to the desk. "I have to admit, I feel most uneasy about this whole situation. I can't help feeling that we should contact Scotland Yard before the trail goes cold, or before the killer strikes again."

Cecily felt a jolt of apprehension under her ribs. "I sincerely hope we won't have another stabbing. I think as long as we leave the gang of thieves alone, they won't disturb us again."

"They could disappear before the police get involved."

"I intend to have a talk with someone today who might be able to help us. I'm hoping to get some answers that will help clear this matter up entirely."

"I hope you're right." He smoothed his hair back at his forehead. "I have the utmost admiration for everything you have accomplished in the past, Cecily. You know that. But this time I can't help feeling that you are treading on very thin ice. If you're right, and there are stolen goods down there and those thieves get away, when Scotland Yard finds out that you knew what was going on right under your nose and could have had them apprehended, you could be in serious trouble with the law."

He wasn't telling her anything she didn't already know. It was a chance she had to take, until she knew for certain that her suspicions were justified. "And if I'm wrong, and the police investigation disrupts Pansy's wedding and Christmas for everyone all for nothing, I will never forgive myself. I'm sorry, Kevin, but I must ask you to remain silent until we know for certain what is going on and just who is involved."

His mouth twisted in a wry smile. "You know I can deny you nothing. Just understand that I'm not at all comfortable with the situation."

"Thank you, Kevin." She sought to change the subject. "Will you be bringing Angelina to the pantomime tonight?"

Kevin visibly shuddered. "I sincerely hope not. That child has the loudest voice I've ever heard in one so young. She's at the questioning stage, and I'm quite certain that she would sit through the entire presentation, demanding answers for everything that is going on onstage."

Cecily chuckled. "Well, I should be happy to see her. She is growing up so fast."

"She is indeed." To Cecily's relief, Kevin seemed more relaxed after talking about his daughter. "I must leave." He pulled a pocket watch from his vest pocket and grimaced. "I'm late for surgery. My patients will be anything but patient."

Cecily shook her head at the feeble joke. "They'll be happy to see you. Most of them only come to your surgery to hear your expansive compliments."

Kevin laughed. "You flatter me, Cecily." He started for the door, then paused, turning back to look at her. "By the way, Walter Pinstone told me that Jacob lost his wife and two children several years ago when their house caught fire. He blamed himself for being away from them at sea so much. Walter said that Jacob was never the same after that."

Cecily caught her breath. "Oh my. I'm so sorry. No wonder he was so cantankerous all the time. How sad."

"Yes. I thought you'd want to know."

"Thank you, Kevin. That explains a lot." She watched him leave, wishing that she'd known about Jacob's tragic past. She would have been a lot more tolerant of his attitude. Poor Jacob. He had suffered such a terrible loss, and then to lose his own life that way, how very sad.

She had just picked up her pen when the office door flew open and Pansy rushed in, apparently forgetting to knock first in her haste. She almost lost her balance as she dropped a curtsey, and Cecily didn't need to see the maid's tearful face to know that something had badly upset her again.

Cecily's first thought was that someone else had been murdered. Stricken with guilt for having delayed the investigation, she waited for Pansy to give her the bad news.

Pansy seemed too out of breath to speak. One hand pressed to her throat, she opened and shut her mouth like a fish gasping for water.

Cecily laid down her pen and clasped her hands to prevent them shaking. "What is it, Pansy? What's happened?"

"I was looking in Lilly's drawer for hairpins," Pansy got out at last. "She's got a *knife* in there." Her voice had risen to a squeak. "A great big one! It was hidden underneath her petticoats."

Cecily stared at her, trying to comprehend Pansy's words. "A knife?"

"Yes, m'm. It cut me. Look!" She held out her hand so that Cecily could see the small dab of blood on her thumb.

Cecily's relief that there wasn't another dead body lying around made Pansy's distress seem almost comical. "Oh, I'm sorry," she murmured. "You must ask Mrs. Chubb to attend to that."

Pansy sucked on her thumb, her wide eyes beseeching Cecily to say or do something that would ease her anxiety.

Cecily struggled for a moment to find something to say that wouldn't set off a major barrage of rumors. "I'm sure there's a reasonable explanation," she said, hoping her soothing tone would help calm Pansy's panic.

Pansy, it seemed, was not to be so easily reassured. "What if there isn't?" She tipped forward, forgetting her place enough to lean her hands on Madam's desk. "What if Lilly killed Jacob and that other bloke with that knife?"

Cecily blinked. "I'm sure she didn't. I'll certainly have a word with her, but——" She broke off as a sharp rapping on the door made them both jump.

The door opened and Lilly stepped into the room.

Pansy uttered a little shriek, but Cecily ignored her, her attention on Lilly's white face. Was this more bad news, perhaps?

"It's Alice," Lilly said, sounding almost as distressed as Pansy. "She's gone."

Pansy moaned. "Not another one."

Cecily felt a cold stab of alarm. "What do you mean, *gone?*"

"She's left. All her things are gone. Her drawer and her space in the wardrobe . . . it's all gone." Lilly waved a hand at the window as if that were where Alice's things had disappeared.

"Did you kill her, too?" Pansy demanded.

Lilly stepped back, her eyes wide with shock. "What? No, of course I didn't. I didn't kill anybody. What in blazes are you talking about?"

"All right." Cecily got up from her chair. "Both of you, calm down. Pansy, go and tell Mrs. Chubb that Alice has apparently left the premises. You'll just have to manage without her."

Pansy stood frozen to the spot, her face a mask of fear.

"Now, Pansy," Cecily said gently. "You need to get to the dining room to help with breakfast."

Lilly turned to the door. "I'll go."

"No!" Cecily softened her tone again. "I need a word with you first." She looked back at Pansy. "Please, Pansy. Mrs. Chubb needs your help now, more than ever."

As if stirred by the words, Pansy nodded and headed for the door, giving Lilly a wide berth as she passed by her.

As the door closed, Cecily sat down again. "I hear you're hiding a knife in your drawer."

Lilly scowled. "Pansy told you, didn't she? So that's why she thought I'd killed Jacob. What was she doing going through my drawers?"

"She was looking to borrow some hairpins. She didn't mean to snoop."

Lilly's expression changed to concern. "*You* don't think I killed him, do you? Or the other bloke? I didn't even know him. I would never kill anyone unless I was fighting for my life." She drew a cross on her chest with her thumb. "On my mother's grave, I swear I didn't kill anyone."

"It's all right, Lilly. I believe you." Cecily leaned forward. "You don't need to hide a knife here. You're perfectly safe. No one is going to hurt you while you are under my roof."

"I bet Jacob thought that, too."

Cecily winced. "Jacob probably poked his nose into something he shouldn't have. I promise you, Lilly, I will make sure you're protected."

Lilly nodded slowly, obviously less than convinced. "All right, m'm. But is it all right if I keep the knife?"

"If you must. You might, however, want to find a better hiding place."

"Yes, m'm. Thank you, m'm." Lilly escaped from the room, leaving Cecily staring thoughtfully at the door. Things were getting complicated. The sooner she talked to Fred Granson the better.

She glanced at the clock hanging above her filing cabinet. So far Mr. Granson had proved elusive. She had spent some time the day before searching for him, but no one seemed to know where he was. She had no idea what he was doing with his time, but obviously he wasn't spending it inside the Pennyfoot. Which only made her all the more certain that he was involved with whatever was going on down in that tunnel.

Making up her mind, she got up from her chair. One thing she did know, Granson took breakfast in the dining room every morning. She would wait for him to leave and waylay him in the hallway. It was unlikely that he would admit anything to her, of course, but she was hoping that something he said would confirm her suspicions enough that she could go to the authorities and have them deal with it without involving the Pennyfoot too much.

As for the murders, it would be up to the constables to solve that part of it once they had the thieves under arrest, thus relieving the country club from any involvement. Except for Fred Granson, of course. She would have to cross that bridge when she came to it.

Sighing, she left the office and headed purposefully for the dining room. One way or another, she intended to corner Mr. Fred Granson that very morning. All she could hope was that she would learn something useful. Time was running out. She could not, in good conscience, delay this investigation much longer if there was a possibility that someone would get away with not only a large haul of stolen paintings, but also the murders of two innocent people. If she couldn't get anything out of Mr. Granson, she could see no other alternative but to tell P.C. Potter what she suspected and deal with the consequences.

She was halfway down the hallway when Gertie rushed up to her, her face creased in anxiety. "Oh, there you are, m'm. I was just coming to see you."

Alarm bells went off in Cecily's head for the third time that morning. "What is it, Gertie?"

"It's that new guest, m'm. Mr. Granson. Mrs. Chubb sent me to the wine cellar last night. Pansy and Alice were too upset to go back down there and Lilly had a bad foot so me and one of the maids had to go. I hate going down there and

Mrs. Chubb knows that, but she didn't know what else to do 'cause none of the other maids know how to find the bottles, so I said I'd go."

"That was good of you, Gertie."

"Yes, well, we had just got to the door when it opened and Mr. Granson came out of the wine cellar."

Gertie's voice, high-pitched with excitement, gave Cecily chills. "Are you sure?"

"Yes, m'm. He stood right in front of us. Gave us both a shock, I can tell you."

Cecily did her best to sound unconcerned. "Did he say what he was doing down there?"

"He said he was looking for a special bottle of wine." Gertie shook her head. "What I want to know is how he got in there. Mrs. Chubb had to give us the spare key out of the safe because the other one got lost. Do you think Mr. Granson stole it?"

Cecily didn't know what to think, but it wouldn't do to share her doubts with her chief housemaid. "I very much doubt it, Gertie. Someone must have left the door unlocked. Probably the constable. Obviously Mr. Granson isn't aware of our restrictions. I shall make sure that he is informed of them."

"Yes, m'm." Gertie still looked uneasy. "He's in the dining room right now."

"Thank you, Gertie." Cecily watched her leave, then called out after her. "Was Mr. Granson carrying a bottle of wine when you saw him?"

Gertie paused. "No, m'm. Not that I could see, anyway."

"Thank you, Gertie." Turning her back on the maid,

Cecily rounded the corner of the hallway, nearly colliding with the gentleman in front of her.

"Did I hear my name mentioned?" Fred Granson's eyes didn't match his smile. "Is there something I can help you with?"

Cecily took a moment to catch her breath. "Actually, there is, Mr. Granson. My housemaid tells me that she saw you leaving the wine cellar last night. I'm curious as to why you were there."

Granson's gaze seemed to burn into her face. For a long, agonizing moment he was silent. Just when Cecily was beginning to think he would refuse to answer her, he said quietly, "Mrs. Baxter, I think it's time you and I had a little talk."

Her heart skipped, and she looked past him down the corridor. People were leaving the dining room, squeezing past them with murmured greetings and apologies. "I would welcome that, Mr. Granson. There's no time like the present."

He glanced over his shoulder. "Perhaps somewhere a little less crowded?"

"The library should be empty this time of the morning." She would have suggested her office. However, the vision of him coming at her with a knife was a little too vivid for comfort. Her office was far too small to offer a means of escape, should that be necessary. At least in the library she'd have a fighting chance.

"Then perhaps you would join me there now?"

"Of course." She led the way, conscious of his presence close on her heels. Every nerve in her body prickled with apprehension, yet she managed to keep an appearance of calm as she closed the library door.

Taking an armchair close to the fire, she beckoned him to be seated, her mind already planning a route of escape. She'd made sure to sit closest to the door, should she have to make a run for it. Even so, hampered by her long skirt, she wasn't sure she was nimble enough to evade the husky man if he should lunge at her.

Granson seemed disinclined to sit, preferring to stand in front of the fireplace, his hands deep in his pockets.

That made Cecily all the more nervous. She realized she was unconsciously twisting a button on her blouse enough to tear it off, and immediately dropped her hand. "Mr. Granson, I have a great deal of work to take care of, so I would appreciate it if we could make this as short as possible. I would like to know why you were in my wine cellar and, in fact, how you managed to get the door open without a key. I locked that door myself."

"Yes," Granson murmured. "I do owe you an explanation, and I apologize for not confiding in you before this. I was hoping to save you a great deal of worry. I realize now, however, that with the death of your maintenance man, this must be a major concern for everyone."

His words intensified her anxiety. "How did you hear about Jacob's death?"

"I make it my business to know such things."

Cecily frowned. He didn't talk like a criminal. She waited, still not quite certain of his innocence and still poised for flight.

"My name is not Fred Granson." He pulled a calling card from his pocket and handed it to her. "It's Harry Clements. Gerald Evans's partner."

Cecily stared at the words *private detective* stamped on the card. Surprise, relief, and a stab of annoyance kept her silent for a moment.

"When I received a telegram from my partner," Mr. Clements continued, "I decided to join him in his investigation. I thought that two heads would be better than one, and with my help, we could clear up this case before Christmas and then we'd both be free to enjoy the holidays. Imagine my shock and distress to arrive at the Fox and Hounds, only to learn that Gerald had been killed."

Recovering her voice, Cecily looked up at him. "I'm so dreadfully sorry. That must have been a shock."

"It was. Ours is a dangerous profession, but somehow you never think of actually being murdered. Gerald was on the trail of a gang of art thieves. He tracked them down to the southeast coast, and while in a public house in Brighton, met a man who told him that he'd been approached by someone wanting to hire him to ship some goods to France. The pickup was in a cove just outside Badgers End."

"I see."

"Gerald seemed convinced that the Pennyfoot Country Club was somehow involved, though he never got a chance to tell me why. He took a room here to investigate and lost his life. I decided to take his room in the hopes of hunting down the thieves, who I believe are responsible for my partner's death."

All her suspicions being confirmed only unsettled her more. "So what does all this have to do with my wine cellar?"

Harry Clements stared at his shoes for a moment. "I did some research and found out about a tunnel below this building, the entrance of which is in a cove. The perfect place to hide stolen goods. I went to investigate the beach entrance, hoping I would find the stolen paintings there. I found the entrance blocked with boulders and rocks."

"Blocked?" Cecily stared at him in surprise. "I had no idea."

"It appears that the boards shoring up the entrance had given way. I found blood stains on the rocks. I think that was where Gerald was killed. Which makes me believe that he was at the point of discovering the stolen artwork when he was confronted by the thieves."

Reluctant to let him know that she had already surmised as much, Cecily tried to sound shocked. "Are you saying that there are stolen goods stored in the tunnel below the Pennyfoot?"

"Precisely, which means," Clements said quietly, "if the paintings are stored down there, they became trapped down there and the only way to get to them and get them out now is through your wine cellar."

Cecily shook her head. "I don't see how that can be achieved without being discovered."

"Most likely they will remove the artwork at night. I believe they have an associate helping them from the inside."

"The inside?"

"Inside this building. I'm sorry, Mrs. Baxter, but you may very well have a killer under your roof. Someone who is breaking through the wall to open up the trapdoor in your abandoned card room to retrieve the paintings."

Cecily raised her eyebrows. "You have done your homework."

Clements smiled. "It pays to be thorough."

"It sounds as if your partner was just as well-informed."

His smile faded. "Gerald must have been getting too close. I know he'd been investigating the wine cellar. I found brick dust in the wardrobe in his room. Your maintenance man was probably killed for the same reason."

Cecily made a mental note to remind the maids to do a more thorough job of cleaning a room. "If you're so certain about this, why haven't you contacted Scotland Yard?"

Clements made a sound of disgust. "Scotland Yard had ample opportunity to apprehend the criminals. They had advance notice of the theft and botched the job. Gerald and I were hired by a member of the art gallery's trustees. The members were afraid the paintings would be shipped abroad and lost before the Yard caught up with the thieves. According to what this chap told Gerald, the pickup is supposed to take place at midnight on Christmas Eve."

Cecily caught her breath. "That's tomorrow night."

"Right. If I don't find those paintings by tomorrow afternoon, I'll have to call in the local authorities. Which means I'll lose a pretty hefty stipend."

"So what are you going to do?"

Clements twisted his mouth in a wry smile. "It looks like I'll be paying a visit to your tunnel."

"But that's dangerous. Two men have died already because of that dratted wall. Besides the fact that the thieves could be down there, the tunnel isn't safe. The entrance has already collapsed, by what you've told me. The damp must be rotting the beams. The rest of it could go at any time."

Clements shrugged. "That's why we get paid such a high fee. Or I should say *I* get paid, now that Gerald is gone." He shook his head, as if he still couldn't believe his partner was dead. "With all the bills left for me to pay, I'm going to need that money."

"Well, you don't have to go down there alone." She crossed her fingers, hoping she was doing the right thing. "I can send some of my footmen down there to help you."

"That's not a good idea." He got to his feet. "I hate to tell you this, Mrs. Baxter, but I'm afraid you can't trust anyone in the Pennyfoot. An operation like this could only guarantee success if the thieves have someone planted in this building at all times. I can't risk tipping them off."

Somehow she'd known all along he was going to say that. "I wish you would let us help you." She got up from her chair. "Or at least, bring in P.C. Potter. I don't think you should be dealing with this all alone."

"Don't worry, Mrs. Baxter. I'm quite capable of taking care of myself. Gerald mentioned the fact that there are three members of the gang, and I feel confident I can outwit them. I must ask you not to mention all this to anyone else. As I said, we don't know who we can trust. The fewer people who know about it, the better."

"Very well. But I don't like the idea that someone here in the Pennyfoot is helping those criminals." She looked up at him. "I don't suppose you have any idea who that might be?"

"None. I did think it might be your maintenance man, until he turned up dead. I'm so sorry about that."

"It's not your fault." She led him to the door. "I wish you luck, Mr. Clements."

"Granson. I don't want anyone else to know who I am."

"Of course. Mr. Granson." She paused to stare into his

eyes. "You will let me know just as soon as you find out who it is helping those thugs?"

"Of course." He reached past her to open the door. "Rest assured, Mrs. Baxter, he will be apprehended. As will the rest of the gang. One way or another."

She nodded without too much conviction. "I sincerely hope you are right."

CHAPTER 16

Gertie bounced down the kitchen steps, heaving the heavy basket of dirty linens on her hip. It had been a long time since she'd had to change the bedding, and she'd forgotten how much she hated the task. Thanks to Alice's disappearance, not only had she spent half the morning struggling with sheets, blankets, and eiderdowns, she'd also had to empty chamber pots. That was a job totally unfitting for a chief housemaid.

Not that she minded filling in now and then when they were shorthanded. But chamber pots? What the blue blazes was that plumber doing that he couldn't get the water running in the guest lavatories? Plumbers were supposed to know how to mend bleeding water pipes. Just wait 'til she set eyes on him again. She'd bloody give him a piece of her mind.

As if she'd conjured him up, Bernie appeared at that moment from the laundry room door.

Before Gertie could question why he was in there, he blurted out, "Someone said Alice is gone."

Gertie raised her eyebrows. True, she'd seen the two of them talking together, but she had no idea they were that fond of each other. Or maybe it was just Bernie who fancied Alice. Gertie couldn't imagine what the shy, fearful young woman would see in someone like the flighty plumber. "Yeah, she's gorn." She pushed past him. "Not that I'll miss her that much. She wasn't much help when she was here. Just like you. When are you going to get those bleeding lavatories working again?"

"Do you know where Alice went?"

"No, I don't, and I don't care."

She'd flung the words over her shoulder. Just as she reached the laundry door, Bernie called out softly, "Let me know when you get tired of that bloke you're seeing."

Gertie rolled her eyes. What a rotten sod he was, moping over Alice gone one minute and making eyes at her the next. She was tempted to tell him that Clive had proposed last night, then decided it was none of his business. Besides, she didn't want anyone to know just yet.

She'd had a tough time keeping her happiness to herself so far. Especially around Pansy, who had become like a sister to her. But tomorrow was Pansy's wedding day, and somehow it didn't seem right to make her big announcement now.

Shaking her head, she bumped open the door with her hip and swept inside.

Bernie had disappeared when she came out again, and good riddance to him. She marched down the corridor to the kitchen, still fuming over the cheek of that bloke. Just let him get in her way again and she'd give him what for. Pushing open the door, she saw the back of a familiar figure talking to Mrs. Chubb. "Charlotte!" She rushed over to hug her. "You're back?" Just in time she saw the cast on her friend's arm and drew back. "Oh, blimey. You can't work like that."

Charlotte laughed. "I'm not even going to try. Dr. Prestwick said it will be at least a month or two before I can come back to work. I just came by to wish you all a happy Christmas."

Mrs. Chubb sighed. "It looks like we'll be doing some more hiring after Christmas."

Charlotte looked worried. "What about Alice? I thought she was helping out."

"She's gorn." Gertie walked over to the dresser and opened a drawer. "She took all her things, so it doesn't look as if she's coming back. Not that she had much."

"Maybe she got her memory back." Mrs. Chubb went on kneading a lump of dough. "She might have just woken up, realized who she was, and gone home."

"Without thanking us for taking care of her?" Gertie made a rude noise. "That's the bleeding thanks I get for saving her from the orphanage?"

Mrs. Chubb clicked her tongue. "That Alice is a troubled person. We should make allowances for her and be happy she's home again."

"*If* she's home again," Gertie muttered.

"Well, where else can she be?" Mrs. Chubb's expression changed to alarm. "You don't think something bad happened to her? You know, like—" She broke off, apparently concerned about saying too much in Charlotte's presence. In an obvious effort to change the subject, she added quickly, "There's been enough bad things happening lately, what with Charlotte here falling down the stairs. It's a wonder you weren't more badly hurt."

"That's what Dr. Prestwick said." Charlotte wandered over to the table, licked her finger, and dipped it into a bag of icing sugar. "He said I was lucky it was only my arm and that it was a clean break."

She stuck her sugar-coated finger in her mouth, and Gertie waited for an explosion of wrath from the housekeeper.

She was disappointed when Mrs. Chubb simply moved the icing sugar out of reach. The housekeeper flattened the dough into a thick pancake. "Madam said she was going to put a lamp in that corner on the stairs. She blames herself for you falling, Charlotte. She says it's too dark in that corner and that's why you tripped."

Charlotte shook her head. "I didn't fall because it was dark. I tripped over something on the stairs. I saw it as I fell. It was soft and wooly, like a blanket or a shawl."

Mrs. Chubb stared at her. "That's strange. I was there right after you fell and I didn't see anything on the stairs. What did this blanket look like?"

Charlotte frowned in concentration. "It was dark blue, and I think it had a white bird or something appliquéd on one corner."

The housekeeper uttered a shocked gasp. "A duck. It's a white duck and that's my shawl! The one I gave to Alice. What on earth was it doing on the stairs?"

Gertie had been following the conversation, and felt goose

bumps creeping up her arm. "What's more, what happened to it after you fell?"

"That's a good question." Mrs. Chubb wiped her hands on her apron. "I think I need to have a word with Madam." She hurried out the door, leaving Charlotte staring after her.

"What's the matter with her?" Charlotte demanded, reaching for the bag of sugar. "She's acting like the end of the world is coming."

Gertie quickly recovered. Deciding there was no point in upsetting Charlotte, she murmured, "Take no blinking notice of her. She always gets this way at Christmas. It's all the extra work."

Charlotte looked guilty. "Oo, 'eck. That's my fault. I should be here working with everybody."

"It's not your fault you fell down the stairs." Gertie had a very good idea whose fault it was, but for once she kept her mouth shut. She would have given her next week's salary, however, to know what Mrs. Chubb was telling Madam this very moment.

Upstairs in Cecily's office, Mrs. Chubb refused the offer of a seat. "I have to get back to the kitchen," she said, sounding out of breath. "We're just about to serve the midday meal. I just wanted you to know that Charlotte's here, and she said she tripped over a shawl on the stairs when she fell. *My* shawl. The one I gave to Alice."

Cecily frowned, thinking back to the moment she reached Charlotte at the foot of the stairs. "That's odd. I don't remember seeing any shawl. Perhaps Lilly picked it up. She was there when Charlotte fell."

Mrs. Chubb shook her head. "Lilly had nothing in her hands when she rushed into the kitchen to tell us Charlotte had fallen down the stairs. I don't think she would have taken the time to bring a shawl back to her room before letting us know . . ." Her voice trailed off, as if she'd just thought of something upsetting.

Cecily peered up at her. "What is it, Altheda?"

"Well, m'm, I know Lilly didn't like Alice very much. Pansy told me that Lilly was complaining about Alice keeping her awake at night, talking in her sleep. Something about being in Paris and worrying about someone called Gwen."

Cecily frowned. "What are you suggesting?"

"Well, m'm, I don't like to say as much, but it is possible that Lilly stole the shawl from Alice and left it on the stairs hoping Alice would fall over it. Alice was supposed to empty chamber pots that morning, but when I found out she was supposed to be leaving for the orphanage, I ordered Charlotte to take over the job. Lilly wouldn't have known that at the time."

"I certainly hope you're wrong, Altheda, but I'll look into it. Meanwhile, I'd appreciate it if you'd not mention any of this to anyone else."

"Oh, of course not, m'm." Mrs. Chubb pressed her fingers to her mouth. "Mum's the word."

Cecily waited until the housekeeper had bustled out of the room before reaching for the telephone on her desk. While she waited for the operator to put her through to Dr.

Prestwick's office, she mulled over Mrs. Chubb's comments. She just couldn't imagine Lilly deliberately trying to hurt someone. Even someone she didn't like. There was another possibility, however, and one she was rather anxious to pursue.

Kevin's nurse answered her, and informed her that the doctor was out on his rounds. She would have him give Mrs. Baxter a ring just as soon as he returned.

Cecily replaced the receiver on its hook and stared at it, deep in thought. She wasn't too happy with the way things were beginning to shape up. She could only hope that Mr. Clements would be able to find the paintings and the thieves, and everything would be cleared up and finished by the next day.

They were running out of time. Tonight, Phoebe's pantomime would be presented. Tomorrow was Pansy's wedding. She simply didn't have time to deal with a gang of art thieves who may or may not be using her underground tunnel to store their ill-gotten goods.

With that, she left her office and headed down the hallway to the dining room. She had promised to meet Baxter there, and right now, all she wanted was to sit and relax for an hour or so and enjoy her husband's company.

Baxter would be most surprised to find out that Fred Granson was actually Gerald Evans's partner. He wouldn't be at all happy to learn that the detective was positive someone in the Pennyfoot was helping art thieves transport their loot abroad. That news could definitely wait until after she had enjoyed her meal.

After that she'd worry about the smugglers and who in the Pennyfoot Country Club was helping them.

Pansy had just finished wiping the last dish and was putting it away in the kitchen cupboard when Mrs. Chubb called out her name. "I sent Lilly out to the stables to order a carriage," she said. "She should have been back by now. Run out there and see what's holding her up. That girl will never keep a job if she doesn't buck up and get a move on. I've never seen anyone slouch around the way she does."

Happy to be escaping the kitchen for a while, Pansy was out the back door before Mrs. Chubb had finished speaking.

Sprinting around the corner, she came to an abrupt halt. Across the courtyard, Lilly was watching Henry, who was skipping around with Tess dancing at his heels. Henry held out one hand with a meaty bone in it, encouraging Tess to leap for the tasty treat. It wasn't that so much that caught Pansy's attention. It was more the way Henry was tripping around on his toes.

Samuel's words came back to her. *He walks like a girl.*

Lilly seemed just as fascinated by the sight. She edged forward, and it was then that Henry saw her. He stopped in his tracks, lowering his hand so that Tess was able to snatch the bone from him.

Henry paid no attention to the dog. His focus was on Lilly, who was walking toward him, a wide grin on her face.

Sensing a confrontation, Pansy slipped around the back of the coal shed to the side of the stables, so she could hear the conversation.

"Whatcha doing?" Lilly called out.

Henry just stood there, a frozen look on his face.

Lilly sauntered up to him. "All right, Henry." She placed a hand on her hip. "Why don't you tell me why you're pretending to be a boy?"

Shock rippled through Pansy, and she pulled back, afraid that her gasp would give her away.

Henry's voice floated on the wind, thin and high-pitched. "I don't know what you're talking about."

"Yes, you do."

Pansy held her breath as she peeked around the corner again.

Lilly had her back to her, while Henry was too busy staring at Lilly to notice Pansy just a few feet away from him.

"I know you're a girl, so you might as well tell me why you're pretending to be a boy."

Henry sounded as if he were about to cry. "You won't tell no one?"

Lilly tossed her head. "Give me one good reason why I shouldn't."

Staring at Henry now, Pansy wondered why she hadn't seen it before. Of course he . . . she was a girl. She was much too pretty to be a boy. She waited, along with Lilly, to hear Henry's answer.

"My name is Henrietta," Henry said at last. "My dad wanted a boy and was all ready to call me Henry. My mum died having me, so me and Dad were all alone. He brought me up, and taught me all the things he would have taught a boy." Henry jerked her hand at the stables. "Like mending motorcars."

Lilly shook her head. "I still don't understand."

Henry's voice rose on a note of desperation. "Me dad's ill. He can't work no more. I needed money to take care of him and I can earn a lot more mending motorcars than I can working in a hotel or a shop."

Lilly still looked baffled. "So?"

Henry raised her hands, palms up. "Who the heck would hire me to mend motorcars if they knew I was a girl?"

Pansy wanted to tell Henry that Madam probably would if she knew the whole story.

She was about to jump out from her hiding place when Lilly said, "You're right. They'd probably say you can't work with the guests' motorcars. Charlie would have a pink fit if he knew you were a girl."

"So you'll keep my secret? *Please?*"

Pansy held her breath again.

After a long pause, Lilly dug her hands into the pockets of her skirt. "Awright, I won't say nothing."

"Thank you." Henry sounded close to tears. "I don't know what I'd do if I lost this job. My dad's illness is costing so much money."

Lilly's voice was muffled when she answered, but Pansy was close enough to hear every word. "Don't worry," she said. "I'll keep your secret. I've got one of my own, so I know what it's like to keep a secret."

Henry sniffed. "You do?"

"Yeah, but it's far too dangerous to tell you about it."

"Dangerous? For who?"

"For both of us."

Lilly started to turn, and Pansy quickly drew back, out

of sight. There had been something chilling in Lilly's words that warned her to stay out of sight.

She jumped as something cold and wet touched her hand. Looking down, she saw Tess's big brown eyes staring up at her. She smiled, and laid a hand gently on the dog's head. She stayed that way until Lilly had left for the kitchen and Henry was safely inside the stables. Then she hugged Tess and quickly made her way back across the courtyard. It seemed as if everybody had secrets lately. Henry, Lilly, Alice—she felt as if she didn't know anybody anymore.

Except her Samuel. Thinking of Samuel swept all her doubts and worries away. Soon she'd be Mrs. Samuel Whitfield. What she needed to do now was go back to her room and try on her gown one more time to make sure it looked perfect. Because everything had to be perfect on her wedding day.

Skipping the last few steps, she started to softly hum the opening notes of the "Wedding March."

By the time the guests were filing into the ballroom to attend the pantomime, Cecily still hadn't heard from Kevin Prestwick. Concerned that something might have happened to him, she was vastly relieved to see him stroll into the foyer, a radiant Madeline clinging to his arm.

Madeline had outdone herself with her wardrobe. She wore a flowing gown in ivory silk and lace, the skirt of which was embroidered with tiny bunches of green holly and bright red berries. In her hair, which fell past her shoulders in smooth dark waves, she had pinned a sprig of mistletoe.

Knowing that Madeline sewed her own clothes, Cecily was most impressed by the delicate handiwork. "You look magnificent," she told her friend, noting that only Madeline would dare to attend a sophisticated occasion with unpinned locks. She seemed unaware of the scandalous glances aimed at her from a few of the women patrons, no doubt in retaliation for the admiring stares from their male escorts.

"You look most becoming yourself," Madeline observed. "I adore the silver trimmings on your gown. They show up beautifully on that dark blue satin."

Having worried that the glittering silver beads and rickrack might be seen as pretentious, Cecily smiled her delight. "Thank you, Madeline. You have made my evening." She turned to Kevin, resplendent in his black frock coat and white bow tie. He wore a red waistcoat that gave him a festive appearance. Together the Prestwicks made a most impressive couple.

"I was a little worried when you didn't give me a ring this afternoon," she said, giving him a fake look of disapproval. "I thought you might have met with an accident. The streets are so busy this time of year."

Kevin looked puzzled. "Was I supposed to ring you?"

Now it was Cecily's turn to frown. "You didn't receive my message?"

"I did not." Kevin uttered a sound of exasperation. "I gave my receptionist the afternoon off, but Esther, my nurse, was supposed to take any messages."

"Well, yes, it was your nurse with whom I spoke." Cecily laid a hand on his arm. "No matter, Kevin. It wasn't that important. I just wanted your opinion on a matter concerning one of my staff."

"If you'll both excuse me," Madeline said, lifting one side of her skirt, "I'll go along to the ballroom. I want a word with Phoebe before the presentation begins."

"Of course." Cecily smiled at her. "I'll see you after the pantomime."

"I'll be right along," Kevin assured her, then turned back to Cecily as Madeline disappeared down the hallway. "Now, what is it you wish to know?"

Cecily glanced around. Guests were still descending the stairs and wandering across the lobby. "Perhaps my office? I promise not to keep you for more than a few moments."

Kevin held out his hand. "After you, my dear."

Smiling, she led him to her office, leaving the door ajar as she entered the room. "It's about Alice," she said, coming straight to the point. "She seems to have disappeared. No one has seen her since last night."

Kevin stroked his chin. "No doubt she has recovered her memory and has returned home."

Cecily pursed her lips. "If so, that was rather uncharitable of her. After all, we did take her in and provide room and board for her. A note of thanks would have been appreciated."

Kevin gave her a rueful smile. "I agree. You must understand, however, how traumatic such a revelation would be to someone who up until that moment had no idea who she was or where she came from. The shock of discovering her life again could quite well have sent her on her way without any further thought other than to get back home and put her family out of their misery."

Cecily nodded. "I can understand that."

"No doubt you will hear from her once she has recovered from the ordeal."

"Well, there is just one more thing." She told him about Charlotte's fall and what had caused it. "I have a suspicion that Alice might have left the shawl there on purpose, so that Charlotte would fall."

"Why would she do such a thing?"

"I was sending her to the orphanage that morning. She was adamantly opposed to the idea. I think she caused Charlotte's fall so that there would be a vacancy in the staff and she could apply for the position."

Kevin looked skeptical. "That would have been a rather drastic measure, don't you think?"

Cecily shrugged. "Alice was feeling desperate. I think she would have done anything rather than leave the security of the Pennyfoot."

"Well, if you're right, then there should definitely be consequences. Charlotte could have been killed in that fall." Kevin sighed. "First we have to find Alice to get at the truth. That won't be easy, since we know nothing about her."

"I know." Cecily turned for the door. "That's something I shall have to work on after Christmas. Right now all I'm concerned about is the fact that we may have a killer lurking somewhere down in the tunnel. I've been waiting to hear from . . ." She paused, remembering her promise to Harry Clements. ". . . someone who may well be able to help in that respect. I'm hoping he will be able to settle the matter without involving me or the Pennyfoot."

Kevin raised his eyebrows. "If he can do that, whoever he is, then he has my utmost respect."

Unwilling to say more, Cecily opened the door. "We must get along to the ballroom. Your wife will be anxiously waiting for you, and my husband is no doubt gnashing his teeth. He doesn't care for Phoebe's presentations, and only my presence keeps him in his seat."

Kevin grinned. "That sounds familiar. I confess that Madeline might very well say the same thing about me."

"Then you and Baxter should both be ashamed of yourselves. Phoebe goes to a lot of time and trouble to present the Christmas extravaganza."

"She does, indeed," Kevin said solemnly. "I shall endeavor to sit back and enjoy the performance, come what may."

Cecily led the way down the hallway, hoping that Phoebe, for once, would get through an entire presentation without some kind of calamity.

Reaching the door of the ballroom, she saw Lady Elizabeth standing just inside, beckoning to her. The aristocrat was fashionably dressed in gold lace, her skirt slightly higher than Cecily was accustomed to seeing, as dictated by the latest fashions coming out of France.

The shorter skirt revealed the woman's slim ankles, her feet encased in gold leather shoes with a tiny heel and gold ruffles adorning the buckle. Cecily had to drag her gaze away from them as she approached.

"Lady Elizabeth, I trust you are well?"

"Quite well, thank you." The woman looked down her nose at Cecily. "I do have a complaint, however. Accustomed as we are to indoor plumbing, we are finding the lack of it here most inconvenient. Pray tell me that the lavatories will be in service shortly?"

Cecily gaped at her. The problem had completely escaped her mind. Fighting back her outrage at the incompetent plumber, she forced an apologetic smile. "I am most dreadfully sorry, Lady Elizabeth. Unfortunately our usual competent plumber is indisposed, and unable to make the repairs. I will certainly have a word with his replacement at the very first opportunity. I promise you, every effort will be made to solve the problem at the earliest possible moment."

Lady Elizabeth appeared unappeased by the news. "I certainly hope so." She lifted a lorgnette to her eyes and peered at Cecily through the lenses. "I should hate to have to return to London to spend Christmas Day in more comfortable surroundings."

"I assure you, Your Ladyship, I will do everything in my power to see that the lavatories are restored."

The woman sniffed, then turned and swept off, no doubt to complain to her husband.

Cecily sighed. The plumber had already left for the day. Spying Gertie by the refreshments table, she hurried over to her.

Gertie looked anxious when Cecily reached the table. "Is something wrong, m'm?"

"I just wanted a word with you." Cecily looked over her shoulder to make sure they wouldn't be overheard. "I need to speak with the plumber. Do you know if he is still here?"

Gertie rolled her eyes. "No, m'm. He left an hour ago. Good bloody riddance, too. He's a bleeding rake if you ask me." Seeing Cecily's expression, she hurriedly added, "If you'll excuse the word, m'm. I don't know how else to describe him."

Cecily cleared her throat. "I was merely wondering if he was close to repairing the lavatories. Perhaps I should ask Mrs. Chubb."

"I wouldn't bet on anything with that bleeding rotter," Gertie said darkly. "It's no wonder he hasn't done with the lavs yet. He's always hanging around downstairs. He's been making eyes at every woman he comes across. Even Mrs. Chubb."

Cecily hastily suppressed a grin. "I see."

"He was even chatting up Alice." Gertie leaned across the table to straighten a plate of sausage rolls. "I couldn't believe it when I saw her talking to him. I thought she was afraid of every bleeding bloke."

"Alice?" Cecily took a moment to absorb this surprising news. "When was this, exactly?"

Gertie frowned. "Let me see. It were yesterday afternoon. I know I was surprised to see them together. Bernie seemed upset that Alice was gorn this morning when I saw him coming out of the laundry room. Yet in the next minute he's bleeding making eyes at me." She shook her head. "Some men should have it cut off, that's what I say."

Cecily wasn't sure what Gertie meant by that, but she knew better than to ask. Besides, what her chief housemaid had just told her was most intriguing. She made a mental note to talk to the plumber first thing in the morning. She had quite a few questions to ask him.

Later, seated next to her husband in the front row, she settled back to enjoy the pantomime. At least, as much as she was able to enjoy it, considering all her worries. The constant threat of a catastrophe onstage seemed minor in comparison, though she could tell that Baxter was on edge, waiting for the inevitable.

It came almost at the end of the performance. Phoebe was a huge enthusiast of the plateau, and most of her presentations, whether they called for it or not, included one in the grand finale. It usually came in the form of dancers balanced precariously on the shaking shoulders of their accomplices.

In order to obtain a perfect plateau, all participants had to remain motionless without so much as twitching a muscle, which meant that perfection was never achieved for more than a second or two at a time. More often than not, the plateau ended with most of its participants sprawled upon the ground.

Despite Cecily's efforts in the past to dissuade Phoebe from attempting the perilous maneuver, the determined woman had ignored all advice or pleas. It was a fitting end for a successful performance, she had insisted, completely ignoring the fact that it seldom had worked, and that she was in danger of causing serious injuries.

Up until that moment, the pantomime had been amusing and quite respectable, with some of the saltier lines omitted by Phoebe's inimitable sense of decorum. Dick Whittington's cat looked more like a street beggar in a moth-eaten fur coat, with a long, stringy tail that dragged on the ground behind her. She made up for the tatty costume with her exuberance for the part, which involved a lot of prowling and mewing around the stage.

Cecily had just begun to hope that this presentation would go off without a hitch, and even Baxter looked more relaxed, when Phoebe announced the plateau.

Cecily heard her husband mutter something under his breath and crossed her fingers. With a good deal of luck, maybe this time the plateau would be successful.

CHAPTER
❈ 17 ❈

Up on the stage, four of the sturdier dancers formed a circle, outstretched arms creating a link. As the orchestra began playing a soft, tranquil version of "O Little Town of Bethlehem," the four slowly sank to a crouch, whereupon two dancers clambered rather ungracefully onto their shoulders.

They, too, crouched, allowing the cat to climb up on their shoulders.

Phoebe's shrill voice could be heard in the wings above the orchestra, shouting instructions.

Slowly, faces turning red and bosoms heaving with the effort, the four dancers at the base of the plateau straightened their knees, with the other three clinging to them. Phoebe's voice penetrated the music again, and the two dancers in the middle began to rise.

Cecily briefly closed her eyes.

With much wobbling and clutching, the two dancers slowly rose to a weak smattering of applause from the audience.

Then came a shriek from the cat. Her voice rang out, loud and clear. "Get your flipping foot off my bloody tail, you stupid sod!"

One of the dancers giggled. The two in the middle shot up, and the cat, her tail still trapped under someone's foot, yelled as her furry costume was stripped from her body.

Amid shocked gasps from the audience, Phoebe rushed onstage, just in time to break the fall of the cat as the plateau collapsed. The half-dressed girl toppled on top of Phoebe, while an argument broke out among the rest of the dancers as to whose foot had caused the whole debacle.

Baxter muttered, "Oh, for God's sake," and leapt out of his seat.

By the time Cecily had risen to follow him he had disappeared through the stage door. The curtains hurriedly swished to a close before Cecily reached the door behind her husband. The audience remained seated, some politely clapping, though no one onstage was paying any attention. They were too busy screaming at each other.

Cecily reached the stage in time to see Baxter hauling a howling young woman off Phoebe's still form. "Is she all right?" She rushed forward, concern taking her breath away.

Baxter gently rolled Phoebe onto her back. Her hat was crushed beneath her, and the line of her hair had slipped lower on her forehead. She stirred, and opened her eyes. "What happened?" she murmured.

Cecily hastily retrieved the hat. "Help her up," she

ordered, cramming the hat back on Phoebe's head the moment it was off the floor. She ignored the odd look her husband gave her. As far as she knew, she was the only person in the world, other than Phoebe's son, the Reverend Algernon Carter-Holmes, who knew that Phoebe was completely bald and wore a wig.

Phoebe uttered a soft moan.

"Are you hurt? Shall I fetch Dr. Prestwick?" Cecily peered at her friend's white face. "He's right there in the audience."

Phoebe groaned again. "My presentation is ruined. Again. Can't those stupid little twerps get it right just once?"

Somewhat reassured, Cecily helped the muttering woman to her feet. "Are you sure you're not hurt?"

"Just my pride." Phoebe tugged at her hat, which stubbornly remained lopsided. "I need to go to the dressing room. Are the girls all right?"

Cecily looked around. Most of the dancers had disappeared—most likely to escape Phoebe's wrath. The two who did remain were creeping off the stage as if trying to avoid being seen. "I can't see any dead bodies," Cecily said, then immediately wished she hadn't been so facetious. Under the circumstances, her comment was not in the least amusing.

Phoebe seemed not to notice Cecily's discomfort. "Good. Then I shall retire to the dressing room to lick my wounds and while I'm about it I shall give those hellions a piece of my mind." She picked up her skirt and with as much dignity as she could muster marched off into the wings.

Baxter, who had been standing by in silence all this time, shook his head. "One of these days she is likely to cause some permanent damage to either herself or someone else."

Cecily pulled a face. "I sincerely hope you are wrong about that."

"Perhaps it's time to put an end to Phoebe's fiascoes."

"How can I? They are such an integral part of our celebrations. Everyone looks forward to them."

"Not everyone. I noticed some of our guests were notably absent. Including our detective."

Cecily glanced at her husband's scowling face. He hadn't taken the news well about Harry Clements hiding his identity. Or the detective's suspicions. In fact, he had threatened to report the entire matter to the constabulary, and it was only with a great deal of persuasion that Cecily had managed to change his mind.

"I'm sure Mr. Clements has other things on his mind." She felt a twinge of anxiety for the man. She'd expected some kind of development by now, and the fact that she hadn't seen him since their conversation that morning made her most uneasy.

She just had to put her faith in his abilities. After all, as he had assured her, he was a trained specialist and should know what he was doing. She couldn't help worrying, however, that something awful might have happened to him.

If he hadn't made an appearance by midday tomorrow, she promised herself, she would contact the constabulary and tell them everything she knew. That would still give them time to stop the art thieves from shipping the paintings to France.

It would also mean an unpleasant upheaval for her guests, and possibly for Pansy's wedding as well. As she followed Baxter offstage she sent up a silent prayer that Mr. Clements would find the proof he needed and bring the criminals to justice without having to bring in Scotland Yard and the disagreeable Inspector Cranshaw.

The following morning, right after breakfast, Cecily headed for the kitchen. As usual, the noise level was such that she had to raise her voice to speak to Mrs. Chubb. Amid the rattling of dishes, Michel's off-key singing, and Pansy's heated argument with another maid, Cecily asked the housekeeper where she could find Bernie, the plumber.

Mrs. Chubb jerked a thumb at the back door. "Last time I seen him, he was going out the back. I don't know what for. The lavatories are upstairs."

Cecily, too, was beginning to wonder why Bernie spent so much time downstairs, when he should be working on the second and third floors. "Thank you, Mrs. Chubb. If you should see him, please tell him I want a word with him."

"Yes, m'm." Mrs. Chubb wiped her hands on her apron. "I can't for the life of me understand what's taking him so long. George would have had all of it done in no time."

Cecily nodded. "I'm inclined to agree with you, Altheda. That reminds me, I really should give George a ring and find out how he's coming along with that sprained ankle." She turned to leave, just as an almighty crash rang in her ears.

Glancing back, she saw Pansy staring in dismay at the pieces of a serving dish lying scattered at her feet. One look at Mrs. Chubb's face made Cecily feel sorry for the girl. Wedding nerves of course. She just hoped the housekeeper remembered that and went easy on the jittery bride. Normally she would have been given the day off, but Pansy had insisted on working that morning, since they were so shorthanded. She wanted to help get the ballroom ready for the reception.

Cecily had a suspicion that Pansy, knowing how much she was going to miss everyone after the wedding, was stretching out the last few hours she had left working at the Pennyfoot.

It was more than an hour later when Cecily caught sight of Bernie through her office window. He was crossing the courtyard, and judging from the red patches in his cheeks and the deep furrows on his forehead, the plumber wasn't in the best of moods.

Deciding to waylay him, Cecily hurried down the hallway and across the foyer. She had just reached the kitchen stairs when Bernie appeared at the top of them. He would have brushed past her with no more than a curt nod if she hadn't stepped in front of him.

He came to an abrupt halt, looking at her as if she were a slug in his salad.

She met his gaze, and saw something in his eyes that unsettled her. "Good morning, Bernie," she said firmly, glad that there were several guests milling about the foyer. "I'd like a quick word with you, if you have the time?"

"Of course, Mrs. B." The hostility in his eyes vanished, to be replaced by the usual twinkling mischief.

It was such a fast and extensive switch, Cecily stared at him for several seconds, forgetting what she was going to say next.

Bernie cocked his head to one side. "Is something wrong?"

Cecily hastily recovered. "Oh no. At least, I hope not. Actually, I was expecting the lavatories to be back in service by now."

"So was I, Mrs. B. So was I." Bernie shook his head. "The problem is, it's Christmas, isn't it. I had to order several parts for the lavatories. All worn-out they were. But because of Christmas, it's taking a lot longer for them to get here. I got word, though, that they'll be here by this afternoon. By tonight your lavatories will be in fine working order again. That's a promise."

Cecily relaxed her shoulders. "Well, I'm very happy to hear it. My guests have been complaining and I can't say I blame them."

"Oh. I'm sorry to hear that, m'm. Like I said, the parts should be here later today and just as soon as I get my dirty little hands on 'em, I'll be up there fixing them all up."

"Very well." She was about to turn away when she remembered something else. "Oh, by the way, someone mentioned that you were talking to Alice the other day."

His expression changed at once. It was fleeting, but for a second or two she thought she saw fear in his eyes. Then he was smiling again, and she decided she must have imagined it. "Was I? I don't remember who I talked to, to be honest, m'm. I talk to a lot of people."

Now Cecily felt uncomfortable again. "Well, yes. I only asked because Alice has left the Pennyfoot and since you were one of the last people to talk to her, I wondered if perhaps she mentioned where she was going."

There it was again. She hadn't imagined it after all. That look in his eyes. He knew more about Alice than he wanted her to know.

Bernie shrugged. "Sorry, Mrs. B. I don't remember even talking to her, so I'm afraid I can't help you. Now, if you don't mind, I'd better get back to work." With that he stepped around her and headed for the stairs.

Cecily stared after him, wondering what it was he knew about Alice that he was keeping to himself. Almost as if he was afraid of her. Frowning, she retraced her steps across the foyer and started up the stairs. She needed to talk to her husband, just as soon as possible.

Pansy picked up another potato from the pile on the draining board and started slicing at it with the peeler. Her stomach felt out of sorts, and the last thing she wanted was to be messing about with food. All she could think about was the wedding. How it would feel to walk down the aisle of St. Bartholomew's with all eyes upon her. Samuel would be waiting at the altar, smiling at her. At least, she hoped he would be smiling at her.

What if he didn't like her gown? What if he changed his mind about marrying her and was going to tell her in front of everybody? What if he didn't turn up at the church at all? What if—

"Are you bloody trying to peel that potato or murder it?"

At the word *murder* Pansy dropped the peeler into the sink. Turning to look at Gertie she snapped, "Whatcha making all that noise for? You made me jump out of my skin."

Gertie backed off, one hand over her heart. "Oh, sorry, your bleeding majesty. I didn't know you were so bloody fragile this morning."

To Pansy's horror, tears starting trickling down her cheeks. "I'm not fragile. I'm j-just s-scared!"

The last word ended on a wail and Gertie's grin swiftly vanished. "Here, luv, I didn't mean to upset you. What's the matter, then?"

"She's got wedding nerves," Lilly said from across the room. She held up the silver fork she was polishing. "I know what that's like."

"So do I," Gertie said, putting a hefty arm around Pansy's shoulders. "I done it twice already."

Pansy sniffed. "I keep wondering what I'll do if Samuel doesn't turn up at the church."

Gertie let out a shout of laughter. "Turn up? He'll flipping be there, don't you worry. He can't wait to marry you. He told me that himself."

Pansy brushed away a tear with the back of her hand. "He did?"

"'Course he bleeding did." She dropped her arm. "He's probably worrying himself sick that *you* might not be there."

Pansy felt a smile tugging at her lips. "He needn't worry about that."

"Well, then, everything's going to be all right, ain't it. Your gown is hanging in your wardrobe, your shoes are underneath it, and your veil is in your dresser drawer. Mrs. Prestwick is going to bring your bouquet over, and we'll be setting up for the wedding feast before we leave. It's all going to be bleeding lovely, so stop bloody worrying about it and finish peeling those potatoes."

"I can't wait," Lilly said, dropping the fork onto the loaded tray in front of her. "It's going to be a beautiful wedding and a lovely reception. You're so lucky to have it here at the Pennyfoot. I had mine in me mum's house and we had nowhere for the guests to sit down. We had to move all the chairs outside so's we could get the food set up on tables, and everyone had to eat standing up."

Gertie stared at her. "I didn't know you was married."

Watching Lilly, Pansy was shocked to see the look on the other girl's face. Lilly looked as if she'd just stepped on a rat. Her hands shook, rattling the tray, and she put it down again. "I didn't mean mine," she mumbled. "I meant my sister's wedding." She picked up the tray again. "I've got to get these upstairs." With that, she turned and fled out the door.

Gertie shook her head. "She's a bloomin' strange one, that one. I never know what to make of her."

Pansy sighed. "Well, I just wish the wedding was all over and done with, and I didn't have to worry about it again."

"Don't say that." Gertie patted her shoulder. "It's one of the biggest days in your life. Make up your mind you're going to bloody enjoy it. Remember every moment of it. When things get you down in the future, you can look back on your wedding day and smile."

Pansy looked at her in surprise. "Is that what you do? Remember both your wedding days?"

Gertie laughed. "Nah, I only remember the second one. Even though it wasn't near as grand as the first. The first one is gorn out of my mind. It's dead and buried, where it belongs."

Pansy shuddered. "I just wish we didn't have Jacob's murder hanging over our heads. I don't think I could ever go down that wine cellar again."

"Well," Gertie said cheerfully, "you won't never have to now, will you. After today you won't be working here no more." Her face changed, and she grabbed hold of Pansy, her arms squeezing so hard Pansy could hardly breathe. "I'm going to miss you, luv."

Once more tears spilled down Pansy's cheeks. "I'm going to miss you, too, and Mrs. Chubb, and Michel, and everybody else."

"Here, here! What is all this crying about, then?"

Michel's voice made them both jump. Gertie cleared her throat and stepped away from the sink. "Mind your own bloody business," she growled.

Michel stalked across the kitchen to the stove. "It eez my business when my potatoes are not ready to boil, *non?*"

Pansy gulped. "Sorry, Michel. I'll have them ready in a minute." She began frantically chipping at the potato with the peeler.

"Oh, lay off her, Michel." Gertie gathered up a stack of dishes that were waiting to be shelved. "You'll miss her when she's gorn."

"I shall indeed."

Pansy stole an astonished peek at the chef. He was actually smiling at her.

"You will make a beautiful bride, *ma petite.* Your Samuel, he is the lucky man, *non?*"

"Thank you, Michel." Pansy smiled back, while for once, Gertie had nothing to say.

Cecily opened the door of her suite to find Baxter on his knees, polishing his shoes. "What on earth are you doing?" she demanded, shocked to see him engaged in such a mundane task. "Why didn't you give them to a maid to shine?"

Baxter went on rubbing at the toe of his shoe with a bright yellow cloth. "I'm going to a wedding," he announced. "This calls for special attention to detail. I'm not confident the maids will do the job."

Cecily rolled her eyes. "Obviously you don't have enough to occupy your mind. Perhaps I should set you to work on the year-end accounts."

He looked up at her. "I wouldn't dare meddle with your meticulous accounts, my dear. If you need my help, however, I'm always ready to oblige." He climbed to his feet. "Speaking of which, have you heard anything from our resident detective?"

She frowned. "No, I haven't. In fact, I haven't set eyes on Mr. Clements since I last spoke to him yesterday. I'm beginning to get concerned about him." She walked over to the fireplace and held out her hands to the dancing flames. "I'm worried something bad may have happened to him."

Baxter muttered something under his breath. "Perhaps it's time we notified the constabulary."

"Mr. Clements made me promise not to call in the police. He said he was hired to do a job, and he wanted to finish it, in order to get paid. He insisted that he could take care of himself."

"Well, it seems that he was overconfident in that respect."

She sighed. "You're right. I will take several footmen down with me to the wine cellar and try to find out what's going on."

"I can't let you do that. What if the thieves are lying in wait? Besides, the tunnel isn't safe. You said that yourself."

As usual, whenever her husband attempted to forbid her to do something, it only made her all the more determined.

She raised her chin. "There are only three members of the gang, and I shall make sure they are well outnumbered by our staff. Besides, I hardly expect the thieves to be sitting in the tunnel guarding their loot. Most likely they are enjoying a pint or two at the Fox and Hounds, waiting until tonight to move it. That's if the paintings are there at all, which we won't know unless we go down there to look."

"Those men are ruthless. They have killed two men already. Maybe a third, since your private detective is missing. It only takes one man with a knife to kill another."

"So what do you suggest? I break my promise to Mr. Clements? What if he's simply waiting for the right time to make his move?"

"What if he's been injured, or worse, by a gang of thieves, who are in the process of shipping some very valuable stolen paintings out of the country?"

"So you want me to send for the constable? With a wedding to be held in just a few hours? What if Mr. Evans was wrong about all this, and there are no paintings down there? All the disruption would have been for nothing. I'd at least like to make sure there are stolen goods down there before calling in the police."

He stared at her for a long time. "Very well. But I want to go down there with you. I'll meet you in the foyer in half an hour. That should give you enough time to round up a few footmen."

"Thank you, darling." She hurried from the room, afraid he might change his mind again.

Reaching the foyer, she saw Gertie at the top of the kitchen stairs and called out to her.

Gertie came at a half run, holding up one side of her skirt. "Yes, m'm?" she said, sounding anxious.

"I need you to find Charlie," Cecily said, eyeing the grandfather clock ticking solemnly away in the corner. "Tell him to meet me right here in half an hour, and to bring five of the footmen with him."

Gertie's eyes widened. "Has something else bad happened?"

"No, no, nothing like that. I just need them to help me look for something." Sending up a silent prayer that Harry Clements was alive and well, Cecily headed down the hallway.

She spent the next half hour in the ballroom, supervising the preparations for the reception. When she returned to the foyer, she found the footmen standing around in a small group, muttering amongst themselves. No doubt wondering why she had gathered them together with such little notice.

Baxter hadn't yet put in an appearance. After waiting another ten minutes, mindful of the time ticking away, Cecily reluctantly decided to go ahead without him. He must have been waylaid by something. He would no doubt follow them as soon as he was able. He would just have to forgive her for not waiting for him.

"I know you all have duties to take care of," she said, calling the footmen to attention. "I'm hoping this won't take long. I need you all to accompany me to the wine cellar."

Charlie stepped forward, anxiety creasing his face. "It's not another murder down there, is it, m'm?"

Cecily looked around, thankful to see there were no guests wandering around. "I sincerely hope not. Please keep your voice down, Charlie. We don't want to upset the guests." *Not until we have to, at least*, she added inwardly.

"Sorry, m'm." Charlie beckoned to the rest of the group. "Come on, then. Look sharp and follow Madam."

Deciding the front door would be less conspicuous than all of them trailing across the kitchen, Cecily led the way out onto the main steps. A keen east wind whipped her skirt around her ankles, and she wished she'd stopped to pick up a warm shawl before venturing on this expedition.

Charlie must have noticed her shivering, as he swung off his coat and draped it over her shoulders.

"Thank you, Charlie. Most gallant of you." She pulled it closed around her. "I hope we won't be too long out here."

"Yes, m'm." His questioning look made her feel guilty. All the young men must be wondering why on earth she was taking them all down to the wine cellar in the middle of the day.

She was beginning to wonder herself if perhaps she was doing the wrong thing. Maybe she should have waited for Baxter after all. It was too late now to have doubts. They were at the door of the wine cellar.

She felt in her pocket for her key and fitted it in the lock. Her stomach seemed to drop like a stone when she realized the door was already unlocked. Slowly, she pushed the door open. One look at the wall confirmed her suspicions. The oil lamp was gone from its hook.

Somebody was down in the cellar.

CHAPTER 18

Trying to sound calmer than she felt, Cecily turned to Charlie. "I need you to go back to the kitchen and ask Mrs. Chubb for two oil lamps. Be as quick as you can."

In spite of her best efforts, Charlie must have heard the tremor in her voice. His expression changed, as if he'd just woken up from a nightmare. "Right away, m'm." He spun around and disappeared around the corner.

The rest of the footmen were staring at her, varying degrees of wariness on their faces. Deciding it would be wise to warn them, Cecily closed the door and leaned against it. "I have reason to suspect that one or maybe more intruders may be lurking about down in the wine cellar. Under the circumstances, it might be a good idea to arm yourselves. Go to the coal shed now and find something you can use as a weapon.

There should be enough shovels, rakes, hammers, or whatever you can find there."

All five lads stood staring at her, seemingly frozen to the spot.

"Be quick now," she said, clapping her hands for emphasis. "We haven't a moment to waste."

One thing she did know, she thought, as the footmen scooted off in the direction of the coal shed. There was only one way out of that cellar and that would be past her and her six escorts. She could only hope that they all came out of this unscathed. If not, Baxter would never forgive her.

It seemed an eternity until the footmen returned, all carrying an assortment of garden tools. One young lad brandished a hammer in one hand and waved a saw in the other. He looked a little like the drawings she'd seen of medieval warriors in battle. Any other time she would have been amused at the thought. Right now all she could think about was how effective their weapons would be against a brutal killer carrying a knife.

Minutes later Charlie returned, an oil lamp swinging in each hand.

He wore an odd expression on his face, and Cecily frowned as she took one of the lamps from him. "Is something wrong?"

Charlie shrugged. "I dunno. Mrs. Chubb wanted to know why I needed the oil lamps. I told her it was to go down the wine cellar with you. She said she didn't know why everybody was so anxious to go down the wine cellar. She gave the spare key out to someone else this morning."

Cecily stiffened her back. "Did she say who?"

Charlie shook his head. "Michel came in just then. He

was shouting about something and took her attention away. I thought it best not to wait around to find out, so I just left." He looked around at the group of young men. "Why are they carrying shovels?"

"It's just a precaution, Charlie."

Alarm flashed across his face. "You think Jacob's killer is down there?"

"I don't know what or who is down there. I just don't want to take a chance, that's all."

Charlie gulped. "I don't have a weapon."

"You have the lamp. It should put a decent dent in someone's head if necessary."

Charlie looked at the lamp as if he doubted its ability to do any real damage.

Wishing fervently that Charlie had taken the time to find out who had the other key, Cecily opened the door again. There wasn't time to go back and question Mrs. Chubb now. They would find out soon enough who was down in the cellar. Taking a deep breath, she stepped onto the stairs. "All right, lads. Keep close together and keep a close watch on your surroundings. We don't want to be taken by surprise. Charlie, you bring up the rear. Hold the lamp up high. We need as much light as we can get."

Treading carefully down the creaking steps, she peered into the leaping shadows ahead. She thought she knew what Colonel Fortescue felt like going into battle. Who knew what lay ahead, waiting for them. Were they walking into a trap? Would they be able to defend themselves if all three thieves were armed and ready to kill?

Her thoughts made her legs tremble, and she forced her

mind to think positively. Her footmen were tall, lusty lads and quite capable of taking care of themselves.

She reached the bottom of the steps and halted, bringing her troops to a stop. Ahead of her the aisles stretched into darkness. Whoever had taken the lamp had either turned it out or had gone beyond the wall. She hoped it was the latter. How she wished Baxter had accompanied her. How foolish she was not to wait for him.

"What's wrong, m'm?"

Charlie's voice, coming at her from behind, made her jump. The lamp swung in her hand, sending the shadows swaying back and forth. "Nothing," she called back. "I was just getting my bearings." Banishing her treacherous fears, she started to walk down the center aisle.

The shuffling of feet behind her echoed and bounced off the rows of dusty bottles. The damp, musty smell didn't seem quite as strong as she remembered. The reason for that was apparent as she reached the end of the aisle and stepped out into the open space beyond.

Half the wall was missing.

Although she had anticipated as much, the sight of it sent a chill down her spine. Somewhere beyond that wall lay danger. She should return to the club right now and give the constabulary a ring. It was obvious now that someone was using the tunnel for illegal purposes. She could no longer deny the evidence.

"What happened to the wall?" Charlie said in her ear, once more taking the strength out of her knees.

"Stop doing that," she said, then wished she hadn't spoken so sharply when she saw his crestfallen look. For another second or two she considered going back, then curiosity and a certain amount of resentment took over.

How dare those criminals use her establishment to hide their nefarious deeds! They deserved to be horsewhipped. All she hoped was that they didn't get away with the paintings before the constables could make their arrest.

"It looks as if someone broke his way through there," she said, in answer to Charlie's question.

"Why would he want to do that?" Charlie asked, while the rest of the footmen stood around staring at her, waiting for her answer.

Cecily took a deep breath. "I think that we may find the answer to that in the tunnel underneath."

The footmen muttered back and forth, and once more alarm crossed Charlie's face. "You think Jacob's killer is down there?"

"I sincerely hope not, but it doesn't hurt to be prepared." She was proud of her calm tone, considering her heart thudded so hard against her chest she was certain everyone in that cellar could hear it.

She took a step toward the wall, but Charlie halted her with a hand on her arm. "I'll go first. Theodore and Jeremy can follow me. The rest of you fall in behind Madam." He looked back at her. "You'll be safer if you're in the middle of us."

Right then she could have hugged him. "Thank you, Charlie. Please be careful."

"Yes, m'm. Don't worry. I'll watch it." He looked at the two young men standing beside him. "Ready, mates?"

They nodded, and Charlie stepped through the gap in the wall to the corridor beyond.

Shivering, Cecily followed the three of them into the dark, gloomy hallway. The musty smell was stronger now, no doubt due to the rooms being shut off from air for so long.

Dark patches on the wall suggested mold, and Cecily held one hand over her nose as she followed the three men down the hallway to the card rooms.

Memories flitted through her mind. Once these rooms had been the hub of entertainment in the days when the Pennyfoot had been a hotel. Hidden from the street and the law, aristocrats had eaten, drank, and gambled to their heart's content.

The hallways had echoed with their laughter and the boisterous conversations. The maids had stacked dishes of refreshments on the sideboards, and the rooms had reeked of cigar smoke and brandy. Glasses had clinked while money had changed hands fast and furiously as the cards were flipped across the tables.

Now all was silent, and the empty rooms sat waiting, as if hoping that one day their earlier times of glory would return.

Cecily hadn't seen the rooms since long before the wall had been erected. She braced herself as Charlie reached for the handle of the first one—more for the expected aura of decay than of a human opponent.

It was rather an anticlimax when Charlie pushed the door open and swung his lamp high to reveal an empty room. "There's no one here, m'm." He stepped inside. "So these are the famous secret card rooms. I always wondered what they looked like."

The rest of the footmen crowded in behind him, all looking

slightly bewildered, as well they might. They were looking at four walls and a wooden floor and nothing else. Faded wallpaper hung in dismal strips, a testament to the damp air that seemed to soak into Cecily's bones.

"No one's here," Charlie said, swinging his lamp to cast eerie shadows of the men on the walls.

They looked like ghosts, and Cecily shuddered. For some reason, Madeline's words crept into her mind. *I feel death in the air. Very close.* Pushing the menacing omen out of her mind, she answered him. "Someone's been here." She pointed across the room. The trapdoor, which had been carefully boarded up several years earlier, now stood open. The boards that had covered it lay in a small heap in the corner of the room.

Charlie walked over to hold his lamp over the opening, his voice hushed when he said, "So this is how you get down to the tunnel."

Cecily couldn't answer. Knowing there were rats down there, it was the last place she wanted to go.

Charlie was looking at her, waiting for his instructions. For a long moment she considered letting them all go down without her. After considering it, though, she knew she couldn't do that. This was her idea, however foolish it seemed right now, and she had to see it through.

Squaring her shoulders, she said quietly, "I'm looking for some stolen paintings that I believe might be stored down there. If I'm right, someone may be guarding them right now and won't be willing to give them up. We may well have a fight on our hands. If any of you would rather not accompany me, you may return to the club right now. I must ask you, however, not to mention any of this to anyone."

Charlie swung his lamp back and forth, then lowered a foot onto the ladder. "I'm going down, m'm."

"So am I." One of the footmen stepped up behind Charlie.

One by one the others followed until they were all standing in line behind her stable manager.

Cecily smiled. "I'm proud of you all and most grateful. You will all be well rewarded for this."

Charlie answered with a grin, then clambered backward down the ladder. Just as his head reached floor level, he looked up at her. "You don't have to come down here, m'm. Me and the lads will take care of things."

"No, I want to come." She glanced around at the waiting footmen. "Just wait for me at the bottom."

Hands clenched, she waited for Charlie to reach the floor of the tunnel. Her shoulders relaxed when his voice floated up to her. "Come on, lads. Get down here."

It seemed to take no time at all for the rest of them to get down the ladder. She gave her lamp to the last footman to go down, and then it was her turn.

Cecily hesitated at the dark square hole, then gingerly stepped onto the first rung. It seemed solid enough, and clutching the sides of the ladder, she climbed down to where the footmen were waiting. "Well," she said, only slightly out of breath, "that wasn't so bad after all." The odor down there, however, made her hold her breath for a moment or two.

"Cor blimey," one of the footmen muttered, "there must be dead rats down here."

"Or someone's been using it as a lavatory," someone else suggested.

"Let's move on," Cecily said hurriedly, retrieving her lamp from the footman.

With Charlie leading the way, the procession moved slowly down the tunnel. It had been carved out through the cliffs, and the walls had once been chalk white.

Time and the damp, however, had darkened the smooth sides. A crude network of boards shored up the roof and sides, but large piles of crumbled chalk at the foot of the walls suggested a constant erosion of the tunnel.

It occurred to Cecily that it was probably quite dangerous to be walking through there. She had no right to be putting these young men in such danger to satisfy her whims. She faltered, holding up her lamp in an attempt to see what lay ahead.

She could see nothing but the heads of her companions and their shadows dancing on the roof. "Wait!"

Three of the footmen halted, but Charlie and the other two must not have heard her. They kept walking, and she was about to call out to them again when Charlie suddenly held up his hand.

"There's somebody lying down here!"

Cecily thought at once of Harry Clements. Dear God, had he met the same fate as his partner? "Is he dead?" she called out.

"He's not moving."

Charlie started forward again and she called out, louder this time. "Wait!"

Pushing past the rest of the footmen she reached his side. "I'm coming with you."

Together they walked toward the figure that lay on the

ground. Rocks lay strewn about, as if tossed by a giant hand, and Cecily picked her way carefully, wary of tripping over one of them.

Her stomach lurched when she noticed the dark stain spreading from under the man's head. She swung the lamp toward him, then froze, disbelief and horror holding her captive.

The light had fallen across the man's face. She was staring at the beloved features of her husband.

"Bax!" Her cry echoed Charlie's horrified gasp. She fell on her knees at Baxter's side, afraid to touch him in case she should find him cold and unresponsive. He couldn't be dead. He just couldn't. She wouldn't allow it.

Charlie hovered over Baxter's still body. "So that's who took the key from Mrs. Chubb. Is he dead?"

Glancing at the dark red pool beneath her husband's head, Cecily gulped. How could anyone live after losing that much blood?

"Is that blood?" Charlie squatted down and held his lamp closer. "It smells like wine."

"What?" Cecily sniffed. Until then she hadn't noticed the smell. It did smell like wine. She stuck a finger in the puddle and brought it to her nose. "It *is* wine." Now she could see the shards of glass from a broken wine bottle close by Baxter's head.

Relief and hope made her knees weak and she sank down on the cold ground.

Gently she laid a hand on her husband's chest. The faint beat of his heart seemed to send strength through her fingers, down her arm, and throughout her body. "He's alive," she muttered, and a chorus of cheers answered her.

Cecily clambered up, brushing dust and grime from her

skirt. "We have to get Mr. Baxter back to the club. You should be able to carry him between you. Hurry. We must have the doctor see to him as soon as possible."

"What about the paintings?" Charlie glanced down the tunnel. "I can go down there to look for them."

"No, forget the paintings." All desire to find the stolen goods had vanished. All she could think about now was getting help for her husband.

She watched anxiously as the footmen lifted Baxter and started back down the tunnel. Following closely behind them, she was heartened by the sound of a soft groan from him as they hauled him up the ladder.

By the time they had carried him through the gap in the wall his eyes flickered open, though he seemed unaware that she was there. When the footmen finally got him outside in the cold wind, however, he turned his head to look at her.

She gave him a wobbly smile before hanging the lamp on the wall. "You're going to be all right, my love. I'll send for Kevin as soon as we get back to the hotel." Quickly she slammed the door and turned the key in the lock.

For once he didn't correct her. His gaze swiveled to the men who carried him. "What the blazes happened to me?" His voice sounded weak, and he closed his eyes.

"Don't think about it now." Cecily hurried alongside him, anxiety gnawing at her stomach. "Just rest. We'll talk when you feel better."

He opened his eyes again. "Did you find them?"

"Find what?"

"The paintings. I was looking for them but then I . . ." His voice trailed off and once more his eyes fluttered closed.

She stared at him, heart pounding. Someone must have attacked him. Thank God he hadn't killed him. Maybe he'd heard them coming before he could finish the job. Well, that person was now locked inside with no way to get out. After she'd rung Kevin she'd ring the constabulary. Harry Clements would just have to do without his big stipend.

As soon as they entered the foyer she ordered Philip to ring for Kevin Prestwick. Baxter insisted on walking up the stairs, but accepted the help of his wife and Charlie and leaned heavily on both of them as they made their way up to the suite.

He refused to take to his bed, preferring to sit by the fire to wait for Kevin to arrive.

Once she was certain he was settled, Cecily sat down opposite him. She felt cold, shaken, and immeasurably guilty. So intent had she been on preserving tranquility for her guests and Pansy's wedding, she had unintentionally put many people in peril.

"My head hurts." He raised a hand to his head and winced when it made contact. "Ouch."

"It appears that someone hit you over the head with a bottle." Thank God it was wine and not a knife, she thought, as he sat there looking at her with a dazed expression. He would be dead now, and once more she would be a lonely, devastated widow.

"What? No." For a minute he looked confused, then shook his head, wincing again. "I was carrying a bottle of wine. I grabbed it for a weapon when I saw the wall had been torn apart. It seems you may be right about thieves using our tunnel."

"What happened? You were supposed to go down with the rest of us."

He frowned, as if trying to remember. "I decided to go down to the cellar myself, to see what was going on and possibly save you from running into danger. I saw the trapdoor open in the card room, so I went down into the tunnel. I hadn't gone very far when I heard a rumbling noise over my head. I thought I heard voices, too, but then rocks started falling. I dropped the wine and heard the bottle smash, then pain exploded in my head. The next thing I knew I was being carried back up the ladder."

Cecily stared at him. "You must have been hit by a rock. It could have killed you." She shuddered. "The voices you heard might have been those of the footmen."

Baxter leaned back, his face a mask of pain. "That tunnel isn't safe. If there is someone down there, he's risking his life. Those boards won't hold up that roof forever. The damp must be rotting them. The chalk is soft, beginning to crumble."

"I know." She sighed. "We still don't know if the stolen artwork is down there, or what happened to Mr. Clements. We can't wait any longer. I will have to ring for the constables. Just as soon as Kevin has taken care of you."

"I'm feeling much better." He gave her a wan smile. "I don't need Kevin to come. We have a wedding to attend tonight, and I'm giving away the bride."

"He's already on his way. I'm not letting you go anywhere until he's taken a look at you."

Baxter closed his eyes as if he were too tired to argue. "Well, I think you should go down and ring the constabulary now. The sooner they get here and do what they have to do, the sooner we'll get rid of them and we can get on with the wedding."

Cecily got up from her chair. "That wedding is going on whether the police are here or not. I just wish we knew who has been helping the thieves. Once the word is out that the paintings might have been discovered, there's nothing to stop the accomplice from walking out of here."

"But then we'll know who's missing."

She smiled. "You're right." She reached the door and looked back at him. "Thank you."

He seemed surprised. "For what?"

"For wanting to save me from going down there." She opened the door. "Promise me you won't move until the doctor arrives."

"I promise." He reached for the newspaper that lay folded on the side table next to him. "I'll catch up on the news."

Satisfied that she could safely leave him, Cecily made her way down the stairs to her office. P.C. Potter answered her call and although he didn't sound too happy about it, he promised to come right away. When Cecily explained about the artwork that could be hidden in the tunnel, Potter announced that he'd be bringing members of the coastguard with him.

Cecily replaced the receiver, her gaze on the clock. Almost noon. They had five hours to get this matter resolved. She had waited until the very last moment to call in the constabulary. She hoped Harry Clements would understand that.

She picked up the receiver again. After asking the operator to put her through to George Rutter's residence, she waited for him to answer. Moments later, she heard George's deep voice on the phone.

"I thought I'd give you a ring to ask about your ankle," she said, after exchanging the usual pleasantries.

"My ankle?"

George sounded confused, and Cecily's pulse quickened. "Yes. I understand you sprained it last week. Wasn't that why you couldn't repair the plumbing?"

After a long pause, George said carefully, "I didn't sprain my ankle. When I got to the Pennyfoot three days ago a chap met me at the gate and told me he'd been given the job. I thought it a bit strange, but I was pretty busy so it was sort of a relief to know someone else was taking care of you." Now he sounded worried. "Why? Did he not do a good job? I could come out there this afternoon if you need me."

"Thank you, George. If we need your assistance I will certainly give you a ring later." Cecily replaced the receiver and sat looking at it for several minutes. Then she reached for the bellpull. Moments later she answered a tap on the door and Pansy stepped into the office. "You rang, m'm?"

"Yes, Pansy. I want you to go up to the second and third floor lavatories and see if they are still in need of repair."

"Yes, m'm." Pansy bobbed a curtsey and left the room.

All this time she'd thought there was something odd about the new plumber. He just didn't look like a plumber, though she wasn't at all sure what a plumber should look like. She leaned back in her chair and closed her eyes, picturing his cheeky grin and unruly hair. Of course.

She sat up again. If she hadn't been so preoccupied with everything going on lately, she would have realized it before. Both times she had talked to Bernie, he hadn't been wearing a tool belt. That's what was missing. George was never without his tool belt.

What was it Gertie had said to her earlier? *Bernie seemed*

upset that Alice was gone this morning when I saw him coming out of the laundry room.

What was Bernie doing in the laundry room? According to Mrs. Chubb, the problem had been taken care of downstairs. It was only in the lavatories upstairs that the problem persisted. *Bernie seemed upset that Alice was gone.* Alice had been talking to the plumber, in spite of the fact that she avoided all men. They must have been well acquainted.

Thinking furiously, Cecily stood up and walked over to the window. Alice had arrived at the Pennyfoot just before the problems with the plumbing arose. Coincidence? Perhaps. Or was Alice an accomplice of Bernie's, helping him get into the Pennyfoot by tampering with the plumbing?

Alice had disappeared right after Jacob's body was found. Was she, perhaps, afraid that things were getting too dangerous for her?

Staring at the courtyard below, Cecily recalled the moment Alice had asked for the job. Right after Charlotte had fallen down the stairs. Had she been right in suspecting that Alice caused that fall, thus securing time for her to stay and help Bernie and the art thieves?

Shaking her head, Cecily started to turn away from the window. All this was pure conjecture. She needed evidence, and all she could hope was that the constables would find it in the tunnel.

Just then a movement caught her eye and she turned back. Someone was crossing the courtyard. He wore a cap pulled low over his eyes, but Cecily recognized the jaunty way he walked. *Bernie.*

Wasting no time in making up her mind, she rushed

across the room and flung open the door. She almost barged into Pansy, who was about to knock.

The maid looked startled and backed off a step before stuttering, "The lavatories, m'm. They're all working. Bernie must have mended them. I took down the signs but . . ."

Cecily didn't hear the rest of it. She was already at the end of the hallway. Picking up her skirts, she tore through the lobby, shocking a couple of guests as she flew past them and out the door.

Running as fast as she could, Cecily rounded the side of the building and raced across the courtyard. She was just in time to see the door of the wine cellar closing behind Bernie. So that's where the missing key had gone. In Bernie's pocket. He must have taken it from Jacob when he killed him.

She spun around and headed for the kitchen, bursting through the door just as Michel was about to take something out of the oven.

She heard him yell, then a dreadful crashing noise, followed by another yell from the chef. "My Yorkshire puddings! They are all over the floor!"

"Oh, I'm sorry, Michel." Cecily waved a hand at him. "Pick them up and wash them off. No one will ever know." She ignored his outraged face and looked at Mrs. Chubb, who stared at her openmouthed. "Altheda, I need a padlock. A sturdy one. Right away."

The housekeeper hustled across the room to the dresser and opened a drawer. "I've got two in here, but I don't know if they're that strong." She held up two padlocks.

"Give them both to me." Cecily grabbed them from her. "Carry on, everyone. Thank you!" With that she was out the door and once more running across the courtyard. Reaching the wine cellar she fastened the lock with both padlocks, pulling on them to make sure they were secure. Then, after dusting her hands together, she walked at a more sedate pace back to the front door.

At least one of the thieves wasn't going anywhere, and neither were the stolen paintings if they were in the tunnel. She just had to wait now for the constable and coastguard to arrive and take care of everything. After that, they could all enjoy Pansy's wedding.

CHAPTER
❀ 19 ❀

Pansy stood in the tiny dressing room in front of the mirror, staring at the image of the girl in the white gown. She hardly recognized herself. Mrs. Chubb had done her hair for her, putting tiny white flowers around the bun before attaching the veil.

Gertie had helped get her dressed. Pansy smoothed her fingers down the silky skirt. She felt shivery and shaky, though not from cold. More from nerves.

Everyone was sitting out there waiting for her. This was the last time she'd look at herself as Pansy Watson. The next time she looked in the mirror, she'd be Mrs. Samuel Whitfield. Just thinking about it gave her goose bumps.

She turned to look at Gertie, who was fiddling with Lillian's basket of rose petals. James sat on a chair in his sailor's suit looking bored, his legs swinging back and forth. Gertie and Lillian wore the same color pink gowns, only Gertie's had long sleeves and a lace collar around her throat.

Mrs. Chubb had assured her Samuel was waiting for her at the altar. Gertie was right. It was going to be a lovely wedding.

The faint sound of the organ made her jump.

Gertie looked up and grinned. "It's time."

Pansy caught her breath as she heard a tap on the door.

Gertie hurried to open it, her skirt rustling around her ankles.

Mr. Baxter stood outside, looking handsome in his black dress coat and gray striped trousers. "Is she ready?" he asked, and Gertie stood back to let him look into the room.

Pansy met his gaze and felt suddenly shy. She looked down at her white satin shoes, peeking out from under her gown. "I'm ready," she said, in little more than a whisper.

He held out his arm to her and she walked slowly over to him, feeling as if she were in a dream. One she never wanted to wake up from ever again.

Her hand trembled on his sleeve, and he patted her fingers. "You look lovely, my dear. Hold up your head and sail down that aisle toward your new life. Samuel will make you happy. You can count on that."

She glanced up at him. "Thank you, sir."

"Entirely my pleasure."

They started down the aisle together, with Gertie and the twins following behind. Pansy could feel eyes upon her, but she kept her gaze fixed on the man waiting for her. This was to be her life now. Samuel's wife. She was leaving the Pennyfoot behind, but it would always be there for her. She knew that now. Madam and Mr. Baxter, Mrs. Chubb, Gertie, and Michel were her family. That was something that would never change.

A sense of peace flowed over her as she reached Samuel's side. She could tell by his face that he liked how she looked. Her new life was just beginning. And she was ready for it.

"Well, I'm glad that's over." Baxter sank onto his chair in front of the fireplace and stuck his feet up on the fender.

Seated across from him, Cecily smiled. "You're not going to tell me that you didn't enjoy the wedding?"

"The food was good."

"Oh, come now. I saw the look on your face when you were walking down the aisle with Pansy on your arm. You loved every moment of it."

He smiled back. "I have to admit, it was rather nice to be part of the ceremony. I felt as though I were giving my own daughter in marriage."

"Ah, you see? That's exactly how I feel about everyone here." She sighed, leaning back in her chair. "I'm just so thankful the coastguard didn't take all afternoon to find the paintings."

"They did a good job of rounding up the thieves."

"Well, once Bernie realized there was no escape, P.C. Potter said he was very cooperative. I was right about the thieves waiting in the Fox and Hounds until it was time to move the artwork. P.C. Potter said when he called that they arrested the men without any problems."

"I'm glad to hear it." Baxter leaned forward and picked

up the poker. He shoved it into the glowing coals, making the sparks fly. Flames licked up the sides of the coals, and he hooked the poker back on its stand. "So our little homeless waif wasn't homeless after all."

"No." Cecily locked her fingers together. "Her real name is Gwendoline Carstairs, and she's Bernie's niece. He confessed that her alleged loss of memory was his idea, as well as her so-called fear of men. It protected her from having to answer questions about anything. He'd promised her he'd pay for a year in Paris if she helped him. She lost her nerve when Jacob was killed."

"Well, let's hope we don't get any more lost souls turning up at our door."

"Speaking of which, there's something you should know."

He sent her a glance full of suspicion. "Don't tell me we have another homeless waif looking for shelter."

"Not exactly." She paused, then added in a rush. "It's Lilly. I didn't tell you before because she asked me not to tell anyone, but I had a word with her and we agreed that you should know."

Baxter's frown deepened. "Know what?"

"Lilly is married. She ran away from her husband because he beat her. She has no family, no one she can turn to, and she is terrified her husband will find her and kill her for leaving him."

Baxter raised his chin to stare at the ceiling. "Oh, good Lord." He lowered his gaze. "Why doesn't she simply divorce him?"

"She doesn't have the money to pay for a lawyer. Not yet, anyway, which is why she's working for us—to get the money to pay for one. Even then, she's not sure she wants to take the chance of letting him know where she is. I think she just wants time for things to cool down." Cecily leaned forward and touched his knee. "She needs our protection, Bax. I promised I'd give it to her."

His expression softened. "I sometimes wonder why you didn't turn the Pennyfoot into a home for waifs and strays instead of a hotel."

She had to laugh at that.

"Which reminds me, did Potter say why Jacob was killed?"

"Apparently Jacob found out Bernie was involved in the art theft. He threatened to tell the authorities unless the thieves gave him part of the proceeds. One of the thieves decided to get rid of him instead."

Baxter shook his head. "And that detective chap? He's all right?"

"Yes." Cecily stretched out her feet closer to the fire. "Mr. Clements found the paintings at the end of the tunnel. Then he noticed that someone had been trying to open up the wall close by the one that caved in. He went to investigate, but it must have been unstable. The roof caved in, trapping him and the paintings. Fortunately he wasn't hurt. Just very cold and hungry when the coastguard dug him out of there. They retrieved all the paintings of course. As it happened, the thieves wouldn't have been able to get at them after all. They didn't know that, however. Bernie found out when he got down the tunnel and found it blocked. Of course, he couldn't get out from the wine cellar again since I'd padlocked it."

"That was quick thinking."

"Thank you, dear."

"So Clements won't get his stipend after all."

"Well, from what P.C. Potter told me, it seems the art gallery had offered a nice reward for the return of the paintings. Since Mr. Clements was instrumental in finding the actual whereabouts of the stolen goods, he will be able to claim the reward."

"That should satisfy him." Baxter reached for the poker again. "So all's well that ends well."

She sighed. "It so nearly wasn't. When I saw you lying there with what I thought was blood pouring out of your head, I can't tell you how devastated I felt. I never want to feel that way again." She paused, part of her still resisting the decision she'd taken so long to make. A decision she could put off no longer. Every instinct told her it was time. Drawing a deep breath, she asked quietly, "Is the offer of your job abroad still open?"

She saw his eyes widen and knew she'd shocked him. "As far as I know. Why?"

She tried to sound casual. "Oh, I thought we might discuss it, once the Christmas season is over. It might be time for a change of view. I rather like the idea of traveling to different countries, setting up hotels. We might even run into Michael or Andrew. I haven't seen my sons in such a long time."

His eyes were full of hope as he leaned forward. "Do you really mean that?"

Again she paused. "Let's wait until after the New Year to talk about it. Christmas is not a good time to make decisions. I do think, however, that it could be a great adventure for both of us."

He smiled with his whole face. "That's good enough for me. Happy Christmas, my love."

He held out his hands and she clasped them. "Happy Christmas, darling, and may the New Year be a bright one for all of us."